Also available from Kris Ripper

Rocky Fitzgerald

One Dead Vampire
Two Black Cats

Queers of La Vista

Gays of Our Lives
The Butch and the Beautiful
The Queer and the Restless
One Life to Lose
As La Vista Turns

Scientific Method Universe

Catalysts
Unexpected Gifts
Take Three Breaths
Breaking Down
Roller Coasters
The Boyfriends Tie the Knot
The Honeymoon
Extremes
Untrue
The New Born Year
Threshold of the Year
Ring in the True
Let Every New Year Find You
Every New Beginning
Surrender the Past
Practice Makes Perfect
Less Ordinary

Kith and Kin

New Halliday

Fairy Tales
The Spinner, the Shepherd, and the Leading Man
The Real Life Build
Take the Leap

The Home Series

Going Home
Home Free
Close to Home
Home for the Holidays

Little Red and Big Bad

Bad Comes First
Red Comes Second

Erotic Gym

Training Mac
Teasing Mac
Taking Mac

Stand-alones

Gun for Hire
Fail Seven Times
Runaway Road Trip
The Ghost in the Penthouse
Hold Fast

THE LOVE STUDY

Kris Ripper

LA GRANGE PUBLIC LIBRARY
10 W. COSSITT AVE.
LA GRANGE, IL 60525
708-215-3200

WITHDRAWN

carina
press

3 1320 00513 0559

If you purchased this book without a cover you should be aware that this book is stolen property. It was reported as "unsold and destroyed" to the publisher, and neither the author nor the publisher has received any payment for this "stripped book."

DEC - '21

carina press®

Recycling programs
for this product may
not exist in your area.

ISBN-13: 978-1-335-94319-4

The Love Study

Copyright © 2020 by Kris Ripper

All rights reserved. No part of this book may be used or reproduced in any manner whatsoever without written permission except in the case of brief quotations embodied in critical articles and reviews.

This is a work of fiction. Names, characters, places and incidents are either the product of the author's imagination or are used fictitiously. Any resemblance to actual persons, living or dead, businesses, companies, events or locales is entirely coincidental.

This edition published by arrangement with Harlequin Books S.A.

For questions and comments about the quality of this book, please contact us at CustomerService@Harlequin.com.

Carina Press
22 Adelaide St. West, 40th Floor
Toronto, Ontario M5H 4E3, Canada
www.CarinaPress.com

Printed in U.S.A.

F
RIPPER

THE LOVE STUDY

Chapter One

Here's how my friends describe me to new people: "This is Declan. He left his last boyfriend at the altar, so watch out."

It's mostly a joke. Mostly. Not that I left my last boyfriend at the altar—that part's definitely true. But *watch out* is just a playful warning. Besides, I swore off romance after that. No one really has to watch out for me.

It was ages ago. The leaving-Mason-at-the-altar thing. The swearing-off-romance thing is ongoing. Though I guess "This is Declan. He swore off romance, so watch out" has less of a ring to it.

Leaving your boyfriend at the altar is the kind of meltdown no one gives you the chance to grow out of. Six years later my friends are still merrily using that line at parties. Case in point: Ronnie and Mia's Christmas recovery party, where the sparkling apple cider I was valiantly drinking in place of alcohol wasn't even close to taking the edge off my mood. And that was *before* Mia grabbed my arm and whispered, "There's someone I want you to meet, they're new."

I love Mia, but she is absolutely one of those *I found true love and now everyone else should too* types. I had just opened my mouth to protest when I caught sight of The Only Human I Didn't Already Know and shut it real fast.

Average height, shoulder-length dirty blond hair, angular chin with a few spare whiskers, and red-framed glasses. Who on earth wears red-framed glasses? Were they one of those people who had multiple pairs and matched them to their outfits? But no, no red anywhere else, all the way down to their plain black shoes.

Please don't let them be one of those people who wears fashion glasses. I adjusted my prescription lenses and prepared to judge. If those frames were the real deal, though, I was already intrigued. Because seriously: who wears red-framed glasses? Maybe I shouldn't be quite so quick to tell Mia off. She only had my best interests at heart, anyway. That and fulfilling her desire to play a romantic matching game with every human she knew.

She leaned in. (Goody; gossip.) "They've only been in town a few months and I think they might be perfect for Mason. Don't you? Not too tall, not too built. Smart, but not intimidating. They have a YouTube advice channel, so there's no way Mason will feel inferior, right?"

"Oh, burn." I secretly loved it when lesbians got catty, but one must maintain appearances.

"Hush, you know what I mean. He's so sensitive about relationships."

The thing about that whole unfortunate leaving-Mason-at-the-altar fiasco was that Mia had been in the limo when I'd opened the door on the way to my own wedding, seen all those faces staring at me, panicked, watched Mason's grin freeze (then wilt), and pulled back into the limo like a turtle into its shell. An effect I immediately ruined by crying dramatically, "Get me out of here!"

I've done a lot of guilt for that moment, but I think for her own penance, Mia plans to fix Mason up with everyone she knows until one sticks...to his crotch. Or I guess his heart. Whatever. She's gonna marry his ass off as soon as he falls in love with someone for longer than two hours.

He's weirdly commitment-averse for someone who desperately wants a partner. Can't imagine why. Cough, cough.

Now that we were close to The Only New Person in the Room, I could see that they were wearing prescription glasses. Damn. Mason arguably deserved first pick of the proverbial fish in the proverbial sea. It was an ethical principle. And I was an ethical man. I sighed and hoped this particular fish was... I didn't quite wish they were awful. I just hoped they were awful *for me*, to save me the pain of wanting them only to watch them drift off with one of my best friends. To the altar. Where they would undoubtedly not leave anyone standing, ever, with a grin wilting on his face.

"Sidney, this is Declan. He left his last boyfriend at the altar, so watch out." Mia beamed as if she hadn't said this dozens, if not hundreds, of times before.

I readied a perfect *I am not an asshole* expression and shook their hand. "It was years ago and I haven't been anywhere near an altar since, I promise."

Sidney's hand was cold, but their smile was warrrrrm. "I'm not interested in altars, so you're safe from the temptation. Good to meet you."

"Yeah, you too. You might be careful around Mia, here. She's in a bit of a 'fix everyone up' phase since she got engaged." *So there, lady.*

Unfortunately Mia didn't seem the least deterred. "It's not

fixing people up, it's just introducing them. We have this friend Mason I think you'd really like."

"Why?"

She blinked. "Why what?"

"Why do you think I'd really like him?"

"I guess because...he watches a lot of YouTube?" Mia, cheeks pink, continued quickly, "And he's a lovely person, and you seem incredibly kind and well spoken, and—sorry, are you exclusively into women? Or nonbinary folks? Did I get that wrong?"

I bit down on my tongue trying not to laugh.

Sidney's expression landed somewhere in the *my, what a fascinating specimen you have here* zone, but they didn't look annoyed. Just detached. "I'm not exclusively into anyone, no. It's more a skepticism about the process by which people decide other people would fit well together." They shrugged. "I don't mean to be rude, but I'm not looking to be set up with anyone."

"Totally get it and I'm sorry I assumed. Do you want to meet some people, though? Aside from the ones at work?" She nudged me. "We get together for drinks once a week. It'd be low pressure and more queers. If you're...into that sort of thing."

This time I did laugh, then plastered both hands over my mouth.

Sidney genuinely smiled. "I am into queer people, yes. Definitely. Drinks sound good. Thank you for inviting me."

"You're so welcome! Ronnie will be thrilled too!"

Ronnie and Mia were more or less joined at the hip. Not that I judged. Whatever makes people happy, right? Especially when they're your friends.

"Anyway, why don't you two do phone numbers and Twitter things or whatever, and Dec, if you want to give

Sidney Mason's info too, that'd be great." She waved. "I need to go check on food, but I'll see you around."

They leveled a look at me. "She's not going to let go of this setting me up thing, is she?"

"Honestly, it's been a year and a half since she and Ronnie decided to get married and we keep thinking she's going to stop doing this, but so far she hasn't." My strong ethical principles forced me to add, "Anyway, everyone likes Mason. It's a pretty safe bet that you will too, even if you don't want to date him."

"I don't date people."

That simplified matters. I hid my ~~disappointment~~ relief by forcing a laugh. "Oh, me neither. Mostly. Well. Not for a long time. I mean, it didn't seem like I was mature enough after thinking I was going to get married and then freaking out? So I figured I'd stick to getting laid, since that was safer. Like…" I focused on the gentle sweep of their hair back from their face as if it would introduce a new topic of conversation. It didn't.

"See, that sentence seemed like it was going to be followed by another thought." Their eyebrows very slightly inclined. Which I noticed because I was already staring at their face.

"Um, sorry, I realized I was basically spilling my guts to a stranger. You are totally not obligated to listen to me ramble. Only my oldest friends are contractually bound to deal with me being a hot mess." Cue self-deprecating smile.

Sidney's hands twitched outward, as if expressing a shrug without actually shrugging. "You don't seem like a hot mess to me and I don't feel obligated. What were you going to say?"

What the hell. If Mia and Ronnie were folding them into The Friend Group (or at least having them audition), they'd probably end up seeing me pathetic eventually. "Just, for a long time my not-dating policy worked? But lately it's kind of getting…old. I'm about to turn twenty-nine. And I'm not wigging about thirty or anything. But I am thinking maybe I should…at least try again. With the dating thing." I wrinkled my nose. "Then I think that's a horrible idea because oh my god where do you even start? Apps? Bars? I have no idea where people meet to date instead of hook up."

Their eyes were light brown behind their red-framed glasses and I felt a bit exposed under their gaze, like maybe the glasses had a filter that could read my thoughts. Right when I was starting to shift uncomfortably, they cleared their throat. "I have an idea. It might be a bit obscene, though."

I batted my eyelashes at them. "I enjoy the obscene."

"Would you be interested in coming on my YouTube channel? It's an advice show. I do one livestream and one pre-taped show each week."

"Er…"

"An interview would be cool, but what if we did a series? You could come on once a week and talk about your recent dating adventures. I could find you the dates if you wanted, since you'd be supplying me with content." Now their hands sort of danced in explanation. "I get a huge volume of emails asking for advice, but the format gets old. This way we could combine direct dating experience with advice. And if you're trying to get back into the dating thing anyway, maybe it's two birds with one stone."

My brain flooded with words and images—everything from *danger, Will Robinson* to a vision of Sidney and I shaking hands for the camera at an awards show where we'd just won for "Spectacular Advances in Dating Advice"—but I couldn't seem to speak.

"Yeah, you're right, it's a terrible idea." Their eyebrows were now a straight line behind their red frames. "Excuse my shameless desire to exploit your emotional turmoil for views. I was approached by this company that's doing a thing I actually think…might be good? So I've been considering doing a sponsorship deal with them and this, um, slightly obscene idea might be perfect. If you…were interested. In retrospect, I think maybe ambition makes me a crummy human being."

"Oh, no, I didn't… I didn't think that at all. I mean, I guess yes on the exploiting thing, but that doesn't bother me. I was more…processing."

"If it makes it any less gross, if I dated, I would absolutely mine my dating experiences for views." They frowned. "Okay, no, that doesn't make it less gross. Sorry. This is a nonideal first impression."

"I like your glasses," I blurted. "Just, that was my first impression. Well, actually I thought, *Those better not be fucking fashion glasses*, and then when I saw they weren't I was impressed. They look really good on you. Not everyone can pull off red frames."

"Oh. Um." They straightened their shoulders. "Thank you. And I know, fashion glasses feel…slightly ableist somehow? I tend to overthink things, so maybe they're harmless, but it feels a little weird that something I need in order to see is someone else's sartorial accent."

"Exactly! Yes. That's exactly it. But also I'm never saying that to anyone, because I don't want to be an asshole cis white guy who makes shit about them."

"Agreed," they said solemnly. "Let us never mention this to anyone else."

I held out my hand.

They held out theirs.

We shook in one sharp downward motion as if sealing the deal. I couldn't help but note that their hand was no longer cold.

"Please forget I even brought up my show? I feel like an ass for mentioning it."

I didn't quite bat my eyelashes again, but I allowed a hint of flirtation into my voice. "That's a little awkward since I was just going to ask you to tell me more about it."

They offered a rueful smile. I couldn't tell if they'd picked up on my timid flirtation or not. "It's called Your Spinster Uncle. I do a livestream each Monday and post a taped show on Fridays. People write or call in and I answer their questions."

"Like Dan Savage?"

"More like Iron Man meets Professor McGonagall, teasing and stern. I do answer a lot of dating questions, but also a lot of family and school and work questions. More and more I answer a lot of…" They paused long enough for me to start brainstorming ways to salvage the conversation. Then they kind of sighed. "I think we have a distinct failure to address legitimate mental health issues in this country. I'm seeing more and more stuff that makes me wish people had free access to real therapy instead of schmucks on the internet."

I swallowed hard, taken by surprise. In the months following my derailed attempt at a wedding I'd gone to therapy. And it had helped. (Apparently the bit in the limo when we were driving away and I couldn't breathe or speak and my heart was pounding so hard I thought it was going to break my rib cage was a *panic attack*. And I thought I'd just been wigging out like a baby.)

Right, focusing. "Me too. I mean the thing about therapy. I'm not endorsing your assessment of yourself as a schmuck. I don't know you that well yet." I would have gone for a cheeky smile, but I didn't quite have the levity to pull it off.

"In the interests of, um, absolving my current schmucky-ness, that's why I'm interested in this sponsorship. The company does therapy online so people in rural areas who need specialties not offered where they live have access to those services. Or even maybe you're the only trans person your therapist has ever seen, so they probably won't be able to meet your needs as effectively as someone who works with queer and trans people as a regular part of their practice. Ditto kinksters or people in polyamorous relationships." They paused. "Um, I'm not trying to pressure you into it. Sorry. I just wanted to explain why you mentioned a very basic thing and I jumped on it and tried to seduce you into coming on my YouTube channel."

There was something so completely charming about their rambling speech. Also points for using the word "seduce." I wasn't *not* feeling seduced. What the hell. "I think we should do it. Your series idea. I mean, it can't possibly make dating *worse*, right? And maybe it will help someone?"

Sidney pushed their hair back with one hand and stared at me steadily, almost as if part of them was being cool and part of them was totally nervous. "Are you sure? It was a ludicrous idea."

"I kind of like it. Plus, you said you'd find the people for these dates, right?"

"I could," they said carefully. "If you gave me some idea who you were interested in. Only if you're sure this wouldn't be terrible for you. And ethically I should tell you that I would be making money off your, um…" They cast around for a word. "Off your romantic journey. If you will."

Across the room Mia kissed Ronnie's cheek and Ronnie beamed. I knew I didn't want the exact relationship they had, but some deep thing inside me wanted that spark of desire, that casual affection.

"I think we should try it. And I'm pretty easy. All genders, all ages." I considered it. "Okay, over twenty-one. Not that

I'm a huge drinker but I think I'd feel self-conscious around someone who couldn't."

Sidney's lips twitched as if they weren't sure if they should smile or not. "Are you serious right now?"

"Dude."

There. They smiled. "Okay."

"Good. And it's okay I called you 'dude'?"

"Yes. Thank you for asking."

"All right, then. That's settled. We're doing a YouTube thing." I gulped. "Oh god, what did I just agree to?"

They patted my arm. "Leave it to your spinster uncle. I'll take care of everything."

I forced myself to ignore the tingling still alerting my brain to the presence of their hand on my skin. "But wait, isn't it better for ratings or something if the dates go really horribly? You have a conflict of interest!"

"Maybe, but it's better for my fans if you have good experiences you can share with them. Even if they're also awkward or strange at times. I'd love it if people came away from this series thinking that maybe things weren't so bad out there in the world of romance."

"Let's...aim low," I managed. Romance. Oh god. I had definitely not been mature enough for this sort of thing with Mason. But that was years ago. Decades in developmental time. The mid-twenties changed everything. Didn't they? "Um, what if I'm like really, really bad at this? What if I fail you? That's sort of my entire track record right now."

Sidney's hand tightened on my arm. "You can't fail. If our goal is to do some shows, get word about this company out there, and facilitate you going on a few dates, there's no metric for failure there. There's no pressure. Anyway, why don't you think about it for a few days? I'll propose it to the sponsor and we can talk more when we see each other at drinks with Mia. All right?"

I looked at them, beyond the red frames, into eyes that were darker suddenly than I'd thought they were. "I left my last boyfriend at the altar. Are you sure you want to commit to a YouTube series with me?"

"I told you, I'm not interested in altars. I think we're safe."

It was probably just a mark of how weird the night had been, but I found myself thinking *we're safe* in Sidney's voice for the rest of the party and feeling a phantom warmth on my arm where they'd touched me.

Chapter Two

Drinks with the Marginalized Motherfuckers almost always happened at The Hole.

Technically it was The Hole in the Wall, which the gays called—obviously—The Gloryhole. Most people just called it The Hole. To be honest, it kind of resembled the proverbial hole, all brown wood paneling and a vague sense that it was bigger than expected once you were poking around in it.

Marginalized Motherfuckers didn't have to poke around; we had a favorite table, a second favorite table, and a third choice, which Oscar had decreed could not be considered anyone's *anything*-favorite. Despite Mia's openness with Sidney, very few people ever stuck around long after we asked them for drinks. It had become an unfunny joke, The Drinks Curse. When you sensed a relationship was heading toward a dead end you might gently inquire, "When are they coming for drinks?" Shorthand for "When are you gonna give up already?"

Apparently heading that off at the pass, here Sidney was, at drinks before even meeting the man Mia wanted them to spend the rest of their life with. Alas, very tragic, the end before the beginning and so forth.

I realized I was about to launch into a round of verse about death and volunteered to buy the first round since no one else had shown up yet. "If a random stranger demands to know if you're you, it's probably Mason or Oscar," I assured them.

They stood up. "How about I get the drinks and you wait for your friends?"

Which I supposed was a reasonable plan. Though I'm always uncomfortable when someone new buys me a drink. I know that's a little backwards, but it ends up making me feel indebted to them in an endless-cycle-of-debt-repayment-debt-repayment way. *No, but you bought last time. Yes, but you bought the time before that.*

I realized Sidney had said something. "Um, sure, thanks."

One corner of their mouth crept up. "I asked what you wanted."

"Right. Shit. Sorry, I'm a little distracted." I didn't even know why. It was just drinks. And Sidney, while attractive and smart, didn't date people, which was handy since neither did I, historically speaking. "I'll have a Coke, thanks."

"I'll be right back."

I was still watching their retreat when Oscar popped in as if from the ether. "That the one Mia wants to set up Mase with?"

"Seriously, how the hell do you do that?"

He frowned in Sidney's direction, hovering over our second favorite table without taking a seat. "That's the new person, right?"

"Yeah."

"I don't think I want to talk to new people today."

I weighed a couple of replies—I didn't think Sidney would be a drag on Oscar's anxiety too badly, but drinks in general was a drag on his anxiety, so I also didn't want to dismiss the possibility—before shrugging. "Next week?"

This got me a kiss on the cheek. "Thanks, Dec. Make my apologies."

"Sure. Love ya, kid."

His hand flapped in a wave as he melted back into the crowd.

Sidney returned with what looked, to my trained eye, like two Cokes. Damn, I should have told them they didn't have to abstain just because I was. "We're going to be one person down tonight," I said, accepting the glass. "Oscar is sitting this one out."

"Make that three. I just got a text from Mia that said she and Ronnie have some urgent responsibility having to do with Ronnie's sister."

"Ooooh. Such intrigue."

They cocked an eyebrow at me from behind their glasses. "Is it?"

"Kind of? Like, it's a big deal her sister agreed to be maid of honor, especially because half of her family still dead-names her to her face."

They grimaced. "That's awful."

"Yeah, it's super shitty. So the wedding is a big thing to start and—" My eyes caught on Mason. My sweet, gorgeous, slightly melancholic ex.

We'd called ourselves the Marginalized Motherfuckers as a joke because for a while in college every conversation we had revolved around...marginalization. Which doesn't sound like fun, and we wouldn't do that again, but I think it was probably a developmental stage we all had to go through. And it brought us together as a family in a way that talking about, I don't know, Kant or chemistry or something probably wouldn't have.

Mia was the Korean one (also a lesbian!), Ronnie was white (but trans!), I was white (but queer!), Oscar was half-white, half-Mexican (and gay!), and Mason was the self-appointed token black guy (and pansexual!) approaching the table with a guarded smile.

"Hey, Dec."

I sprang up to give him a hug. "Mase! We've been abandoned by the other Motherfuckers. But look, Sidney's here!" I made an extravagant Vanna White arm motion in Sidney's general direction because apparently I couldn't stop being a jackass.

"I'm Sidney Worrell. Nice to meet you."

"Mason Ertz-Scott."

They shook hands, both of them looking like models for different things. Mase would be Suave Young Businessman on His Way to an Important Meeting, and Sidney would be Nerdy Person at Cafe Table Staring Contemplatively into Their Coffee. Not that I spend a lot of time coming up with stock photo descriptions for real people or anything like that.

Suave Young Businessman and Nerdy Person at Cafe Table both sat down again, which meant I did too. Except now Mase didn't have a drink. This would be the perfect opportunity to give them a chance to chat, right? I sprang back up. "Beer, babe?" Horror at the slip almost stopped my heart. "Oh my god I haven't called you that in years, what is wrong with me? Sorry. Do you want a beer?"

"You're buying me a drink *and* calling me 'babe'? I sure hope you're planning to text me in the morning, Casanova."

"Oh shove it—" I broke off. Because Sidney. "Just for

that I'm getting you a light beer!" I—okay—*flounced* off in the direction of the bar, ignoring his laughter behind me.

I'd at least stopped blushing by the time I returned to the table, though the reprieve was short lived. They were talking about Sidney's video series idea.

"Wait." I set a beer (not light) in front of Mason. "You're calling it *The Love Study*? That sounds terrible."

Mase punched my arm.

"What? It does! I mean…doesn't it?"

Sidney nodded, not quite in agreement, more like they knew what I meant and were acknowledging it. "I think it gets across the crudest sense of what we're trying to do in the fewest number of words. It abbreviates decently, though I did try to think of a name that could be spoken, like AWOL. The Love Study is short, to the point, and easy for people to remember. Which makes it perfect for YouTube."

"Yeah, but…" I took a disconsolate sip of my Coke. "Doesn't it sorta make me sound like a tool? I'm the subject of—" I made my voice into Dramatic Movie Announcer Voice "—*The Love Study.*"

Mason giggled, momentarily pressing the back of his hand against his lips to stifle it before giving in and flat-out giggling, the monster. "Honey, you've been the subject of plenty of love studies before. Maybe Sidney will get somewhere when the rest of us couldn't."

"Hey! Uncool!" Blushing again. "So uncool."

"Well, look," Sidney said, ignoring our childish byplay. "The name isn't set in stone, though I'd probably have to run a new one by the sponsor, and—"

"Oh, you got the sponsorship?" I interrupted.

"Yes. But I'm sure I can find someone else if you're not into it. I don't want to force you into anything you're not comfortable with."

"No one's comfortable with dating," Mase mumbled.

Sidney turned on him. "You could do it too! You could both be part of The Love Study. We could compare and contrast your experiences, and the fact that you have a history with each other only adds—"

"Not gonna happen."

"Er, sorry, I...lost control for a second there. Forget I asked."

He waved. "You seem like a perfectly nice person and everything, but I'm not going to date for the benefit of your audience. I have a hard enough time dating for my own benefit." Mason, the man I'd once almost pledged to spend my whole life with, slumped and sipped his beer.

I reached for his hand. "I'm really sorry. Again."

"I know. And it wouldn't have been good. I know that too. I want, like, romance and flowers and shit. You aren't even a little interested in that stuff, which I thought was a compromise I could make, but in reality it would have hurt me too much. It's just *endless* trying to meet new people." His eyes narrowed on mine. "Plus, you didn't tell me you were dating again."

"I'm not. In practice. It's more sort of...theoretical. At this point. Until Sidney puts me in front of their audience, or whatever." Also, right, Sidney. I looked over to find them watching us, something I couldn't quite make out in their expression. Not quite sadness, not quite longing? Yearning, maybe, but only at the edges.

A second later it was gone. "Okay, not talking about your experiences I get," they said to Mase. "But do you think you could come on the show to speak to Declan's past experiences? What made him the man he is today, something like that?"

"Oh sure. If we're just roasting Declan, count me in."

I stuck my tongue out at him.

"Maybe not *roasting*. I find the…cultural context of having left someone at the altar fascinating. What it means to so publicly commit, especially for queer people, and then to so publicly break up."

"Ha, yeah, I can totally star as the poor loser who got dumped on his wedding day and never recovered." He gestured to himself. "I'm basically Ms. Havisham right now."

I hit him. "He's lying, don't listen to him."

He leaned forward to say, confidentially, to Sidney, "I sleep in my wedding gown every night. It's tragic."

"Oh my *god*." I did *stop it* eyes at him. "Seriously, he's just messing around."

Sidney looked from one of us to the other, eyebrows slightly raised. "I've always wondered if more people wish they hadn't gone through with a marriage when they did. Or wish they had when they didn't."

Mason and I traded glances. "Not us," I said.

"Nope. I could have seriously throttled this asshole six years ago, and I'm pretty sure our friends would have helped me hide the body, but in a way, he saved us a world of pain. Or at least made it come all at once instead of unraveling for years as we grew to hate each other."

"You don't seem to hate each other now." They pushed their glasses up and I had to stifle the urge to mirror the gesture.

"Nah, I love the bastard." Mase leaned over to kiss my cheek. "I am so watching The Love Study. I can't wait. I'm gonna make popcorn. Oh! I'll have everyone over to watch at my place. It's going to be *dee-lightful* to see you going on a bunch of stupid dates and then being forced to talk about them."

"I'm not forcing him—" Sidney was saying, right as I

said, "They might not be stupid—" We stopped, both of us looking away.

"Oh yes," Mason murmured. "Yes, yes, yes, I foresee a whole lot of popcorn. We're gonna make a drinking game up for this thing. Maybe we'll make up a drink too. I can't wait."

I pouted. "You're the worst."

"You *left me at the altar*, sunshine."

For a second I tried to think about a comeback that would somehow make gathering our friends to eat popcorn and watch me embarrass myself on YouTube a bigger crime than leaving him at the altar, but…it wasn't. "Yeah, okay, you win. Forever."

"You're damn right I do." As if he felt accomplished now that he'd scored that point, Mason turned to Sidney. "What else do you do, when you're not giving out advice? You work with Mia, right?"

"Yep, though in a different department. I stock groceries. What do you do?"

"I'm a loan officer at a bank. It's exactly as glamorous as it sounds. I'd like to work my way up to financial manager, but it's slow going."

I cleared my throat. "Plus, you don't really want to *be* a financial manager."

He rolled his eyes. "It's a career. I really do want a career."

"A boring one."

"Not everyone can live the glamorous life of an office temp forever, Dec." He took a pull on his beer and since we had company I resolved to leave him alone. "Sidney, you gotta tell me how you moved up here. I hyperventilate if I even think about moving, it's so fucking expensive."

"It really is. I'd been working as a server in a restaurant, and making decent money I guess? But I was skipping sleep to get videos out, and I rented a room in a house mostly because moving is awful, but I had no control over background noise."

"So you were making money but hated your life?"

Sidney laughed low, like the laugh itself acknowledged it was being kind of dark. "It was time for a change, let's say."

"What's your, like, long-term plan? Keep stocking groceries and doling out advice on YouTube until you make enough to do it full-time?"

Which was a super good question and I was a little chagrined I hadn't asked it myself, though I had been sorta distracted by the whole *going on YouTube so Sidney could advise me* thing.

"I'm not sure I have a concrete plan right now. I didn't start out thinking I was actually going to make any money on YouTube. But in the last year I've received more interest from advertisers than before, so at this point it's looking like that might be a semi-reasonable goal."

Mase nodded. "It's hard for me to imagine being comfortable being on video that much. Like, I could come on to poke Dec, but I think if I had a channel of my own it'd be overwhelming."

"It can be, for sure. But I think it helps in a way that I..." They paused. "I guess I've always been really awkward face-to-face? So being on video is easier for me. It's a way of connecting to people that doesn't rely on in-person human interaction. Um. That sounds terrible." Their nose crinkled up. ~~Adorably.~~ In a vaguely intriguing way.

"Yeah, I can sort of see that. Would YouTube be your primary job if you had that option?" Mase gestured with his beer. "In a perfect world, would you do it full-time?"

"I'm not sure...in a perfect world? I think I would be able to quit the store, keep doing videos, and go back to school. Maybe become a therapist, or a psychologist."

Oooooh, I could totally picture that. "Wow, that would be amazing." I poked Mason meaningfully. He'd been thinking about grad school basically since we graduated from college.

"It's so expensive, though," he said. "At least when I've looked into it, it was."

"Exactly. I still have student loans from undergrad, how can I sign up for more?"

They lapsed into a conversation about the ins and outs of financial aid for graduate school and I listened with only half of my brain reporting for duty. I was pretty sure the "humans only use 10 percent of their brain" thing was a myth, but whatever the percent, I was using quite a bit less than that on tracking my companions' conversation.

Mostly I was thinking about how great it would be to have more queer therapists in the world. Or more specifically, how great it would have been for me to have seen a queer therapist after the whole attempted-wedding-freakout thing. Not that my straight AF therapist had been bad! She'd been nice! But I didn't think she'd totally understood the, like…cultural phenomenon that was suddenly being allowed to get married. It was 2015, it was legal, everyone was doing it, so it seemed like we might as well. It wasn't that I didn't love Mason. I loved him *a lot*. I loved him so much that I failed to realize until it was too late that I didn't really want to get married at all.

Then I was there, and he was there, and everyone we knew and loved was there, and I couldn't breathe. The rest of my life was a blur of impossibility because I didn't know if I was going to get through the next thirty seconds. I didn't calm down until the limo was miles away. The therapist eventually told me that thinking you're going to die right where you're sitting is some kind of classic panic attack thing, but I didn't know that then.

What I knew was that not getting married felt better than getting married. So I'd decided to save myself and everyone else the hassle of ever going through that again.

No more romance. Full stop. The end.

If that wasn't the end, if I was going to try doing this again, how could I ever ask anyone to put their faith in me? Most days I could only commit to getting out of bed if I had to go to work. I regularly skipped breakfast because I hit snooze too many times.

I'd left my last boyfriend at the altar. How do you ever prove you're trustworthy if you've done something like that?

Sidney laughed, bringing me back to our second favorite table at The Hole, back to this moment, in which I was nursing a Coke and ruminating over the past. Not the best idea.

I leaned forward and said confidentially to Sidney, "Do you want to hear about the time Mase moaned so loudly we thought the gay history professor was going to bust in on us while we were having sex in the empty office next to his?"

They grinned. "Hell yes."

Mason pulled out all the dignity he could manage while slumped into a bar booth. "I still maintain that he would have joined in, which means technically I should have been *louder*. He was super hot."

Sidney and I laughed. After a second Mase gave up the stoic act and grinned. Weirdly, I thought old Sidney might make it back to drinks again. Maybe the trick was not banging any of the Motherfuckers. *Good plan*, I thought at them, and started another story.

Chapter Three

I wasn't sure what to expect, walking up to Sidney's apartment for the first time. A huge building? A duplex? An old-fashioned boarding house with a landlady who forbade overnight visits from "members of the opposite sex"? (I'd always wondered if that rule ever worked out in favor of queers. Obviously the "opposite sex" deal had been debunked as an actual thing, but I still liked to imagine queers having sexy overnighters while their hetero counterparts languished with only the pleasure of their preferred hand for company.)

The apartment ended up being a lot closer to boarding house than skyscraper. The building was a converted single-family home, and Sidney's apartment was a studio. Since "studio" sounds better than "room with a sink, a toaster oven, and a very small bathroom."

I'd done some research—I'd meant to only check out a video or two, but three hours later I was still watching—and

I was a little surprised that the actual space was so small. I'd imagined they had a whole room set aside for filming, but the recording area was only a corner in what would have been the living room part of the single room. Two folding shades were posted around what I assumed was their bed. Most of their videos were in their last apartment, so maybe that had been...bigger?

Apparently I was just, like, standing there taking it all in while they watched. "Um, sorry, I know I'm almost late, I meant to get here earlier because I didn't know if we needed to do a sound check or something, but I got held up at work. Sorry."

"We're okay on time. What held you up at work?"

I waved a hand. "My boss keeps offering me a permanent position. Some people just won't take *no* for an answer." It was a weak joke and they didn't bother laughing politely. "I'm a temp, see? I've been with this same agency for almost five years. Getting a permanent job is supposed to be the holy grail, but I enjoy what I'm doing right now, so."

Insert coin, listen to Declan ramble.

They didn't seem bothered. "What I'm hearing is you have a fear of workplace commitment."

"Oh my god. Um. I never thought about it that way before." Jeez, talk about a head case. "But no, it's more like your thing with dating, right? You don't do it because it didn't work for you and what you're doing now—by not dating— is working for you. Right?"

"Hmm. Not quite, I don't think? My not dating practice is more of a guideline than a rule."

"Oh." For a long moment we just looked at each other. I wanted to know so much more. It probably wasn't the right time to bombard them with a thousand questions. Was it?

No, I told myself firmly. "But for real, what's our plan? We don't need a sound check?"

"Nope. I used to have guests regularly, so I think the set-up will be okay. This is a new place, but I can't see how having a guest will throw everything off." Their right shoulder—no—my right side, their *left* shoulder rose in a rather charming half-shrug. "Then again, the whole thing might fall apart. I've committed worse crimes on YouTube than the sound being a little wonky. Do you need the bathroom or anything before we start?"

I was tempted to say yes just because I'm a nosy bastard and always want to poke around in people's bathrooms, but we probably did need to get started with the actual…shoot? Show? Stream? Whatever it was. I shook my head.

"Sweet. Let me show you where we'll be sitting."

Since I'd already seen other videos I thought I had a pretty good idea of what I was in for, but they surprised me again. Big lights were set up, pointing at an L-shaped desk, which sectioned off a corner of the room. And: "Dude. Is that a fucking green screen?"

"Yep."

I did a theatrical double take at them. "You are so pro right now."

"You can get the fabric on Amazon. Do you want to see the graphic I designed for the series?"

Did I? Considering I was still feeling tool-like for making myself the subject of a dating advice show, I wasn't sure. Except I was also totally curious. "Show me."

Their eyebrows did a little hop, as if I'd said something suggestive. "Okay, come this way. Welcome to my studio."

"Yeah, like, the place is kinda small, and the hot plate kitchen gets old, but you seem to have everything you need, so hey."

"I meant the place where I record and edit videos."

I winced. "Uh yeah. Me too? No, sorry, I meant your apartment."

"It's okay."

I wanted to believe they were trying not to smile, but the thing about the expression a person makes when they're trying not to make a different expression is that it could be almost anything. And why not smile? Smiling was good! Which meant it was more likely they were trying not to scowl. Or no, I couldn't picture Sidney (or anyone) scowling with those glasses on.

I sat down in the chair they weren't standing in front of. Good clue. They sat down after I did, like a gentleman. "So, uh, this is where the magic happens?" Three minutes until their thing was scheduled to start, I couldn't help but notice.

"Yep. Are you nervous? A lot of people are nervous the first time they're on camera. Especially a livestream. The important thing to remember is you're safe. No one is looking at you."

"You mean except you?"

They paused. "Okay, good point. I'm looking at you. It might seem a bit strange if we did a whole video and I never looked at you."

"I'm okay with you looking at me. And I don't know if I'm nervous about that or—" I made a too-hot-soup hand gesture. "You know. It's just a new thing, I guess."

"I understand." They did a thing on their computer and pulled up an image. Light pink background with white dots at random intervals and the title THE LOVE STUDY at the top in an *X-Files*-style typewriter font. "What do you think?"

"Oh." I didn't know what I'd expected but it was kinda... classy. "I like it."

They nodded. "Good. Pink is not my thing as a general rule, but I was playing with backgrounds and I wanted something a little subtle and a little evocative." They switched windows to—*oh god*—a shot of us, then they did something else which made it look as if we were sitting in front of a very pale pink wall with white dots on it and THE LOVE STUDY printed at the top.

"Wow. Okay, that's cool. Seriously cool. Like magic."

"The first time I set up the green screen and got it to work felt like magic to me too." They turned squarely to me, both eyebrows rising above the line of their glasses. "You ready to do this?"

"How would I know if I wasn't?"

"As long as you're not going to vomit, you're probably within the normal bounds of 'ready to record.'"

I ran a hasty internal check. "Nope. Stomach contents staying where they are."

"Good. All right. Here goes. I'll hit the button and it will count down from three, then we'll be live. When we're live, it will always say 'live' right here in the corner." They pointed to a spot on the screen. "I'll be monitoring questions as we go, but we don't need to address all of them. Talk about whatever you're comfortable talking about, say 'off-limits' about anything you don't want to talk about. Okay?"

Deep breath. "Okay."

"And talk to me, not the camera. You can look at the camera, of course, but I think it will be less overwhelming if you treat this like we're just having a conversation."

"Um, us and your legion of followers?"

"My *legion* of followers, ha. Yeah. You still with me?"

"Yep."

"Let's go." They clicked a thing. The numbers three… two…one were superimposed over the picture of us against the pink background. A little red circle appeared right where they'd said it would with the word "LIVE."

And *poof*: I was on YouTube.

"Hello and welcome to Your Spinster Uncle, the advice show where we combine forces to answer questions sent in by viewers like you. Today is a very special day because we're starting a new series called The Love Study, in which we'll explore dating and queerness and all the complexity therein through the lens of one person's personal experience. And the subject of that study is our very important guest, Declan. Everyone say hi to Declan."

I waved at the camera. "Um. Hi, everyone. I'm, uh, Declan. Obviously."

If I had wondered what it looked like when Sidney smirked—and I'm not saying I had—my answer would have been on their face when I reintroduced myself seconds after they'd first introduced me.

Oh god, five-point-two seconds on YouTube and already blushing. I hoped my friends were drinking to that.

"Our first order of business is getting to know Declan, and then composing a dating profile so we can find him dates." They turned slightly more toward me. "I have a few questions for you to that end—and I'm sure everyone else does too—but before we do that, why don't you tell me a little bit about your dating history. And can I share with the audience how we were initially introduced?"

How we were...oh right. "Okay."

They held my gaze for a long moment, as if making sure, then looked at the camera. "I met Declan through a mutual acquaintance, whose first words about him were to tell me he'd left his last boyfriend at the altar. Before anyone reaches for a pitchfork, I've met the so-called jilted fiancé and they remain close friends. Sometimes we make plans that don't work out, y'all."

That seemed like a point to the audience that I didn't think had much to do with me, so I kept my mouth shut and focused on the way they were talking to me but not excluding their viewers, which was cool. They also had a slightly different tenor to their voice, maybe a little lower, almost practiced. Did they rehearse for their show? I should ask later.

"But here you are, submitting yourself to The Love Study." This time the smirk was only on the side of their mouth facing away from the camera. (Impressive smirk control there.) "Tell us what's led you to this moment."

"Um, well, I didn't really date. For a long time. I mean since then. That was what you might call a *low point* for me and relationships." I hesitated, creepily aware of all the people who might be watching.

"How did it change your approach to dating?" Sidney asked gently, as if tossing me a lifeline.

"Right, I guess I just stopped. Figured sex was good enough and I didn't have to mess with romance. Which it was, don't get me wrong. Sex is good. Super good." Shit, shit, shit, I could practically hear Mason laughing and shouting, *Drink!* "Um, but yeah, I don't know, it seemed like I wasn't adult enough for romantic relationships so I just didn't go there. Like, other people wanted to go out for fancy dinners and I wanted, I don't know, to stay home and bake cookies together."

Sidney nodded. "That makes a lot of sense to me. It's a frustration I've heard expressed before, that romance as we've constructed it seems alienating on some levels."

"Yeah, like, I don't know how to want things I'm not really into. I mean, marriage is great for the people who want it? But if you want something else, it's harder."

"Okay. Do you consider yourself personally against marriage? Do you think you might eventually find someone you'd want to marry?" They spread their hands out in front of them, an open sort of gesture. "How do you feel about the role of marriage in your life now?"

"Um." I contemplated. Oops. Probably not supposed to have long thinking silences on YouTube.

They cracked a smile. "Only the easy questions, right?"

"Ha, yeah. I haven't thought that much about all this. I know that what I was doing before, six years ago, didn't work that well for me. And I didn't know I could...not do it but keep dating. So then I spent six years not-dating. And now... I don't really know what I want." I made a face. "Um, sorry."

"Don't be sorry, that's perfect. That's what we're conducting The Love Study to find out, right? What you really want."

Were we? Did that make me more of a tool?

They knocked one of their knees against mine below the camera's range and when I looked up, their eyes were bright and clear in the white lights. "Should we move on to the questions?"

"Yeah. Sounds good." I shifted in my chair, ignoring the screen showing me a mirror image of the movement.

"I have a few questions, and I'm sure you all have a few questions. Remember our aim is to find out what Declan's looking for. You've already said all genders and all ages over twenty-one—sorry, young'uns—so tell us something you'd consider a date dealbreaker. Could be anything."

"Fashion glasses," I said promptly.

They grinned.

The show only lasted twenty minutes. I couldn't believe it when I looked at the clock. "I feel like I've been talking in front of that camera for an hour."

"It either feels long or short to people. Sometimes it flies by. Sometimes it drags." They hit the button on the monitor of their computer. "Sorry, if that's up I'll just keep messing with things and watching the comments."

"Oh my god, I forgot about the comments. Are people destroying me?"

They shook their head. "Well, it's YouTube. You always have some percent of people who are doing death threats and rape threats and spewing homophobia. And some percent of people who are glowing adoringly. The middle ground is where things get interesting."

I made a vigorous *go on* motion with my hands.

"People like you. You're charming and attractive and friendly. My brother has accused you of ageism, but he's mostly joking."

"Ohmygodyourbrother?" My whole body contorted totally without my permission.

"He comments as YourSpinsterOwl, which is a nickname I used to call him when he was a baby because his eyes were so big and he watched everything." They waved a hand. "Don't worry, he's eleven and therefore well below your dating pool."

"Aww, he's eleven and he watches the show? That's super cute."

"Yes, it's...one of the reasons I felt I could move. Now that he's old enough to message me and Instagram at me and comment on videos, we won't lose touch. Um. Anyway." Their voice got slightly higher, as if they were flustered. "A rather larger portion of my regulars have volunteered to be your dates, which I probably should have expected but didn't, so that's interesting."

"Hey!" I pinched up my face in comic anger. "You thought people *wouldn't* want to go out with me? That's super cold, Sidney."

Their cheeks colored. "I didn't mean that. I meant, er, the volume of people who specifically volunteered surprised me a little. Not because of you, because of them. Some of them like to pretend they're wizened old cynics, but I think you wooed them with your talk of hating long walks on the beach."

"I like the beach! Listen, I think that was entrapment. I never said I didn't like the beach! Just it's often really windy and sand blows in your face and gets, like, *everywhere*, and sometimes you get cold and want to go inside, so—" I broke off. "Are you *teasing* me right now?"

That smirk again. Oh jeez.

"Maybe a little."

I sat back in my chair and shook my head. "YouTube doesn't see the side of you that gets off on me tying my tongue in knots. You know that only makes me want to provoke you, right?"

"You've only been on one show, I don't think you can say what I show to YouTube."

"Except I've watched a bunch of your videos, so I think I can."

They froze. "Oh. You did?"

"Uh, yeah." Who agrees to go on a show and doesn't watch it? "Do your other guests not watch it?"

"I'm not sure. I didn't think you would."

I wasn't sure how to parse that and didn't want to lose the thread. "Well, I did. So I know a little bit, and I think you hide some of yourself. Which is cool, except I like that. Uh. This. Thing. Wait."

They glanced up. "You like me teasing you? I could *definitely* do that on camera if you wanted."

"Hang on. I think I had the upper hand for a minute here, but I've lost it now."

"I'm pretty sure any impression that you had the upper hand was an illusion. How was it, though? Not too traumatic?"

I almost reassured them without thinking, but forced myself to stop. A lot of people asked questions without being invested in the answers, but if I'd learned anything in the last half hour, it was that Sidney really liked thoughtful answers. "Not traumatic. I guess parts of it were a little...awkward? When I remembered people were watching. But most of the time it felt the way you said, like you and I were talking, which is super happy. Easy. Happy-making. Um." *Mayday, mayday.* "Anyway, I showed you mine, now you show me yours—long walks on the beach? What's your perfect vacation?"

"Oh." They fiddled with their little wireless mouse, also red, like their frames. "A bed-and-breakfast out in the country, somewhere that's not in the US. Lots of space to walk, not too many people. Interesting ruins to explore optional but preferred."

"God, that sounds incredible. Not the big commercialized ruins, though, right? The ones on the side of the road that you walk through feeling almost like you're the first one to ever see it?"

"Exactly. You can have that fantasy that you're going places no one else has gone. Even though you know it's not true, it still sounds compelling to me."

I nodded. "Maybe when you make your first million on YouTube, right?"

"It's on my 'made my first million' bucket list. Travel, afford grad school. The usual things."

A very slightly strained silence fell. Not super strained or anything. For two people who barely knew each other it was pretty comfortable, with just a whiff of strained.

"So," I said. "I guess I'll see you next week?"

"Sure, depending on when you can set up a date."

Jeez, I'd almost forgotten I was going to have to *go on*

dates in order to justify coming back to chat with Sidney each week. Downer.

"I think we should go with transparency," they were saying, "which should be easy enough since your dates will be in some sense generated by the show. I'll set up a basic profile and sort through whoever, um, applies? Signs up? Volunteers? I'm not sure what verb to use here that doesn't make you seem like a fire truck to ride at the state fair."

My jaw dropped.

"Sorry, that was awful. I didn't mean *ride*." When they tried not to smile it kind of softened their face somehow, as if whatever combination of muscles was required to not-smile rounded off the edges of their usual expression.

I made my voice very prim. "I'm not against being ridden."

They sputtered.

Mission accomplished. Now it was my turn to be smug. Sadly, I had nothing clever to follow up with and had to rely on boring logistics. "So you'll just email me and some poor jerk who gets stuck with me for an evening?"

"Why do you think they're a poor jerk? I'm not conning strangers on the street into dating you, Declan. They're volunteering. We don't even have a profile set up yet and people are already in the comments arguing that they'd be good for you."

That was…hilarious? Ludicrous? Batshit? "Um. You, um. Have everything under control?" I'd heard scary things about YouTube comments. And *seen* scary things in YouTube comments.

"I feel relatively confident. I gave this a lot of thought because, essentially, however many people you go out with will know your general location—and mine. But I think a few things are in our favor. You have a car, so you can travel around a bit, which means we can keep your actual home base, um, shrouded in mystery."

"Ooooh. I've never been shrouded in mystery before!"

"I'm sure that's not true. But yeah. I'm going to make suggestions about where to meet people based on what's convenient for them and inconvenient for you, essentially. I probably should have warned you about that in advance, my apologies."

"No, all that sounds good. And I think I should not have sex with people. Sorry, TMI, just I've been thinking that for the purposes of this—of the study, the series—I wouldn't add that into the mix on these specific dates." I couldn't tell by their expression if that was waaaaaay too much information.

"Maybe play it by ear" was all they said. "But we don't have to talk about sex on the show regardless."

"Okay." Was that a *We should not talk about sex on the show*? Or a *We don't have to talk about sex on the show if you, Declan, are uncomfortable talking about sex on the show*? I was usually an open book when it came to sex, but I'd never been on You-Tube before this, so maybe that changed things. "I mean, are there...rules? Like. Will your sponsor flip out if I'm all 'And then I got laid!' Um. Not that I'm going to do that. Just that I want to know if there are rules. I definitely don't want to risk your, you know, professional reputation by me being a dumbass."

"Talking candidly about sex does not make you a dumbass. And no, it wouldn't be an issue for the sponsor at all—I made sure before I started working with them since the tone of the show is sex positive, and you can't be sex positive if you're avoiding all mentions of sex."

"Oh good. Okay, then. Just making sure. Because for real when I have good sex I totally want to shout it from the rooftops like HELLO I MIGHT BE A SEX GOD OVER HERE."

They smiled widely, their eyes crinkling. "You might be a sex god? I'll, um, make a note of that. For the show."

I gulped. Uhhh. Oh god. That seemed flirty. Was that flirty? I couldn't think of anything appropriately flirty-but-not-too-flirty to respond. Shit! Awkward. Since I couldn't think of anything to say, I stood up and, also awkwardly, shifted from foot to foot. They stood too, the smile lingering on their face. A weird impulse seized me and I held out my hand to shake.

They took it.

I gave them one sharp shake, as we had when we'd agreed to never whine about the potential ableism of fashion glasses. "Thanks for hosting the first YouTube video I've ever been on."

"You're a natural. The first time really stretches the walls of your comfort zone, but after that it's easier to relax and enjoy it."

Was that…innuendo? I bit my lip and puzzled over it, but their poker face was amazing.

For about thirty seconds.

They laughed. "Sorry, I couldn't help myself. Thanks for coming on. I'll text you when I've sent the email with name and contact info for lucky date number one."

"Lucky, please. Whoever they are, they should be getting hazard pay for going out with me."

Sidney's eyes narrowed, making them look darker. "I can't tell yet if you believe that or you're trying to be cute and self-deprecating, but I'll figure it out eventually. Good show, Declan."

"Good show, Sidney." I tipped an invisible hat.

They tipped an invisible hat back and walked me out.

Chapter Four

My job is pretty unglamorous. I mean, it's not the *least* glamorous job. It's not like being a sewage worker or something. (Not that I have anything but the utmost respect for sewage workers, but it's not exactly glam, though that would be cool. Imagine those jumpsuit things, but in hot pink with little glitter accents around the cuffs and neckline. That'd raise morale. I guess you'd have to have a variety of colors: hot pink, neon green, gold for the supervisors. Gold might be a good idea, depending on what stuff they're walking around in. I'm just saying. Gold might be a good way to prevent stains from showing.)

Maybe I shoulda been a sewage worker. Or at least a wardrobe consultant for sewage workers.

Instead I pursued a degree in philosophy and worked my way through college doing administrative jobs. Show me a pissy copy machine and I will sweet-talk that thing like nobody's business.

Things I enjoy about working office jobs: offices tend to have a predictable hierarchy and a familiar rhythm. Whether it's a small business with twenty employees, or a huge one with two thousand, sweet-talking copy machines is pretty much the same.

What I especially like about temping at offices: never feeling like I'm trapped in the same desk with the same tasks seeing the same faces hearing the same voices *forever.* I love being able to move around and start new jobs. Not every job is great, but if you're only there a few days or a few weeks, you don't care.

Having said that, I've been shifting around covering different jobs at the same actual business for six months now. I suspect my acting boss keeps switching it up on me so I don't go back to the temp agency and demand reassignment. She for sure knows that I'm not about being a permanent employee because I've been very clear about that.

But Deb has a plan and she's not shy about it. Not in a creepy way. In a "maybe if I give Declan what he wants, he'll finally agree to be a real boy" way. We understand each other. I was convinced that she only kept me on because she liked having another queer around until my friends pointed out that she's the HR director and that's not how HR directors roll. At which point I was forced to acknowledge that it's possible I might be good at my job. All the jobs. All the jobs she's assigned me, anyway.

Somehow she always finds me when I'm eyeing the clock because the Motherfuckers are meeting up for drinks and I need to leave the very second my shift is over. It's as if she's got a sense about when I'm worried about being late and is helping me overcome that fear through exposure therapy. When she tracked me down toward the end of the workday the week after the first episode of The Love Study, I was just finishing up carpet cleaning confirmation calls (yes, that's a thing). I hadn't even known the company did carpet cleaning until I'd moved to cover a maternity leave in this department.

Okay, truth: I ~~have no fucking clue~~ only sort of understand what it is the company does. It's big, there are a lot of departments across three floors of a building downtown, and the only thing I reliably know how to get to is Deb's office, which is in a cluster of cubicles on the middle floor.

And yes, cubicles come in clusters. Like cats.

She walked up to my temporary desk right as I was finishing the final confirmation call, smiling at me as I said goodbye to what sounded like either a very old man or a very old woman (or a very old nonbinary person).

"You're excellent at customer service," she said when I finally put the phone down.

"Don't try to butter me up, Deb. Hey, did Anne get what she needed from—" I waved my hand "—uh, the book restoration place? I meant to ask you last week."

"Origin of Book, yeah, thanks again for that."

"Sure. Glad to help." Deb's partner Anne is basically that scary lesbian professor that you secretly wanted to have sex with just one time because yeah, she was terrifying, but terrifying in a *hot* way. I was genuinely glad to help. Any time you could tell the lion how to get a thorn out of its paw while standing a safe distance away was a total win.

"I'll keep that in mind." When Deb said that it sounded vaguely ominous. "Do you have a minute to talk?"

"Um…sure." Oh, fuck. She was pissed I wouldn't take her up on her offer and she was firing me. No, she couldn't fire me. Getting rid of me. Sending me back into the temp pool. Which was what I wanted! I liked being in the temp pool! Except I also liked working for Deb, and if she was legit going to send me back for not agreeing to work for her for real, maybe I'd been too hasty. I'd thought we were playing. Going back and forth, with her trying to seduce me, and me playing hard to get. It wasn't right that she'd changed the rules and now was going to dump me before we'd even properly consummated our business relationship. This wasn't fair at all.

I opened my mouth to say that but she started talking first and I shut it.

Which turned out to be a *really* good thing.

"We have an event coming up that needs a coordinator. The things I need done are well within the scope of your current duties, but it would be a bigger project than you've ever taken on for me before, and it will require planning over a longer period of time. In all honesty, Declan, I'd need a commitment from you that you'll see it through to the end." As if anticipating my protest—which was in no way coming because I was still realigning from getting the whole thing wrong—she held up both hands. "I'll iron it out with the temp agency, but I wanted to make sure you were on board. It wouldn't be a contract, just a verbal commitment. I trust you to stay if you say you will."

My emotions were in something of a tizzy (technical term). Relief that she wasn't dumping me warred with irritation at that manipulative *I trust you*, which warred with, like, feeling humbled that she trusted me. Deb wasn't blowing smoke up my poodle skirt; if she said she trusted me, it was because she did.

A wildly inappropriate desire to wear a poodle skirt to the next episode of The Love Study just to see Sidney's face intruded into my awareness. I forced it back and focused on Deb.

"How long term?" That seemed like a reasonable question.

"The event is six weeks away."

I nodded. Although the panic was receding, my freak-out response to the idea of being sent back to the temp pool seemed to indicate that I wouldn't mind continuing to work for her that long. "I can commit to six weeks. As long as you square it with the agency."

"It would be a long-term assignment. The first month you'd be covering other positions part of the time and de-voting a certain number of hours a week to the event. The last two weeks at least would be full-time coordination."

"Sounds good."

She ran a hand up the buzzed back of her head and took a deep breath. "After our conversation last week I thought for sure you'd say no."

"I, uh, thought you were dumping me. I was prepared to beg you not to."

"Good god, no. Though I'll file that away for future ref-erence." She leaned back against the wall outside the cubby where I was currently holed up. "You were going to beg me to keep you on, huh?"

"It would take a real bastard to hold that against me, Deb."

She smiled. "How unfortunate for you that I'm a bastard. Oh, and one more thing."

My spidey sense went to red alert. "What's that?"

"I might assign you a staff at some point. I did check with the agency and they said you'd had prior supervisory expe-rience, so that would be perfectly appropriate."

"A staff?" I echoed. My *"prior supervisory experience"* was being lead intern at a literary magazine that only ever had one issue (and it wasn't the one I worked on; they went bank-rupt two months after I got the gig).

"You'll be fabulous. Have a good night, Declan." The woman winked at me. Had the freaking *cheek* to wink at me.

"You too." Because what else do you say?

Chapter Five

The Motherfuckers were meeting up at Mason's apartment. I only realized why when he let me in and called, "Places, places! Everyone find their mark for the reenactment!"

This was to be a Declan roasting. I accepted my glass bottle of sparkling water—they'd spared no expense—and located Sidney in the fracas.

I smiled at them as we hovered in the kitchen while my ridiculous friends giggled and assumed exaggerated poses. "You made it to drinks again."

"I think I was lured here under false pretenses." At my questioning eyebrow, they explained, "Mia promised it would be fun. But now..."

I followed their gaze to where an envelope had been taped to the top of the TV screen. On the envelope, in painstaking block letters, was THE LOVE STUDY. Jackasses. I couldn't help but move slightly closer to Sidney. For the sake of reassuring them, naturally. "I think it'll be fun once we weather the storm. Let them get it out of their systems." They didn't seem convinced and it occurred to me that they might think my friends were mocking the show. "Um, this is totally just them teasing me. They already like you. Well, everyone who's met you likes you and Oscar doesn't like anyone." Shit, this seemed less reassuring than I'd intended. "I just mean they're not *trying* to be jerks."

Sidney's gaze drifted across the room to the TV again before returning to me. "I don't think I'm taking it personally. Still, it's a vulnerable thing, what you're doing. I guess I feel…a little protective." Their eyebrows drew down. "Of the show, you know. And you as an extension of that. Of how I feel about the show."

Oh boy. Sidney felt protective. Of *me*. Like, that was cool. Even though I knew the Motherfuckers had no bad intentions, it was nice that Sidney was thinking about me as a person who was kind of risking something. "Um. Thanks."

"I hope that doesn't seem condescending or anything?" They were full-on frowning now.

"Oh, no, not at all." I wanted to add more, but Mason cleared his throat loudly and said, "Silence in the peanut gallery, please." He glanced around at everyone, all apparently frozen in place. "And, action!"

"I'll never forget where I was when Dec introduced himself to the camera for the first time," Ronnie intoned, half bent over the bowl of chips. "It was a magical moment."

I hid my smile behind the bottle.

Mason raised his hand with the remote and let it hang there. "I'll never forget where I was when Dec blushed bright pink on YouTube for the first time."

Everyone giggled while I did my best not to blush bright pink in Mason's living room. (Not for the first time.) Sidney's arm shifted until it was barely touching mine, and if my friends being embarrassing meant Sidney comforting me, it was a small price to pay.

"My favorite part was when Declan told the whole world he hated the beach and the commenters collectively lost their shit." Mia sighed in reminiscence. "It was a beautiful thing to watch."

Oscar, ever the rule breaker, craned around to look at us. "So, you two. What's going on there?"

Shouts of "Ooooooooh!" and "Oscar, dammit!" filled the room. I took this as a cue that we were allowed to sit down. I climbed over the back of the couch and slid in between Oscar and Ronnie, silently bemoaning the lack of places for Sidney and I to sit together, though when they sat cross-legged on the floor I wished I'd thought of that.

Ronnie patted my leg. "We're just teasing, you looked good. I wasn't sure what to expect but you honestly looked like yourself having a conversation. It was neat, you know? Seeing a Motherfucker on YouTube."

"Let's hear it for Mr. Big Shot!" Mason called, lifting his beer.

"To Mr. Big Shot!" the others cried. Sidney missed the shout, but lifted their Coke in a salute.

I slunk lower in my seat. "Oh, shut your faces."

Oscar poked me. "I can't believe you stepped out into the dating world for five seconds after six years and immediately found someone you liked. You dog."

"I haven't even been on a date yet!"

He rolled his eyes and did an incredibly unsubtle chin-raise in Sidney's direction. "Hello."

I elbowed him and Mia smacked the back of his head. "Quiet, Oscar."

"It's true, though." Mason held out his hand to Oscar for

a fist bump. "I've been out here the whole time and I can't even get a third date."

They shared mutual sighs. Desperately attempting to redirect away from my maybe not that imaginary having-found-someone-I-liked-ness, I reached for my phone to pull up the information about my actual first date. "Excuse me, this is the human I'm going out with this week." I brandished my phone open to the email Sidney had sent as if it was a shield that could protect me (us) from my friends.

Then I realized I might be breaking a Love Study rule and did a wide-eyes silent question in their direction, but they smiled, so I figured it was okay. It was a moot point anyway, since the Motherfuckers were already gathered around my phone like it was a campfire in December.

"Oh, she's cute!" Mia.

"She lists multiple *Call of Duty* games as her favorites, dealbreaker." Oscar.

"She loves *Sword Art Online*, win." Ronnie.

Mase grabbed the phone and read through the whole thing. "Okay, okay, I'm seeing it. Sidney, you think Dec will get along with this woman because she's passionate and has a good sense of humor?" He looked up. "For someone who just met Declan, you sure seem to *get* him. He's totally into passion and laughter."

They nodded, not seeming too weirded out by the fact I'd shared their email with four people without explicit permission. "I'm glad that made sense to you. I wasn't exactly sure how to phrase it."

"Who's not into passion and laughter?" I asked.

Oscar raised his hand.

"You don't count."

"Why? Because you don't want to date me?" He pulled an Extreme Sad Face.

I punched him in the arm. "You don't count because you *try* not to be into passion and laughter."

"What? I am insulted, sir! Weehawken—"

"At dawn!" the rest of us—minus Sidney—cried out.

"Ugh, we're the worst," Mason muttered, falling back into the couch on the other side of Oscar. "How am I ever going to settle down with someone when no one can be expected to put up with the Motherfuckers?"

Mia and Ronnie looked at each other.

He waved a hand in dismissal. "Already tried it."

I reached around Oscar to pat Mase's hand. "Sorry again about that."

"It's fine. I just don't see how anyone who's not us could ever put up with this."

Mia gestured at Sidney. "You've hung out with us a few times. We're nice, aren't we?"

"Sure…"

Dead air. We all looked around at each other.

Sidney laughed. I really liked their sense of humor. And that they were willing to troll the Motherfuckers a little even though they were only just getting to know us. They said, still smiling, "I mean, yes, of course I think you're nice. Or I wouldn't be here. It *is* hard for a lot of people to relax when getting to know the friends of the person they're dating, though. Maybe the key is not to wait so long that it becomes A Thing?"

"Drinks Curse," I said, nodding. "Truth."

Their eyebrows arched delightfully. "*What* is the Drinks Curse?"

Mase leaned forward. "Right, here's what happens, and I guess it's basically all me now that these two are getting married and Oscar refuses to let us meet any of his beaus."

"I *do not* have *beaus*."

"Anyway, I'll be dating someone I like, and I'll think, *Now's the time. Now's when I introduce them to the Motherfuckers.* So I'll invite them to drinks. And within a week, no shit, every time, we'll break up. Drinks Curse." He sat back. "Invite your person to drinks, and you *will* break up. Every. Damn. Time."

Oscar raised his hand. "It happened to me once and that's the last time I tried. It's not my fault you keep expecting a different result."

"Well, what else am I gonna do? Never introduce anyone to you guys? Actually…"

"Fat chance," I told him.

"Do what I plan to do. Take a break from dating and live vicariously through Dec dating on YouTube," Oscar suggested.

Ronnie leaned around me to look at him. "Sorry, had you been dating and I missed it?"

"Bite me."

"Honey, you wish."

"Children!" Mia said.

"Also," Mason mused, looking at my phone again, "well done setting Dec up with a Black gamer girl, Sidney."

Mia rolled her eyes. "She's probably a woman. Unless Sidney has Dec's interests drastically wrong."

"Sorry, I meant woman." He looked up at me. "You know, 'cause you're so into Black folks."

Despite knowing I was playing directly into his tease, I defended myself. Incoherently. "Oh my god, *I am not.* I mean obviously I'm into—I meant I'm not into—I don't *fetishize*—"

"Mason, stop triggering Declan's white insecurity." Mia lowered her voice. "White people are so sensitive."

Everyone laughed but me. Because: still busy sputtering

nonsensical half statements. In front of Sidney. Who was smiling benignly.

Mase, assuming the air of someone taking pity on me (so I was immediately suspicious), said, "Hey, there's some good porn on this—"

I snatched back my phone. "You monster. Don't you dare mock my phone porn. Phone porn is sacred."

Oscar held up his beer. "To the sacred nature of phone porn!"

"Amen!"

"Okay, but seriously, how is this going to go down?" Ronnie twisted to better look at me, then down at Sidney. "You send Dec an email with some random's face and info and Dec calls up the random and makes a date?"

"Excuse me," I interrupted. "First: she's not random. She volunteered. In fact—" I lifted my chin imperiously "—Sidney says a lot of people are interested in dating me."

"A lot of people are interested in being featured on You-Tube," Oscar corrected.

"Hey!"

Ronnie patted my knee. "I'm sure plenty of people are interested in dating you, darling."

"It was actually hard to choose from all the people interested in going out with Declan," Sidney said, riding to my rescue. "There were quite a few."

"See! I'm in high demand."

My friends variously giggled and coughed into their hands.

"And *second*," I continued, ignoring them, "I have already set up a date with #1. We're going out for dinner Friday to some place in Berkeley that's supposed to be not too expensive."

"Ah, yes, always a good sign." Mason nodded sagely. "Prioritizing 'not too expensive' over, say, learning the name of the restaurant."

"Where in Berkeley?"

"And whose idea was the place, yours or hers?"

"Did she seem nice?"

I buried my face in Ronnie's arm. "She seemed nice, I don't know where, her idea because she lives in Berkeley. Do you guys really think people only want to go out with me because I'm going to talk about them on the show?" I appealed to Sidney. "That's not true, right?"

"Not all of them." Oscar considered it. "But probably most."

Sidney shrugged. "There's some danger of that, but overall I'm not concerned. I would feel comfortable saying that most of the people who expressed interest were genuinely into you—or at least the idea of going on a date with you."

"Plus," Mia said, poking Oscar, "Sidney's had this show for three years. They're probably really good at separating the opportunists from the people who are sincerely interested."

"I'd like to think so, anyway."

That sounded reasonable. Right? I looked at them to make sure they were for real, but they were always for real. "Okay. Thanks."

"And the idea—at least my idea—isn't for you to fall madly in love with the first person you go out with. That would be detrimental to the point of the show."

"It would?" I asked meekly. "Are you sure? Because it sounds kind of okay to me."

My friends laughed.

"I just mean that what I really want to dig into is what dating, specifically queer dating, realistically looks like. To counteract some of the less helpful messages I think people receive from this culture."

Ronnie raised her fancy soda water. "That's awesome. I mean, I got super lucky since Mia and I were already friends, but if we hadn't gotten together, I would have had, like, no clue how to date humans."

"This is over-complicating a simple thing," Oscar muttered. "Go to bar, get partially drunk, bring home random, fuck, send them away, and scene."

Mase sighed heavily. "That is *not* dating. But man, I wish that's what I wanted because it sounds relaxing."

"How can bringing home randoms all the time possibly sound relaxing?" Mia did an exaggerated shudder. "Ugh, my nightmare. I'm with Ronnie—if it wasn't for us working out, I'd seriously hate everything about relationships."

I traded looks with Mase and Oscar. "For the record, we're also really happy you guys worked out. We kinda hated everything about your relationships before Ronnie too."

She gasped. "Oh, you'll see how it is having your dates evaluated by the Motherfuckers, Dec. Just wait."

"The Motherfuckers and literally everyone else." Mase rubbed his hands together. "This is gonna be amazing."

Shit, shit, shit. I glanced at Sidney, who raised their eyebrows at me. "I, um…"

"Don't get iffy now, sunshine," Mase said. "You are strapped in to this roller coaster. Dating is the big climb where the thing goes *tick-tick-tick-tick-tick*. If you're super fucking lucky, maybe someday you'll make it to the top and go over the edge."

"Um. Maybe I'm missing something but I'm not super hot on that metaphor."

He did a hand motion of a roller coaster dropping off the edge and crashing into the couch. "That's your future. Welcome to the ride."

Mia kicked him, Ronnie hit him, and Oscar nodded in total agreement. Sidney merely looked back at me and smiled.

Even crashing head first into the couch might not be so bad if Sidney was waiting to hear all about it.

I stayed later than everyone else, helping clean up, enjoying the bone-deep familiarity of Mason's company. I told him about Deb's project and request for a verbal contract.

"Sidney says I'm afraid of commitment."

"Preaching to the choir. I know exactly how afraid of commitment you are, *babe*."

Like I said: have blushed in Mason's living room before. Will do again. "I still can't believe I called you that. I was so nervous. It felt like I was chaperoning a blind date between you and them."

His brow furrowed all disbelievingly. "Wait, what?"

"That was Mia's plan. Fix you up with the first new queer we've met in months."

"Wow. I can't decide if I'm more touched or offended."

I shrugged. "She has good intentions. It's like she has some kind of compulsion to marry everybody off."

He tilted his head to the side and tapped his chin as if deep in thought. "Um, nope. Just me. She never tries to set you and Oscar up with people."

"Yeah, but until five minutes ago I didn't date, and Oscar's..."

"Oscar," he finished. "Well, maybe I don't want to be set up with people."

I waited.

"Okay, I kind of do. Fuck, I don't know. Everything seems hopeless. Maybe if this thing with Sidney works out they can set me up too."

"Oh my god, *there is no thing with Sidney*. Jesus! We did one twenty-minute video and now everyone's convinced we're soulmates! What is that, contagious?"

He eyed me with way too much speculation. "Pardon me," he said delicately. "I meant this thing where they're setting you up with dates. I *meant* if they set you up with someone you hit it off with, maybe they can do the same for me." Then he just looked at me, mouth an unimpressed line.

Oops. I hunched deeper into my chair. "Umsorry."

"Uh-huh."

"I may have jumped the gun there."

"Me thinks the lady doth protest too much. I saw the way you looked at them tonight." He gestured between me and an imaginary floor-sitting Sidney. "You like them."

"No!" I protested. "I mean, yes, I already said I like them. Obviously. I'm not, y'know, pining for them."

"You're crushing on them."

"I'm really not."

His unimpressed lip line got even thinner.

"Maybe just the *slightest tiniest little bit*. But that's it! It's the fun kind of *very minuscule* crush, not the actionable kind."

"Oh, tell me another one, baby boy. Why wouldn't it be actionable? You like them, they like you."

"Listen, you're making too big a deal of this. I'm a guest on their show. It's a professional relationship, not a personal one." Though I couldn't help but think about how they'd said not dating was a guideline, not a rule.

Mason rolled his eyes. "Riiiiight."

I was too lazy to find something to throw at him. "I'd throw something at you but nothing's within easy reach."

"So sad." He glanced at his phone and made a face. "It's late and I'm getting old. You crashing here or going home?"

It was tempting. Mase made really good morning coffee.

"I'm feeling the need to act responsible. And also to wear clean clothes tomorrow."

"Yeah, big change for you, first day of a new work commitment."

I gasped. "How dare you ruin this for me! Calling it a commitment! You need a spanking, mister!"

He stood up for the sole purpose of wiggling his ass in my direction. "Come and get it, Mr. Big Shot."

"Tut tut. Don't try to lure me into your clutches." I dragged myself out of the chair and picked up my sweatshirt. "Thanks for hosting drinks, it was a nightmare of affectionate humiliation."

He kissed my cheek. "Anytime. Text me when you get home."

"A dick pic, right?"

"Maybe just a link to some of that stellar phone porn."

I punched him on my way out the door.

Chapter Six

Date #1's actual name was Destiny, and we met up at the restaurant she'd suggested. She was shortish with a shaved head and she was rocking a pair of rainbow boots I immediately wanted. (A friend had made them for her, but she offered to send me a link to the tutorial they'd used.)

As far as first impressions went, we liked each other and weren't wildly uncomfortable, which meant...so far so good?

I had the gourmet nachos plate, which included roasted red peppers and a cheese I couldn't identify but found ecstasy-inducing. I had to control my mad enjoyment for fear of scaring Destiny, who was handling her food a lot more casually.

First dates are probably universally awkward. I hadn't gone on a lot of them. It wasn't the same in college where people hooked up and maybe that developed into A Relationship, or directly after college in the brief time I'd gone out before Mason and I got all serious.

We did some small talk type questions—where are you from (she was local), what do you do (vet tech), what do you like to do (both of us liked cosplay)—and it wasn't *too* awkward. On a scale of "watching an embarrassing part in a movie and making a face because: awkward" to "watching an embarrassing part in a movie and leaving the room to play Sims until the scene is over because: awkward," small talk with Date #1 was probably right around "squirm a little in your chair but still have the presence of mind to eat more popcorn" awkwardness.

Within acceptable range for a blind date, in other words.

We had more games in common than we did anime, so we laughed about best characters/weapons/lines of dialogue. You can tell a lot about a person by their favorite lines of game dialogue. Destiny's favorite *Overwatch* line was Zenyatta saying, "I am on fire...but an extinguisher is not required."

Mine was the ever-cheery Tracer saying, "The world could always use more heroes." I got the impression from Destiny that this marked me as something of a sap.

Then came the cosplay conversation, which was where things began to deteriorate. Or okay, where *I* began to deteriorate.

Look, I don't show my Princess Leia pictures to just anyone. Well. There was that one time in Walmart, but it was Halloween-related and thus justified. I may also make sure I have them pulled up at Pride, but who doesn't want to be a princess at Pride?

The point is, we were talking about cosplay, and it was totally appropriate to show Destiny my sexy cosplay pictures. And no, I did not go as slave Leia (because Leia's hot, but that whole scene where she's chained up being rape-threatened by Jabba the Hutt is super squicky), but I did find a skintight white bodysuit with a hood to go with my Leia wig. And my gun, of course.

Destiny laughed when I showed her my pictures. "Aww, you look cute as Leia. That wig looks weirdly good on you."

"Right? I legit considered growing my hair out. Then I realized that I'd never have the patience to actually do the double-braids-double-buns thing so there was probably no point." I took back my phone and pushed the last of my nachos to the middle of the table for sharing. "I've shown you mine, now you show me yours. What's your favorite cosplay character?"

"In general? Maybe Jessica Rabbit. I've seen some not-skinny-white-girl Jessica Rabbits who made me want to go there."

"Oh my god, you should! That would be great! But you haven't done it?"

She took a chip and scooped up some black beans and red peppers. "Not yet. I like the challenge of reinterpreting a character who's not meant to be sexy as a more appealing figure. Jessica Rabbit starts there, so it's less of a leap."

"Ohhh. That's really cool. What's your favorite character to do that with, then?" Since she was still paying a lot of attention to the chip, I had the impression maybe she didn't want to tell me. Which was weird? So I did the thing I always do when I get nervous: I rambled. "I mean, not that I'm asking for sexy cosplay pictures of you at all. Obviously. Because I wouldn't. Photographs not required! I was just wondering how you'd done that in the past because I've never thought about it and now that you've said it I'm intrigued. Like, I guess you can probably pick any character and sexify it? Not in a creepy way, but in a sort of reclaiming way, or an interpretation, like you said. I'm sure you wouldn't be able do that with children's characters or something because that would definitely be problematic but probably with most characters there would be some opportunity to kind of play with how you were portraying them to change the way they were, you know, portrayed." I cringed and shoved another chip in my mouth. *Stop. Talking.*

"A friend of mine did sexy Splinter once," she said after a minute. "From Ninja Turtles."

Still feeling self-conscious, I managed to say that sounded cool.

We picked at the last of my nachos in awkward silence.

What if she thought I'd been asking for sexy pictures of her? That was awful. "I really wasn't pushing for pictures. I mean. If that's…how it seemed."

"No, I got that. I just don't want to talk about how I cosplay."

"Okay." Because what else was I going to say? On the one hand, why was it a big deal to tell me how she cosplayed? Then again, if my argument was it's no big deal, then why couldn't I let it go? Plus, maybe it *was* a big deal. In which case she should totally not share it unless she wanted to.

And I was being a big jerk about that decision.

Ugh.

"Um, so, any other favorite lines? I once melee'd the hell out of someone as Mercy and she said, 'You might not want to tell your friends about that,' which I thought was hilarious."

Destiny looked up. "Have you heard D.Va say, 'Boom shakalaka! She's on fire!'?"

"Oh my god, no, but now I seriously want to."

"I think I hear it once every fifty hours of gameplay or something, but it's really funny when she says it."

We went back to talking about games for the rest of the nachos.

This time I wasn't *almost* late for The Love Study. I was literally late.

"Sorry, sorry, sorry," I mumbled to Sidney as they let me in. "I swear I'll be on time next week."

They didn't seem at all perturbed by me walking in three minutes later than we were supposed to start filming. "No biggie. I once forgot an entire show when I first started livestreaming; being a little late won't hurt anyone. Everything's ready to go."

I shrugged my bag and jacket into a pile beside the door and slid into the chair I'd been in last time. My mirror image slid into a chair on the screen. Sidney's image slid into their chair.

"Ready?"

"Ready." Still kind of panting from running down the block, but sure, ready.

They smiled at me before hitting record and turning toward the camera. "Welcome to The Love Study. The series about love, dating, and the pursuit of queer companionship in a bleak and hopeless world. I'm your spinster uncle Sidney, and this is my series co-host, and our volunteer for the dating trenches, Declan."

"Ooooh, we have an intro," I said without thinking. Then I winced. "Sorry, forgot we were, like, live."

"What do you think of the intro? I'm trying it on." A glance at the camera. "Comment your thoughts." Back at me. "Does that accurately represent your pursuit? I meant to run it past you before we started."

"Then I was super late." I experimented by also looking into the camera. "Um, sorry I was late. I haven't worked out the best way to get here from my job yet." Shit, was that okay? I did *ahhhhhh*-eyes at Sidney and they chuckled.

"You weren't that late. But the intro?"

"Um, yeah, I definitely feel like I'm pursuing queer companionship. I hope that doesn't come off anti-het. I'm not against dating straight people!"

"I think it is possible to queer relationships even when

straight cis people are involved in them." I couldn't tell if they were teasing, but I thought the smirk was threatening again. "Should we get to it? You had your first date of The Love Study this week."

"I did!"

Sidney smiled and their smile did that weird thing again where it made me feel all warm and fuzzy. "I came prepared with questions, but I thought you could start by telling us a little about it. No names, of course."

"Totally agree on the no names part. It was…it was good…"

"I feel like I should have flashback sequence music to cue up for this moment."

I shot them a mock glare.

"Maybe start by telling us what went well?"

"Right. Okay. I'll… I'll do that. So our dinner was, like, really delicious…"

DATE #1: NERDY GAMER GIRL WHO WOULDN'T TELL ME WHO SHE COSPLAYS AS

I sketched out a little bit about meeting Destiny and the acceptable level of awkward. "Then came the cosplay conversation, which was where things began to deteriorate. Or, okay, where *I* began to deteriorate."

Sidney cleared their throat, bringing me back to the show. "I've heard a lot of things, but I'm not sure I've ever heard anyone cite talking about cosplay as a reason for a date going wrong."

"Not cosplaying in general! And it didn't go wrong so much as…get briefly tense? Which I think, with the benefit of hindsight, was entirely my fault. The date itself I would categorize as pretty good." I looked into the camera. "Seriously, Date #1, if you're watching, I think we had a good time. Right? Uh, don't comment. I mean, obviously do if you want to, but if you don't, that was a rhetorical question."

"Have you cosplayed before?" Sidney asked.

"A few times, with friends." I batted my eyelashes at them. "I make a very fetching Princess Leia."

They laughed. "Do you have a hairpiece of some kind for that?"

"Yes! I even bought a Princess Leia wig, with the two side buns."

Sidney, eyes still full of mirth, said, "Declan, you have hidden depths."

I flushed at the roughly ninety-three dirty jokes my brain popped up in response. "Umm…" *Say something, make a sentence, any sentence that is NOT about your "hidden depths."* Was all of YouTube making jokes about my ass right now? Probably not, right? "Anyway, I'm all for cosplay, but after I shared my Princess Leia story—and I might have, uh, offered photographic evidence—Date #1 totally refused to reciprocate with cosplay stories. Okay, no, sorry, she did talk about cosplay, but she wouldn't show me any pictures or tell me about her favorite characters and obviously that's her choice but I don't know, it made me feel weird."

"Because you had already shown her a picture of yourself?"

"Umm." Was it better or worse to say *Umm* instead of sitting there like a lump on live YouTube? "I guess I just figured we'd both be kind of sharing? And then it felt like we weren't."

"Ah yes. A vulnerability clash in which one person has shared more than the other and feels uncomfortably exposed." They nodded. "That's a familiar conflict."

It was a little disconcerting to have my seemingly irrational weirdness about not being told someone's favorite cosplay character so breezily diagnosed. "It wasn't exactly a *conflict*."

"An imbalance, then?"

"…maybe?"

"How did the date go on from there?"

"Well, I guess I was…more miffed than really made sense. Which I didn't do a very good job at hiding." I glanced toward the camera again. "Uh, I'm really sorry, Date #1. Apparently I was feeling vulnerable after showing you my sexy Leia outfit. Anyway, it didn't end badly, at all. I don't think there were mad sparks in either direction, but I could see us being Xbox friends and playing *Overwatch* together."

Sidney nodded. "That seems like a positive outcome for meeting a stranger. I thought it might be helpful if we end each episode with the same three questions, in order to have a standard sort of metric by which to judge each date."

"Give 'em to me."

Another little quirk of their lips. "Question one, if you're comfortable rating this: Did you feel you had physical chemistry?"

"Yeah. She was super cute and she didn't seem to find me repulsive, so yes. Wait, do we have an actual scale?"

"Say, one to five."

"Okay, I'd say four. With five being, like, *I was so powerfully attracted to them that I couldn't stop thinking about touching them.*"

"And one being *Find them repulsive?*"

"Exactly."

We smiled at each other.

"Question two: Was there intellectual chemistry?"

"Oooh." I paused to think about what it meant to have intellectual chemistry with someone. "I think so? We like a lot of the same stuff, I guess."

"I'm trying to get more at a sense of…being interested in

the same aspects of things even if you're not interested in the same actual things." Sidney straightened their keyboard and brushed a piece of lint away from the space bar, which seemed weirdly fidgety for them. "Like, you can read the same book as someone and still not be intrigued by the same themes. But I think if you have intellectual chemistry you're more likely to be intrigued by similar themes, even if your scope of experience with those themes is different." They frowned. "I thought I had a whole concise explanation for this but it sounds confusing now that I've said it out loud."

"No, I think that makes sense. And actually, maybe not that much?" I considered the *Overwatch* conversation again. "In a way I'm more into character interaction, even in first-person shooters, than I am in the actual shooting. And she's big into killing all the creatures, which is cool, but it's less likely to bring me back to a game than it is a lot of people."

They mimed wiping sweat off their brow. "It seems like you somehow managed to understand what I was trying to say."

"I get it. So on intellectual chemistry, I'd say maybe a two."

"The last question is one I think you've already answered, but let's do it officially: Would you go out on a second date?"

I shrugged. "Date, no. Game, yes."

"Thank you, Declan, for offering your dates up as fodder for our better collective understanding of dating." They turned to the camera. "And thanks to all of you for tuning in to our second episode of The Love Study here on Your Spinster Uncle."

They went into a detailed description of the services offered by the company that was sponsoring the show, and I had to admit, it sounded intriguing. Being able to do therapy without leaving your house was a cool idea and there was an app and a sliding scale and everything. (Which I learned from the ad-read as they talked.) I tried to look politely interested, which I was, so at least that was pretty easy.

"As always, find all the show's social links in the description box, like this video to give us a boost, subscribe to Your Spinster Uncle to find out when new videos are posted, and you can always send your questions in by email. We will schedule another live phone show soon. Thanks for watching and I will spinster at you more next time." They clicked the record button and the little LIVE red dot disappeared.

I waited through the rest of the administrative bits to posting or whatever, studying the apartment. The walls were blank, whether because Sidney didn't hang stuff or because they hadn't had the time since moving, I didn't know. The only picture in the whole place was a frame on the desk of a grinning kid with light brown skin and big dark eyes, who I assumed was the little brother.

The window had a dark shade over it, which I figured was for filming. Outside the bright lights trained on us the rest of the apartment looked a bit dim. The screens still kept what I assumed was a bed closed off (there wouldn't have been room for much more than that), but there were two chairs wedged in between the recording area and the screens with a small rug I could barely see from my spot at the desk. The chairs were armchairs, but small ones. That was the sort of thing Ronnie or Mason might know: what to call a certain type of chair.

Whatever they were, they looked cozy.

"Sorry, one more minute," they said, scrolling through comments. "Uh-oh. They're going feral on me again."

"What does *that* mean?"

They shook their head and turned off the monitor. "Any time I have a likeable guest on more than once, they decide that guest is my one true love. I don't know if you plan to

read the comments, but if you do, just ignore them. They'll
stop eventually."

I couldn't help wondering what that meant. "How, um,
how do they express this fascination?" *And are you repulsed?*
Not that I thought I was anyone's one true anything, but I
couldn't get a read on if they found the idea of me magneti-
cally repelling or what.

"Ship names." They sighed.

"No. Way."

"Oh yes. In my extremely cursory look it appeared that
Sidlan was beating out Decney. For good reason."

"*Deck-knee.* Oh my god."

"Yep." They gestured wryly at the monitor. "Behold my
public. But seriously, ignore them and they'll eventually stop.
Well, most of them will. Arman—" a gesture at the picture
"—will probably keep it up indefinitely."

"That's your brother, right? I mean, I assumed."

"My little owl, yeah." They ran their thumb across the top
of the frame. "Anyway, don't worry about the commenters."

I was way more interested in their brother, honestly, but
I didn't want to get too personal if they...weren't. "It seems
a little, I don't know, bothersome? That people try to ship
you against your will."

"If I were, say, aromantic, I'd find it problematic. But I'm
not, so it's more that they're teasing. Do you want a bottle
of water or something? You did a lot of talking."

As if it took them saying it for me to notice, I was suddenly
aware of my dry throat. "That would be great." I followed
them into the little kitchenette. "How long have you been
doing videos? I think maybe Mia mentioned it but I forgot."

"Three years. Three and a half now." They pulled two
bottles of water out of a refrigerator that seemed to hold

mostly bottles of water and vegetables in various states of decomp and gestured to the seating area.

Yay, I'd graduated to the comfy chairs.

They settled into the chair facing the kitchen, so I took the one facing the window. Obviously both chairs were, more importantly, facing each other. Today Sidney had on rainbow suspenders over a purple T-shirt with a skinny black scarf around their neck.

I forced my brain away from rating our physical chemistry on a one-to-five scale and focused on what they were saying.

"I'd been watching genderqueer and nonbinary people on YouTube for a while and I liked those videos, but I didn't want to do a gender channel. For one, I don't feel as though I have anything to say about gender that's not already being said far better by other people. And for two, sometimes I wanted to see a genderqueer person talking about something *else*, you know? I realized I was GQ years ago. It's great that so many people are processing it in real time on YouTube, but I don't need to do that anymore."

I nodded, thinking about the Marginalized Motherfuckers. "Like processing is a stage, and then you move on?"

"I wish it were that linear. But you process in different ways as you move on, I think. More than you just stop needing to process. Anyway, I had a group of friends in college who called me the spinster uncle and it kind of made sense to build the channel around that idea."

"That's really cool. I mean, obviously it's worked out for you." I let that trail off a little in case they wanted to disagree.

"It's been incredibly rewarding. I've made tons of connections with other trans folks, binary and nonbinary, and other queers, so I'm always happy I posted my first terrible video. I wouldn't keep doing it if no one watched. It takes a ridiculous amount of time to record and edit videos, even now that I'm a lot better than I used to be at not stumbling over my words. The live videos are a bit of a relief from that, though then you don't get a chance to revise your answer to a question."

"I would be terrified to do that. To answer questions without a buffer. I mean other people's questions, like for advice." I shivered a little just thinking about it.

"And here I was going to ask if you wanted to do a call-in episode with me. You can always come to hang out and provide a dynamic interaction. No pressure to answer anything if you don't want to. Or, of course, you can say no. Either way."

A lot of people said they'd be okay with you not wanting to do something but they were secretly not okay with that. Sometimes I was one of those people, because it was sort of aspirational, saying, *You can always say no.* I definitely wanted to be okay with that, but I couldn't always control whether it hurt my feelings a little.

But when Sidney assured me sincerely that I could say no, I completely believed they wouldn't hold it against me.

"I think that might be fun." Being with Sidney in any context was likely to be fun. "As long as you don't hit me with tough questions."

They held their right hand to their heart. "I solemnly swear I will not ask you any tough questions. Your first time, anyway."

"Ah, the fine print! I suspected this was a trick."

They smirked. "Yes, I have a dastardly plan to keep you coming on my show for a long time. The videos with guests get higher views, more ad clicks, and therefore more money."

I covered up my legit *ouch* feelings by pretending to have been shot. "Right in the ego. Here I thought you were having me on because we have intellectual chemistry."

"Oh, we do. I wouldn't propose a series with someone I didn't have intellectual chemistry with." They frowned. "Sorry, did I make it sound like I only want you for financial gain? That's definitely not true. We have a shocking amount of intellectual chemistry. I mean, in my opinion at least."

All the saliva in my mouth dried up. I needed to talk. Say something. Anything. Respond. To what they'd said. Except my mouth was too dry.

"Um, right, so do you want to see who you're going out with this week?" They sounded awkward and a bit self-conscious, like they were also thinking about how they legit just said they wanted me.

My brain whirred in chaos for a moment until I remembered to answer their question. "Um, sure." But seriously, we had intellectual chemistry, hooray! I wondered how much. I'd put it in the four-to-five zone. How much intellectual chemistry did Sidney need to have with someone before inviting them on the show? A three?

"And sent."

Sent? Oh right. I pulled out my phone and obligingly checked my email. White guy, maybe a little older than me, clean shaven, short hair, shirt and tie. "Wow, he's very…conventionally handsome."

"I tried not to hold that against him."

I glanced up. "You don't like conventionally handsome people?"

They shifted, pulling one knee up into the chair and kind of hugging it. "I feel ambivalent about conventionally handsome people on a personal level, but I do think conventional appearances leave something to be desired on both political and imaginative levels."

"Oh." I surveyed my own boring work costume.

"Dude." They eyed me pointedly. "You were wearing sequined ballet flats when we met."

"Oh my god, those shoes are *so uncomfortable*, but they make me so happy!" Hello: they'd noticed my shoes. Hello, hi, that totally happened. Add a point to the *Sidney's not physically repulsed by Declan* column.

"Consider what picture you would submit if you were volunteering to go on a blind date with someone. Would you be wearing your work clothes?"

"Oh, no, definitely not." I paused to consider it. "Lime green T-shirt over a black thermal, jeans, beaded rainbow bracelet, and I'd spend an hour making my hair artistically mussed." I bowed in my seat. "There you have it."

"You should take that picture, it sounds—um—unconventionally handsome. But anyway, the thing that won me over about Date #2 was that he self-describes as 'a queer man trying to forge a path through the warring expectations of gay culture.' Which I thought was rather poetic."

"Aww. Yeah. Totally is. Okay, sweet. I'll get in touch with him." I put the phone away. "Thanks for arranging the actual human component of this. I'd still be going back and forth about even attempting to date if it was all up to me."

One of their eyebrows twitched above their glasses. "You could always set Mia on the case. I'm sure she'd love to find your one true love."

I groaned. "You have no idea. Dear Spinster Uncle, how do I make my friend stop trying to marry everyone off? Love, Declan."

"I've addressed that question before. I'll send you a link."

"It's that common?"

They shrugged. "Alas, the marriage contagion, once limited to heterosexuals, has now infected the queers as well.

There's no known treatment for this malady, but in most cases it does eventually run its course."

"Thank god for that." I raised my water bottle. "To Mia's speedy recovery."

We toasted.

Chapter Seven

Date #2's real name was Gregory. Not Greg, he assured me. Gregory.

Maybe that was the first warning sign, but I didn't notice it at the time.

The first very slight tingle that this date might be a mismatch was when he picked the restaurant and the movie he wanted to take me to.

And he said it like that: "I want to take you to dinner and a movie."

Which I probably should have been into, but I...wasn't. There's this funny tension where people are supposed to be proactive and say what they want, but sometimes that can have the effect of sort of...erasing what the other person might want or think about that thing.

Sometimes it doesn't. Mase and I got together because one night in college when we were walking home from eating dinner he turned to me and said, "I want to kiss you right now." Which was completely hot and I giggled and he kissed me and I kissed him and we kept kissing (not like continuously, but when it was convenient) for years.

So I don't find having a bold partner a turn-off. Like at all. But Gregory delivered the line about taking me to dinner and a movie like it had never occurred to him that I might not be into that. He was stating it as if it was simply how things were going to be, which was emphatically not a turn-on.

Also, I don't think there's much point to going to movies on blind dates because you're not really getting a feel for the other person. Not that I have well-developed notions about what does and doesn't work for blind dates, since this was only my second one, but it never made much theoretical sense to me.

And in practice it was *worse*.

We went to see an independent film that wasn't bad. It wasn't good. For me it was a flat line of vaguely interesting scenery and characters, with a plotline that didn't seem to go anywhere.

Gregory *loved* the movie. And that's another reason movies don't seem like great things for first dates. If I'd gone with a friend, and they loved a movie I thought was mostly blah, we could talk about that. But with a stranger you're stuck either A) not disagreeing too strongly because after all, they might have connected to the movie on some level you can't even fathom because you don't know them. Or B) disagreeing carefully at first, then progressively getting more emphatic as you argue with a total stranger over a movie you probably don't care that much about.

Maybe there are other options, but those were the only ones I saw, so I attempted to go with option A. After five straight minutes of enraptured monologue on how amazing this mediocre film had been.

"...and then, the scene with the corn field, that huge expanse of sameness into the horizon." His fingers tapped the steering wheel restlessly as if he was so passionate about the movie he couldn't contain himself. (I made a mental note to never ever ride with a blind date again.) "The way they expressed the tension between conformity and risk was incredibly poignant."

Um. Or they had no money to film and were stuck with a corn field? "I'm not sure I got all that out of it? I definitely felt like they were...working with some of those themes... but for me it didn't quite go all the way." I didn't exactly know what I meant, but it sounded noncommittal, which was my goal.

"Really." No rising question at the end of it.

"I guess it just wasn't my thing."

"I'm sorry I brought you to a movie you didn't enjoy," he said stiffly.

"It's okay!" *Though for the record maybe collaboratively picking a movie with your date might achieve better results than proposing one and halfheartedly adding, "Unless you'd rather see something else..."*

That was it. Silence until the restaurant, which was thankfully not that far away. He might have been doing the same thing I was doing? Not arguing over something dumb on a first date? But it felt more like since I didn't agree with him that the movie was wonderful he punished me by falling into silence. But that was probably just me being paranoid. Maybe.

Anyway.

All that happened before we even got to this very nice, upscale restaurant, where he not only held the door open for me but also pulled my chair out so I could sit down.

Which was fine? Except it felt awkward and forced and like I'd stumbled into a stage play called *Dating For Men, 1956*.

And *then* he told me he'd be paying and I could get whatever I wanted.

Which is pretty much when I gave the whole thing up as a lost cause. I got the cheeseburger, which had bleu cheese and bacon and caramelized onions and oh my god it was *amazing*. The highlight of the date was that burger.

We spoke somewhat civilly through dinner but I was relieved when he dropped me off at my car. I didn't want to text Sidney with all the details because obviously we were going to talk about it on the show, but I also felt a serious need to be like OH MY GOD YOU WERE RIGHT ABOUT THIS DUDE.

I texted, *You could have held conventionality against this one. #NoSpoilers.*

After which I ~~dawdled hoping they would immediately reply~~ took off my jacket and folded it neatly in the passenger seat, deliberated on what the right soundtrack for Lousy First Date Recovery was (Melanie Martinez won), thoroughly warmed up my car until I needed to roll down a window—

My phone buzzed. My heart did a triple axel.

Oh no! That bad? No, probably don't tell me.

Buzz.

Sorry, Declan! I feel terrible. Maybe I could distract you or something to alleviate my guilt.

Dammit. Why hadn't I waited until I was home to text them? Then we could be having this conversation while I was getting into my flannel PJs and doing other before-going-to-sleep things.

Not *that*. Brushing my teeth! I meant brushing my teeth!

I sent back, *Don't feel bad! It'll be good for the show, having a "bad date" to compare other dates to.*

Them: *That is not my intention.*

Me: *Oh, I know. Of course it's not. But still, it's nice thinking that at least it will have some use as a bad date.*

Them: *Okay. Well, I'm glad it's helpful. But I am sorry about the date. What are you calling this one?*

I contemplated it. *Maybe… Conventionally Handsome Guy Who Likes Pretentious Movies? Or no, that sounds judgey.* I hit send.

Them: *You went to a pretentious movie? I'm sorry SQUARED.*

Damn. I really wanted to keep talking to them. But I also really wanted to, you know, drive home. And it was too soon in our friendship for me to dictate texts. You have to build up to the kind of intimacy that forgives things like *I ducking ate lip gloss.* (It was meant to say, *I fucking hate your boss,* and since I'd sent it to Ronnie after we'd been friends for years, she knew what I meant. Eventually.)

I stared at my phone, willing it to solve my dilemma.

My…phone. Um. Huh. It felt too soon to talk on the actual phone. Was it? We weren't dating. Were there friendship rules about such things? The only people I ever talked to on the phone were my parents and Mia. Mia was huge into the phone. In this situation she'd just say, *Can we call? I'm driving.*

I typed out the message. Then revised it to, *Can we call? I haven't driven home yet.*

And stared at it.

Was this a big thing? It felt big. Then again, I'd spent the last few hours second-guessing whether or not I was an asshole for disliking a dislikeable movie, whether I was weird for not wanting my chair pulled out, and whether Gregory would incorrectly interpret my enjoyment of my burger as enjoyment of our date.

Screw it. Sidney would probably forgive me if I was violating some unspoken social regulation by proposing a phone call.

I hit send. Thus initiating one of the most Sidney-and-me exchanges ever.

Them: *Oh, I'm sorry! I figured you were home. I don't want to distract you while you're driving.*

Me: *I haven't started driving yet. But I…probably should.*

Them: *I'm sorry, I'll leave you alone.*

Me: *No! I mean, you don't want to call?*

Them: *I don't want you to feel obligated to make me feel better for setting you up with a pretentious date.*

Me: *I don't feel obligated! I just thought…um… I just kind of wanted to talk to you for a few minutes? BUT YOU DON'T HAVE TO.*

I gnawed on my lips, willing the phone to buzz. It didn't. It rang.

"Hi," I said, like a dumbass.

"Hi. Sorry. About the date and the awkwardness and keeping you from your bed. Basically everything." Their voice was hard to read without visual cues.

"Omigod, don't be. It's totally okay!" I turned off the heat, put the phone on speaker, and made sure the volume was up as high as it would go. "And the date wasn't, like, traumatic or anything. It was just kind of blah."

Pause. I pulled carefully out into traffic, waiting for them to say something.

"I want to know everything that happened, but I'm trying to restrain myself because I want my questions on the show to be *pure*, like I have no preconceived notions or expectations."

"Yeah, same. It'll probably be better to hash it out on the show."

They made a noise. A snort? A giggle? "Oh, hashing. Sounds fun."

Which...might have been flirtatious? Dammit, I wanted to see their face! "It could be fun, but also, I don't want The Love Study to turn into me bitching about people. I'll have to be, like, *measured* about it."

"I think we can do that. I mean, you can, but I can help."

"Thanks. So, um. What're you doing tonight?"

"I'm listening to a podcast about chocolate while I clean up old videos."

"Ooooh. What does that mean?"

They explained a little bit about hashtags and YouTube changing algorithms, and end cards, and other interesting behind-the-scenes stuff I had no idea existed.

"Hashtag-Sidlan is one of the most popular comments on The Love Study videos. I'm not kidding."

"Wow. They...are they missing the point a little?"

"That depends on what you think the point is. For a generation still watching Disney movies well into their twenties, the point might actually be for you to live happily ever after in partnered bliss, in which case I suppose they're pursuing that goal with the means they have available."

I laughed. "And that means is YouTube comments?"

"It's making me happy I never started a Twitter account. Though there has been some...um... I guess you'd call it 'fan art' on Instagram."

"Holy shit. Of us?"

"Don't look. Swear to me you won't look. It's ridiculous. I'm ignoring them."

I tried not to giggle, but it was one of those times when not giggling turned into explosive giggling turned into *might have to pull over because I can't see for tears* laughter.

"I…did not predict this response," Sidney said after a minute. This time I was pretty sure they were smiling.

"Sorry! I'm sorry. Some of this is pent-up date energy, probably. But oh my god, there is *fan art*. No one's ever made fan art of me before."

"You can no longer say that."

"Wow. That is…wow. I don't even know how to…wow." I wiped my eyes and pulled, with some relief, into my landlord's driveway, parking off to the side where the gate to the backyard was.

"It's absurd. They know they're being nuts, but I'm honestly not sure they can help themselves."

I thought Sidney was still amused by my laughter, but I couldn't tell how much of their protest was about how silly their fans were, and how much was about how silly the very idea of us being together was. I…hoped it was more the former than the latter. But Sidney was so deadpan it was really hard to tell.

"Fan art." I made a big deal out of sighing happily. "*Sidlan* fan art. Wow."

"I'm pleased you don't find it disturbing. There are some distinctly strange aspects to this business, and the presumed accessibility of YouTubers is one of them for me."

"Well, *I'm* not a YouTuber. I just play one on YouTube." I gathered up my jacket and my messenger bag, locked the car, and walked the little gravel path through the backyard to my tiny in-law unit. "I'm home. But I'm super happy we talked."

"I am too. Though I'm sad it was inspired by a lousy date with, uh, Pretentious Guy."

"I'll come up with a better stock photo description for him," I promised. "So I guess…" It's not like I wanted to get off the phone with them. But I did need to do stuff.

Then again, I was probably just going to put on a movie. "Are you busy?"

"Not really. Finishing up work for the night."

"Do you…um…have any interest in buddy watching something? I was going to put on a documentary about divers exploring a shipwreck. I mean, if you have Netflix. Or I could give you my login info. Or not! Totally feel free to say no. Just thought I'd throw it out there in case that sounded good to you." I bit down on my lip and forced myself to continue going through the motions of a normal human just home from a date: hanging up my jacket, toeing out of my shoes, biting my lip so hard it hurt, gripping my phone so tightly my hand shook, you know, *the usual*.

"Oh. Um."

Shit! "We don't have to, no worries, forget I said anything."

"No, that sounds… I mean, I've never done that before. But I'm up for trying."

I explained buddy watching somewhat more enthusiastically than was necessary and Sidney agreed to give it a shot. By then I'd managed to splash water on my face and change my clothes, so I curled up in bed (and hoped they were also curled up in bed, though I didn't want to be a creeper and ask).

I had way more fun during the hour and a half we spent watching a slightly out of sync documentary than I had the entire rest of the night. There was a lot of squealing (me) and exclaiming (them) variations on OH MY GOD DO YOU SEE THAT? and AHHHHH WHAT IF IT BREAKS? when the crew was hauling sunken treasures out of the wreck.

Intellectual chemistry: clearly a five. Not that anyone was counting. Because #sidlan was not a real thing. But just in case I ever needed to rate our intellectual chemistry, I felt very confident doing so. Five all the way down.

Chapter Eight

The weekend flew by, which was fantastic because my standing The Love Study date with Sidney was becoming the highlight of my week.

Not, obviously, that it was a real date. I meant date in the sense that we had a *day* we knew we'd spend time together. In a casual way. A mundane non-date way. Like you have a standing date with your therapist. Wait, no. More like you have a standing date with your personal trainer. Actually, that doesn't work either.

Whatever. On Mondays after work I went to Sidney's apartment and I looked forward to it the rest of the week.

For the third episode of the series I even managed to get there with ten whole minutes to spare. I could tell they were surprised because they seemed flustered to be interrupted in the middle of their setting-up process.

"You brought me chocolates?" They shook their head as

if they were shaking something out of it, the way a little kid shakes a piggy bank. "I mean, us? Are we eating chocolate tonight?"

I brandished my fancy-looking-but-really-from-Grocery-Outlet chocolates. "For you! You said you were listening to that podcast and then I saw them and thought of you. Plus, you're hosting, so technically I should bring a thing, right?"

They looked at me blankly. "I've only ever offered you a bottle of water."

Oh my god, this was excruciating. I could feel my cheeks heating up. Starting the show with a playful gesture totally rebuffed. I'm not mortified, *you're* mortified. "Do you not like chocolate?"

"I like dark chocolate." They were standing very still, eyes on the box in my outstretched hand.

I sighed and tossed the box of chocolates on the kitchen shelf. "I got a mix. You can throw them away if you want, just do me a favor and wait till I leave." Then I pushed through and busied myself fumbling around in my bag and perfectly piling my stuff in the usual place. Being late was apparently the key to not screwing up this whole thing. Good to know.

"I'm sorry," they said from behind me. "The chocolates are...look delicious, thank you. Maybe we can have some after the show? I did a whole livestream once with chia seeds in my teeth, so I don't eat right before streaming anymore."

I turned. "No, but for real, how can you eat chia seeds? That shit is *alien*."

They smiled a little weakly. "I know. I think that's why I like them. There's a sense of wrongness about them that resonates with me."

I experienced this terrible urge to hug them or comfort them or something, which I forced down beneath the humiliation of bringing an unwanted gift to a friend. My brain was super confused about how it felt. "Don't worry about the chocolates, seriously. It's no big deal."

"Let's open them after we do the show." They went behind the desk and started (or maybe resumed) doing stuff at the computer, but leaning over, not sitting down. It seemed strangely unguarded, like the kind of thing they'd do if no one else were there.

My meters were all scrambled from the unwanted chocolates calamity so I couldn't get a good read on whether or not I should sit down. The alternative being to hover awkwardly. "Can I grab a bottle of water? Is that okay?"

"Sure. They're in the fridge."

"Want one?"

"Please."

There's something intimate about looking in a person's refrigerator. I couldn't help but notice that last week's batch of dead and decaying vegetables had been replaced by a bag of wilting spinach and some very flaccid looking carrots. "Um, Sidney? What's up with the produce graveyard?"

They groaned. "I know. I keep thinking I'll do salads or something. Then I don't. And everything turns to mush. The thing is, I really enjoy salads in a restaurant. They're complex and interesting. But I cannot get it up to make a good salad at home. It always ends up being some greens with oil and vinegar on top."

"I think the key to home salads is prep. If you have everything ready to go, you're more likely to make a salad. And it's more likely to be delicious."

"That makes perfect sense." They gestured to the chair beside them. "You ready?"

I handed them their bottle of water and opened my own, so I wouldn't have to do it on video. Just in case it was a stubborn one. Sidney's second chair was beginning to feel like *my* chair, as in, *I sat down in my chair.* That was probably a danger sign of some sort. I put it out of my head while they hit record and did the intro.

"Welcome to another episode of The Love Study. The series about love, dating, and the pursuit of queer companionship in a bleak and hopeless world. I'm your spinster uncle Sidney, and this is my co-host, and our volunteer for the dating trenches, Declan."

I waved at the camera. "Hellooooo."

"So, Declan. You went on your second date in six years."

"I did!"

"Is it like riding a bike?"

"Not exactly. I mean, I didn't really do *this* when I was younger. It's definitely different than dating in college. And I hooked up with my ex when we were like...twenty-one? So I'm a lot older now, which changes things."

Sidney nodded. "I can only imagine it would. Do you want to tell us a little about Date #2?"

"That's why I'm here! Let's do it."

DATE #2: CONVENTIONALLY HANDSOME GENTLEMAN WHO WAS MAYBE *TOO* CHIVALROUS

I spilled the whole date out for Sidney (and the folks at home) like someone who's waited too long to go to the doctor so when they finally do they recite fourteen years' worth of complaints all at once, finally ending with, "So anyway, I got the cheeseburger, which had bleu cheese and bacon and caramelized onions and oh my god it was like *amazing*. The highlight of the date was that burger. For sure." I sat back and took a deep breath.

"Okay," they said. Their expression had gone through

many flavors of contrition and displeasure, but had settled in familiar YouTube-persona neutrality. "All right, um... are you all right?"

"Yeah, sure. No harm no foul. Other fish in the sea or whatever." I was getting tired of my own voice so I took a sip of water.

"It sounds like Date #2 was a little...rough." They were being careful, I thought. I wasn't sure if that was because we were on YouTube and they had to maintain impartiality or because they were good at seeing different sides of situations.

Which, so could I. Eventually. "It was, uh, good perspective. He probably left and told his friends he went out with a caveman who hated art and had a burger at a restaurant when he could have had salmon."

"Should we still do the three questions?" Sidney asked.

"Yeah. It's still a date. It counts." I noted with relief that I was stating, not asking. It had for sure counted. After talking to Sidney on the show it felt even more like it counted, honestly.

"It does. So, on a scale of one to five, how would you rate your physical chemistry?"

"Maybe a three? I think three might be as high as I can go if I'm not into someone."

"That's interesting. You can't feel powerfully physically connected to someone unless you like them?"

"I guess I could feel *attracted* to someone I'd never met, but I wouldn't then say we had chemistry."

"Good distinction, thank you. Question two: How would you rate your intellectual chemistry?"

That one was easy. "Zero. Unless this scale has negative values."

"It doesn't."

"Then zero. Flat line. Dead in the water."

Both of us nodded, not quite in unison, like we'd been rehearsing but our timing was off.

Sidney cleared their throat. "So question three, for the sake of the format: Would you go out on a date with this person again?"

"Nope. Sorry, I kind of feel like I've failed you so far." I gestured at the camera. "All of you."

"By not falling in love with one of the two people you've dated in the last six years?" Their voice was deadpan, but I could see the smirk *in their eyes*. (That's a thing.)

"Okay, that does make it sound like my expectations are skewed. I guess maybe I didn't realize how hard this is. And you're doing a lot of the administration. But just the awkward planning, and the leading-up-to-the-date anxiety, and then the actual date, and no matter how compatible you are with someone if you don't know them there's going to be weird little pockets of silence and times when probably both of you wish you were somewhere else."

They were nodding along. "Exactly. That's *exactly* what the purpose of The Love Study is, though—documenting all of that. Because we live in a culture that wants the heroes to meet in a comedic way, for hijinks to ensue, and then for them to live happily ever after. Without digging into the real meat of how unscripted life unfolds."

I allowed that to sit for a minute before saying, "So... I'm the meat is what I'm getting from this. I mean, am I an FDA-certified hunk-a-burning love? Am I Grade-A? Am I—" another dramatic pause "—a *beefcake*?"

Sidney laughed out loud and turned to the camera. "I think that's a great end note to this episode. Please vote in the comments about whether or not you think Declan is a beefcake." They did the rest of the outro and sponsorship ad read stuff under dire threat of giggling, so I considered the bad date well redeemed by making Sidney laugh.

I waited until the recording had stopped before slipping around them and claiming the box of chocolates. Sometimes the best medicine for extreme embarrassment is embracing the thing that embarrassed you…and eating it. If it's chocolate. "I'm mining the white chocolate out of here unless you tell me not to," I said, going to sit in the armchairs.

It felt a little overfamiliar, but also within the boundaries we'd set. I watched them to make sure they were okay with it, but they only waved distractedly as they did whatever YouTube magic they needed to do before the video would be officially on its own in the world.

"I'm beginning to agree with my friends that everything's hopeless." Since they were still working and I was *working* my way through the selection of chocolates I'd brought as a gift, I figured it wouldn't hurt to casually voice my deepest fears. "Dating. Relationships. I'm sure this guy was perfectly nice and would have been a great date—for someone else. Someone who likes having chairs pulled out for them. And being told what they think of movies."

A click indicated they'd turned off the monitor. A minute later they were sitting across from me and passing me my water, which I'd left on the desk. "And that feels hopeless to you? It seems like it means maybe the person who should be going out with that guy is in the world somewhere going out with someone you'd be more compatible with."

"Is this a chaos theory thing? A butterfly flaps its wings in China and I'm turned off by a guy touching my chair?"

They selected a dark chocolate with precise finger movements I found compelling. Sidney's hands were lovely. Slender wrists, shortish thumbs, clean nails, and everything they did with their hands was deliberate.

"The door-opening, chair-pulling-out thing is…problematic for me," they said finally. "I understand the intent. But at this point I expect someone to ask me if I want a chair pulled out for me instead of just doing it. When it feels like it's part of a script, that they're playing a role, then it doesn't work for me at all."

"That's exactly it." I took another chocolate, though any second now I was going to reach sugar saturation and its accompanying mood crash. "I felt like I'd been cast as the guy who's charmed by chivalry in a movie I never auditioned for. And it's *totally okay* for people to get off on that shit. I just…don't. I tried to! That whole night I kept telling myself I should like it. But I didn't."

"Why? I mean, why did you try to like it?"

"I…dunno. I guess because the people who do have it easier in a way? That script is written, they just have to show up."

"Hmm." They licked their lips and I discovered that Sidney's lips were even more mesmerizing than their fingers.

Had I somehow bought the "special" box of chocolates? I knew pot was legal now, but they'd have to put it on the label, right?

"I think that script makes very few people genuinely happy. What I see more often is the phenomenon you're describing: people making an effort to fit themselves inside a script that doesn't work for them, and then being unhappy with the result."

"So I was right." I picked up a milk chocolate, having finished off the white chocolates. "It's hopeless."

"If you're saying you hope you'll someday want the thing you once ran away from with Mason, then that's probably hopeless. I'm not sure you can *try* yourself into someone else's mold. Actually, I'm entirely convinced you can't, or I would be a totally different person."

"I'm glad you're not. A different person." *Danger, Will Robinson.* Just one more chocolate, mostly to keep me from talking. A safety chocolate.

They smiled. "Thanks."

"Is that—" I swallowed and oh my god, was that my hand reaching for another freaking chocolate? "—is that what happened with you and dating? You didn't like the script so you gave up?"

"Not quite." They pulled both legs up to sit cross-legged, their knees wedged in against the sides. "I value companionship. And intimacy. And trust. I'm not against romantic relationships, I just haven't found a way to adequately queer them to my satisfaction yet. It feels like those things all have these set values that everyone just…knows about. Accepts. Companionship doesn't have to mean a sexually exclusive lifetime commitment that starts with marriage and ends with death, but that is such a strong narrative it's hard to find people who are open to other interpretations."

Which was a good line and all, but… "Um. So you…quit the game? Sorry, that sounds bad. I mean…"

They picked out another chocolate and turned it over between their fingers without taking a bite. "I think part of it was probably trying to find a way to navigate other people's gender expectations, which was harder when I was younger. I haven't had too much trouble with that when it's about sex, but when it's about dating, relationships, it's more of a minefield."

"That makes sense, I think? Obviously it's super shitty. But gendered relationship stuff is…a thing." I considered it. "I've definitely seen that stuff play out even with queer people."

"It would be nice if we were immune, but we're not. And

I'm really sensitive to that kind of thing. It…gets in my head. Like the chocolates." They gestured at the box. "I had this horrible moment of flashing back to dating people who gendered me as a woman and did things like bring me chocolates. Not that you and I—I mean we're clearly not dating. I didn't mean to imply—" They broke off, blushing pink. "I didn't think *you* were doing that. But that's why I acted weird about it. Sorry."

"Oh my god, no, I'm sorry." Buggering badgers, I was an ass. "I absolutely was not doing that. You'd mentioned the podcast and I also enjoy chocolate and I thought it'd be nice. That's all. I swear. Plus—" I held up the chocolate I was currently eating "—you can tell I mostly brought them so you could share them with me. Totally not in any way chivalrous behavior."

They knuckled up their glasses. "I'm sorry I was a little disturbed, it just brought up some memories. I've been in two separate fights about Valentine's Day with two separate people, both of whom expected me to be into it. Eventually those conversations felt so draining and demoralizing I gave up."

I gave them half a second to justify that before saying, "Oh my god. What do you have against Valentine's Day?"

"Nothing. I feel nothing about Valentine's Day. It has no relevance to me at all. It's part of a pre-formed idea of what a relationship is supposed to look like and it means nothing to me."

I couldn't help it. I goggled. "I think it's just an excuse to have a romantic dinner with someone you really like, though?"

"But doesn't that have more significance to you if you do it because both of you want to, than because it's a date on a calendar?" They were leaning forward now, getting into it.

"Maybe? I mean, probably? But I'm not huge into Valentine's Day as a thing, but I don't want to reject it just because a lot of people do it, you know? Like, if it doesn't work for you, that's fine, but that it does work for me doesn't make me The Man."

Their serious expression morphed into a grin. "You should get a business card. Declan Lastname. THE MAN."

"That'd be hot. I could pass them out to all my dates. 'For a second date, please contact Declan Swick-Smith, THE MAN.' Uh, that's my last name, Swick-Smith. Because my folks were into equality."

"That must have been fun in school. I've been meaning to ask you about your first name. It's Irish, right?"

I felt a little glowy that they knew the origin of my name. "Yep. My parents both had legit Irish grandparents, so they're big into 'the home country' and stuff. County Cavan is where my dad's people are from, and Wicklow is where my mom's people are from."

"I've always wanted to go to Ireland," they said wistfully.

"It's on the 'made your first million' bucket list?"

"Yeah." They picked up a demure third piece of chocolate when I'd eaten half the box. "You might be right about Valentine's Day. I think I was fighting about it with the wrong people, who were into it being this big symbolic thing. Maybe it is more about enjoying each other's company and I missed that a little."

"Maybe *a little*," I teased. "It probably *is* a big romantic holiday for a lot of people. But I think it can be enjoyed outside of that. Plus, it's been six years. I'd really like to have someone to enjoy Valentine's Day with. Actually, Mia and Ronnie took care of that this year by scheduling their wedding on Valentine's Day, so that saves all the rest of us the trouble. Wait." I sat more upright. "Hey, do you want to come to the wedding as my valentine? I know it's not for weeks, but it might be fun, don't you think?"

They paused in the act of taking a bite of chocolate. "Um."

God, I was the worst. Way to compound my surprise chocolate sins with romantic holiday atrocities. "Never mind! Forget I said that! Oh my god." Time to drown my further humiliation in more chocolate. I reached for the box, but Sidney leaned forward to grab my wrist. Just lightly.

"I can't come to the wedding. I'll be working. It was…a nice idea, though. I don't deeply desire a romantic Valentine's Day or anything, but all the couple stuff does get old, and it would be nice to have a no pressure arrangement. Do you…want to get together the night before maybe? Maybe for pizza or something?"

"Are you sure? I don't want to, like, force you into being my no-pressure Valentine's arrangement."

They let go of my wrist but didn't lean back. "You aren't. Honestly. Yes, Declan, I will be your pre-Valentine's valentine." They licked their lips a little, as if they couldn't believe they'd just tasted those words. Or maybe like there was residual chocolate on them.

Regardless of why, the sight of their tongue, their lips, shot a spike of heat through my body, starting at my toes and ending at the place where I could still almost feel their hand on my skin. "Thanks. Um. Really. That'll be fun." Now I needed to get the hell out of there before I made a total fool of myself (again).

"I think so too."

"Um, I should go." I stood up. "Thanks for letting me eat most of the chocolates I brought for you."

"I don't like white chocolate anyway, so you did me a favor." They walked me to my pile of stuff, which I managed to variously put on, pack away, or shrug into.

"Have a good week." That felt inadequate. "It was really nice talking to you the other day. And watching the shipwreck thing. All those statues and artifacts and stuff, and the old coins! I hope it didn't keep you up too late, but obviously you control how late you stay up, and know how to do math, so probably it didn't." Dear god, what was I talking about. "Right, yeah, anyway, I should go, bye!"

"See you next week!" they called after me.

The sugar crash hit on my way home and I banged my head into the steering wheel to express my horror. Except it's not as easy as people make it look in movies. I had to scoot back the seat in order to get a good angle and by then the red light had changed and it was uncomfortable to drive and I still hadn't accomplished the level of theatrical mortification I'd been going for.

Why, oh my god, had I asked them out to a wedding and *then* ended the already awkward evening by rambling about shipwreck treasure? Who does that?

Which would be such a good place to bang my head on the steering wheel: *bang, bang, bang.* Did I have it tilted down too low or something? Were my legs too long?

I settled for slumping in my seat and feeling sick. And wondering if I had more chocolate in the house. Still, some tiny part of me was thinking, *Wouldn't it be nice if Sidney touched my arm again?*

And yes. Yes, it would be.

Chapter Nine

I had assumed that all the offices on the top floor of the company were lush executive suites or something, but the top floor was the same as the other floors: clusters of cubicles, conference rooms, administrative areas. Nicer, yeah. They had clients of some sort, I thought, because everything was slightly more posh. But the same basic idea.

Deb was leading me through the maze to what she was calling my new "workspace" for the event project, so I followed her black slacks and tried not to get distracted by the twists and turns. She always wore black slacks and tailored button-up shirts in bold colors. Sidney might dig tailored shirts. They'd look wicked hot in a tailored shirt. I wondered if they were into formal wear at all...

"Welcome to the fish bowl." With a flourish, Deb opened a glass door into a glass-walled room, bordered on three sides by cubicles and on a fourth by a walkway running between the conference room and a wall of windows.

Whoa. Was this all mine? It wasn't huge, but it was…a room. A space. For me. At least whenever I was working on this project. Since no one was using the walkway, I had the illusion of my own windows, looking out on—well, yeah, looking out on the building across the street mostly, but some legit natural light was getting through too.

I sent Deb a very accusatory look and said in my best accusatory tone, "Are you trying to seduce me, Mrs. Robinson? *With your windows?*"

"Yes, Declan. You've figured out my master plan. I'm giving you temporary access to a room with windows in the hopes that you'll never leave me." She pushed in a stray chair and gestured to the room. "It's not huge, but I decided you needed a home base and nobody wants to have a meeting in the fish bowl, so it goes mostly unused."

"What, people don't like the feeling that they're in an aquarium?"

"I have no idea what the designer was thinking. Every other conference room has at least three solid walls."

"Maybe it's the punishment conference room!" I grinned at her. "You can put the troublemakers in here so they can't get away with anything."

"Perfect."

"Hey!"

She smiled. "The opposite tends to happen. This room is something of a psychological dead zone. I'm not entirely sure why, but it's as if people go out of their way to not-notice it, possibly projecting that they wouldn't want to be stared at if they were stationed here."

"That's neat." I looked around with a greater appreciation for the fish bowl. "What I'm hearing is I can get away with anything in here."

"Is that what I said?" The smile stayed on her face, so at least we were playing. "I have someone getting you a laptop and since you'll be responsible for it, I'm also giving you a key to this room. You'll have to sign for that downstairs in Admin."

I blinked. "A key?"

"It seemed the simplest way to ensure no one would disturb your workspace." She shrugged. "We don't have a lot of high value theft around here with all the cameras and security measures, but I'd still rather not leave a laptop sitting in an unlocked room."

"Um. Yeah, makes sense."

She stared at me for a long moment. "It's a temporary assignment. Don't be scared."

"You're giving me a *key*, though." I waved my hands around in a somewhat freaked-out fashion.

"Declan."

I braced for a pep talk about how I could leave at any time after the event, and no pressure, and she was there to support me. I looked at Deb, feeling my heart speed up in anticipation of nodding pleasantly while she mouthed inane inspirational quotes at me.

"If you don't return the key by end of business the day after the event, you're fired. Does that help?"

Not a pep talk. I exhaled. "Actually, yeah. It kinda does. Temporary key holder exclusively for this project, got it."

"Good." She walked to the far right corner. "I grabbed you a small file cabinet and a garbage can. We can requisition anything else you need. I threw some random office supplies in the file cabinet, but you know where they're kept if you need more."

"Got it," I said again.

"Good. You got my email about hours and time codes?"

I was super tempted to say *Got it* one more time, but I was a temporary key holder now, and needed to compose myself as such. So I saluted and said, "Aye, captain."

"Let me know if you have any questions. Oh, good, here's Jack." She went to open the door for the guy walking up.

Pale pale skin, dark dark hair, barely taller than Deb, and I liked his smile for the split second I saw it, before he spotted me. The smile slid off his face like egg yolk slides down a window. Not that I've thrown a lot of eggs at windows. But that's how I've always pictured it: a slick, messy slide.

Unsmiling, this guy was totally Dire Man on Barstool Who's Played "Piano Man" on the Jukebox Seven Times in a Row.

"Jack, this is Declan. Declan, Jack."

We eyed each other. I had no idea why I suddenly felt defensive, but I did.

He turned back to Deb. "Are you pranking me? He's a kid."

Her eyes narrowed. Even though I was smarting from being called a kid, I had enough presence of mind to wince at Deb's expression. Dire Jack's only reaction was his face going very still for a second before resuming animation on its way back toward me.

He sighed as if my very presence was a tremendous disappointment. "Do you know anything about the event we're planning?"

"I, um, don't think we've gotten to that yet?"

"It's the annual stockholders' luncheon," Deb explained to both of us. "Around here we refer to it as 'The Spring Fling,' but don't let anyone important hear you call it that."

Eep. "Okay."

Deb studied us for a long moment. "Jack will be reporting directly to you, Declan."

Boss say what?

"I expect you to collaborate on this event and divide your tasks according to your skills and strengths. Since you have prior supervisory experience, you are the lead coordinator for the Fling. Don't hesitate to contact me if you have questions or concerns about this or the rest of your job duties."

Jack's mouth tensed. Which, um...yeah. Because he was at least five years older than me and now I was kind of his boss somehow? Yikes.

"Got it, captain," I told Deb, thinking, *Oh my god, how am I going to get anything done with this guy hating on me so hard?*

She might have withheld an eye-roll. I couldn't be sure. "I suggest you start by grabbing a desk calendar and stealing a whiteboard from one of the other conference rooms. Declan needs to be briefed about the event and caught up with where you are in the planning, Jack."

Jeez, he'd already started planning and now I was being brought in? This was the worst. Maybe for both of us.

"Understood." Jack's voice was tight like he was clenching his teeth.

"I'm so pleased. Both of you will have keys to this room, but you will be the only ones with keys to this room. If anything happens, you're sharing responsibility for it."

Jack didn't look too thrilled about that, and I couldn't say I was either, but both of us nodded.

"Good. I'll check in next week." She waved and left the room, which was amusing, since we then watched her walk away on the other side of a pane of glass.

"I have two hours to devote to this today," Jack said brusquely. "I will find a desk calendar and some notebooks, you go steal a whiteboard."

When Deb had said it, it sounded playful. When Jack said it, it sounded criminal. "What, from...anywhere I happen to find one?"

"I assumed you would know where they were kept since I'm but a lowly temporary worker and you are a *supervisor*."

"Um." Right. Supervisor. "I guess that makes me a lowly temporary supervisor, then. But okay, I'll go...find us a whiteboard."

He flapped his fingers at me. Not even his whole hands. Like I wasn't worth the effort of flapping his entire hands. All I got was a finger-flap in dismissal.

Ugh. I left the room with some relief.

So far I wasn't impressed with Deb's seduction. Sure, she gave me windows (sorta), but she also gave me a "staff" who finger-flapped and appeared to want my job. And what had I ever done to this guy to make him such an asshole?

It wasn't the greatest of life's mysteries (which is clearly, *What are Tootsie Rolls really made of and how can they be simultaneously so disgusting and so addictive?*), but any hope that I'd figure Jack out in our first two hours together was dashed by his lousy attitude. He threw a lot of information at me, took every opportunity to frown in disapproval, but never stepped over the line to outright insubordination.

Sweet horny hippos, though, he knew exactly where that line was. It was almost an art form the way Jack managed to insult my intelligence, work ethic, and wardrobe without ever saying anything I could write him up for. Not that I planned to write him up. Though he made it tempting.

I almost asked what his problem was. Maybe he'd thought he was going to have a staff? Maybe he just didn't like new people? I briefly entertained the idea that he might have the same sort of anxiety Oscar had (which did give strangers the impression he disliked them when really he was just so hideously anxious that he couldn't look them in the eye or respond to conversational gambits with more than one or two words). But Jack had no problem making eye contact, and he had a lot more words for me than two.

Past a certain point I wished he'd shut the hell up for a second and let me finish a sentence. I'd scrawled a tangled mess of notes across the back and front of two pieces out of the legal pad he'd slid across the table at me before he even seemed to pause for breath.

The one time I seemed to achieve some status above *unidentified slimy thing on the inside of a boot which had now squished between his first and second toes* was when I said I'd draw up a spreadsheet with our various projects, sub projects, tasks, and sub tasks, with who'd been assigned to do them, and deadlines.

Spreadsheets were apparently Jack's mean-guy Achilles' heel. The frosty glare let up just long enough for him to say, "Actually, that might be helpful."

Uh, yeah, that was the point. "Good" was all I said.

The brief, shining moment in which I was not slime between his toes was gone practically before I'd been able to bask in its glow. He went right back to acting as if my lack of knowledge about a bunch of stuff that hadn't been part of my job until today was a personal failure.

I've never been happier to leave work. The key to the fish bowl sat like a lump of lead in my pocket. Was it too late to opt out?

Chapter Ten

The following few days didn't go much better. I whined about my new supervisee at drinks (and received limited sympathy from my friends, the bastards), and was grateful that for the most part I only saw Jack if our mutual event working time happened to overlap. Mostly we kept in touch via email and I, like a good supervisor, monitored the spreadsheet to make sure Jack was doing things. He, like a good supervisee—*gross*—was accomplishing a lot. Way more than I expected. (And more than I was doing, so I had to step up my game.)

If we did happen to see each other in the fish bowl we interacted with cold civility over the surface of mutual antipathy. I kept telling myself I should be going out of my way to be mature since I was kind of his boss, but then I'd see him in person and hear the echo of him calling me "kid" and I'd be annoyed all over again.

I'd mostly stopped moping about the whole thing by the time I met up with Date #3 at a tiny espresso cart on the La Vista Pier.

Mara was genuinely intriguing. Sidney had sent me two photos: one of Mara in a business suit (in which she looked hot and not at all boring or conventional), and another of her hanging off a rock, one foot dangling in mid-air (in which she looked determined, and again, hot). She self-described as "fat, queer, an extrovert on the outside, and an introvert on the inside."

I'd never heard it described that way, but I thought that fit a lot of people really well, even myself. Despite being intrigued, I was also kind of *exhausted* for Date #3. Like, on one hand, yes, I'd only been on two dates, true. But I almost couldn't fathom going on…that many more. Which was of course why Mase and Oscar were always so depressed about dating in general. Because they went on dates. Consistently. And apparently that put you in a position to feel pretty hopeless about dating. Consistently.

Anyway, ennui aside, I was still eager to meet Mara and she was easy to spot: both of us were fresh out of work and she was in a dark gray suit with a bright pink tie. I was smiling by the time I got to her.

We did the usual awkward *So you must be—*greetings and shook hands. She offered to buy me a coffee and I said that would be nice. I got a decaf mocha (she didn't say anything derisive about my decaf order) and she got a double espresso.

Usually I felt inferior in the presence of people who enjoyed espresso straight up (I required a lot of steamed milk and something sugary to go with my espresso, thank you), but Mara seemed really laid back.

"I'm extremely nervous," she said as we began to walk down the pier, the slightest emphasis on *extremely*.

"God, are you? I was just thinking about how chill you were being when I'm bouncing off the walls." I paused. "In my head, I mean. Bouncing off the walls of my skull. So to speak."

"I think I'm good at pretending to be more calm than I am. I'm a lawyer. You can't walk into a contract negotiation and let them see that you're internally a mess of nerves and worst-case scenarios." She sipped her espresso, lips folding in over it. "I was surprised when Spunk emailed me."

"Um. Who emailed you?"

She laughed. "Sorry. Spinster Uncle. We old timers call them Spunk for short."

"Oh my god, *you do*? I can't believe they never told me that. No, I can believe it, and now I'm completely calling them Spunk. That's fantastic."

"It's gone out of style with the younger parts of the audience, but I remember when they were just an adorable baby YouTuber with bad lighting and worse sound."

I clutched her arm, ennui banished. "Tell me *everything*."

"It's all right there on the internet, you know." But she didn't seem bothered by the question. Or my hand on her arm. "At the time one of my partners was transitioning, and we watched like *all*—" again, that slight emphasis "—the trans videos. We came across Spunk when they had maybe six videos out and my partner had a huge crush, so he wrote them an email, and they wrote back. We started watching more, commenting a lot, and eventually my partner drifted away, but I stuck around Your Spinster Uncle."

We'd made it to the end of the pier and found a free space to stand, facing the water. With all the other people looking out at the water, or fishing, and not a few people kissing…it had been a long time since I'd made out with someone like the couple standing against the lamp post… Not that I was staring. Because that'd be creepy.

Focus, Declan. "I kind of wish I'd known them when they first started out," I confessed. "Or…not exactly. More that I wish I'd known them longer than I do. Though sometimes it feels like we've been friends for a long time. But maybe everyone feels that way with Sidney. Um. Spunk." Ha, that nickname was gold.

Mara raised an eyebrow, turning to more fully look at me. "Really? I've always had the impression that they run the opposite way. I've known them for three years and still don't think I've scratched the surface."

"Huh. Or maybe I'm just weird. I mean, for sure I'm weird, but it could be that my weirdness is interfering with my, like, understanding. Or something. So anyway, you're into rock climbing?"

"I'm *obsessed* with rock climbing." Emphasis more pronounced that time. "Have you been?"

I shook my head. "I've never even been to a climbing gym, though I know there's one here in town and my friends go. Do you recommend starting inside where there are pads on the ground or going straight into the danger zone?"

She laughed.

We started walking again, back down the pier and then along the waterfront. The wind was cold and the sun, just starting to set, was still warmish. Mara was smart and funny and this was definitely the first time I'd really gotten along with one of the dates Sidney sent me on. Mara would like the Motherfuckers, and they'd like her. She was sexy and smart, and while I didn't feel a strong romantic vibe, you never knew…maybe that was the kind of thing that developed over time?

We eventually decided to stop at one of the little bistros

on the far side of the street and she regaled me with more early tales of Sidney's show.

"You are one of the more popular guests already, though it doesn't hurt that you're cute and flirty."

"Who? Moi? Flirty?" I batted my eyelashes at her.

She pinched my cheek, which might have played badly, but by then we were pretty comfortable with each other. "This has been a lot of fun, Declan. I'm glad Spunk picked me for the honor of going out with you."

"Oh, hey, honor, I don't know about that. And you never said why you were surprised they did."

Mara glanced away, picking up the crumbs from her croissant sandwich. (I'd already meticulously finger-poked and eaten every stray poppy seed from my poppy seed bagel with cream cheese and lox.) "In the past I've been, uh, strongly anti-dating. It was actually a little hard to compose an email asking them to give me a chance."

"Really?" It seemed like there was more going on there, but also like she wasn't stoked about discussing it. "Well, I'm incredibly glad you did, because this has been by far the most fun date I've been on. Sidney will be excited their devilish machinations were so successful, don't you think?"

She sat back. "Hmm."

Hmm?

I got nervous. Cue: nervous rambling. "You want to go out again, right? I've just been assuming because I'm having a really good time, but you definitely don't have to. I'm feeling a strong four, four-point-five on the physical chemistry score, I don't know if you've been watching The Love Study. Wait, you must have been watching The Love Study. Or we wouldn't be sitting here, right?" Cue: nervous laughter. "But *are* you interested in going out again? Or am I making up that we have chemistry? Which you can tell me, I'm tough, I can take it. It's all in the name of science and YouTube, right?" I took a slurp of my ice water, which was now a glass of ice with a little bit of melt at the bottom, and waited for global warming to put an end to the earth so I wouldn't keep embarrassing myself.

Mara took a deep breath.

Oh my god, I'd gotten it wrong, she was repulsed by me after all, why was I so stupid, and how could I ever think a woman this smart and attractive would be interested—

"I think you might have your eye on someone else, Declan."

I glanced around, wondering who she thought I was looking at. Not the love-struck seniors at the window table (though they were sweetly holding hands and staring into each other's eyes), and for sure not the business casual threesome with their phones out. "I really don't," I said, satisfied I really hadn't.

She uttered an amused *hah*. "I meant Spunk."

"Wait, what?"

"Don't get me wrong, I like you a lot. But your favorite topic of conversation is Spunk, and I think before you go trying to seek out a stranger to date, maybe you should, you know, try dating the person who's right in front of you."

I pouted. "I just tried that and she said no."

"*Figuratively* right in front of you. Right in front of you every Monday evening when you film cute, flirtatious livestreams together."

"Sidney *does not* flirt." Did they? Maybe every now and then. In passing. Casually. Not for real.

Mara eyed me for another long moment. "I've never seen any other guest have such a playful, warm dynamic with them. I'm not sure what all they've told you, and I only know a little from the kinds of things they used to say, but I don't think they're used to…expecting anyone to pay attention to them for longer than a video. And you do. Anyway, I'm happy to see you again, and this has been fun, but if you want my opinion, you should talk to Spunk."

"But…they don't date people."

"Neither do I, usually." She poked my shoulder in what I took to be a big-sisterly way. "You're a little bit special, Declan. And I could be wrong, but I think Spunk thinks so too."

I sat there, stunned, my thoughts slowing down to half time while everything outside it had sped up. Did Sidney like me? Of course they liked me, but did they *like me*? They'd said not dating was a guideline, but what did that mean? I'd taken it as a throwaway line. Maybe it wasn't? I added *Do I have an obvious and pathetic crush on my YouTuber friend, and does all of YouTube know it?* To my list of Things to be Mortified About Later.

"Unless I'm wrong…" Mara said gently.

"Um." I tried my water again, but very little ice had melted since the last time.

She pushed her half-full glass across the table toward me.

"Thanks." When I'd downed almost all of it, I looked up. "The thing is, I don't want to be the guy who thinks he's the exception. And they said they don't date."

"So be the guy who's honest about how he feels and doesn't act entitled to someone else returning those feelings."

I cringed. "But what if they don't? That sounds awful."

"Would it be awful if someone told you they had feelings for you and you had less-strong feelings for them? Or would it be nice to know they felt that way even if nothing came of it?"

Which was, okay, logical. "Except that sounds, like, super scary."

Mara reached for one of my hands (this wasn't quite the hand-holding I'd sorta hoped for at the beginning of our date). "Hey, you know who'd be able to give you good advice about your dilemma?" Slight emphasis on *advice*.

"Yeah." I sighed. "Sidney."

"You could ask them. If you want to." She squeezed my hand. "Either way, do you want to go out for coffee again? And Sidney said you crochet, is that true?"

"Oh, uh, yeah. I mean, I'm not brilliant, but I can follow a pattern."

"Have you been to the yarn shop over on Tice?"

"I don't think so?"

She nodded like *that settles it*. "Let's do a coffee and yarn shop friendship date. Okay?"

"That sounds really nice." I hesitated, knowing it was time to let go of her hand, but holding it just a little longer. "You really think I won't sound like an asshole if I ask them for advice about…about them?"

"I think you could go out with a dozen people, but if you'd rather go out with Spunk, none of them will measure up. And if they say no, at least you'll be able to let that go and give someone else a chance."

I couldn't tell if Mara put herself on the list of people who didn't measure up, or if she was making a general statement. Either way, she had a point. "Dating is way more complicated than I remember it being in college."

She laughed. "Isn't everything?"

We walked back to the parking lot, talking a little more about Sidney, but I managed to stop being so self-absorbed and ask some actual questions about Mara too. It was by far the least awkward I'd felt, and we even hugged when we were saying goodbye.

"Can't wait to see the show!" she called as she was getting in her car.

The show. Sidney. Me. My no-longer-deniable crush.

Oh dear. I had three days to come up with some clever way to broach the subject with them. Go, team.

Chapter Eleven

I panicked sitting in my car down the street from Sidney's apartment and called Mason, completely forgetting that he was hosting Motherfuckers gatherings to watch The Love Study. So basically: I called everyone.

"I'm panicking." That was me.

"Do you want a pill?" Oscar.

"He goes live on YouTube in five minutes, it's too late for a pill." Ronnie.

"Hush, both of you." Mia. "Dec, take slow breaths, okay?"

I tried that, but it didn't help. Until—wait a minute—it helped a little. "What if they reject me live on YouTube in five minutes?"

"It will take longer than that for you to ask them out." Oscar. "What if they reject you live on YouTube in *fifteen* minutes?"

"Oh my god."

"Slow breaths!" Mia.

"Ow!" Oscar.

Good, at least someone smacked him for me. Probably Ronnie.

"Y'all, be quiet." Mason took the phone off speaker and the background sounds of my friends got much more distant. "Dec, listen to me for a minute."

"Listening." I concentrated on inhaling.

"You're going to go and say hello and sit down like you always do."

"Right."

"And if you want to tell Sidney about the date as usual, you can."

"Okay."

"If it feels good, you can ask them out. If it doesn't, don't."

"I was thinking I might ask them for advice. Like hypothetically, if I wanted to ask out a friend who wasn't into dating and I wanted to make sure I was doing it respectfully."

"Mmm." Was that a good *mmm* or a bad *mmm*? "That could work. Will you regret it if you don't go for it?"

I squeezed my eyes shut. "Totally. But maybe I should wait until we're not live? Because what if they feel like I put them on the spot?"

"If you do it hypothetically, and they answer you hypothetically, I think you're still doing the show. Once the video's done, then you can follow up and take their advice." His voice was so comforting. "Honey, they like you. Anyone can tell that."

"I'm terrified," I whispered.

"If they blow you off, do what you always do: crack a joke and change the subject."

"Hey!"

"Stop being a silly goose and get your ass in there, you're late. Go get you some, son!"

The others shouted variations on the theme of me going to get me some and I hung up on their laughter.

Mason knew me really well. I *would* regret it if I didn't say anything. Also, I *was* late. Again. Dammit.

This time they smiled and opened the door wide for me to step inside. "Everything's ready for us."

Us. I dropped my stuff. "Sorry I'm always late. I should have warned you before you committed to the show."

"It doesn't bother me. You're here. That's what counts."

We nearly crashed into each other on the way to our chairs, awkwardly separating and laughing it off. *Not* an auspicious start to the show.

Oh god. Oh god oh god oh god. Was I really going to do this?

DATE #3 HOTTIE WITH THE DOUBLE SHOT WHO WAS COOL AS A CUCUMBER

Sidney hit the button, the LIVE red dot appeared, they did the intro. My pits were sweating. My temples were sweating. My palms were sweating. I might literally (figuratively) melt into the chair.

"People who misuse 'literally,'" I blurted out. They were looking at me, it's not like I interrupted, but they definitely hadn't said anything that made that a reasonable reply. "Sorry, dating dealbreakers. Fashion glasses and people who misuse 'literally.' I mean, I do sometimes? But only *for effect*. You know. Ironically. Um."

Somewhere my friends were shouting at a screen. Possibly throwing popcorn.

"Did Date #3 misuse 'literally'?" Sidney asked, with a *humor the unhinged guest* smile.

"Oh no. No, not at all. Date #3 was fabulous. Physical chemistry: four-plus. Intellectual chemistry: five. Second date: kind of? We're going out again, but it's sort of not exactly a date-date? More of a friendship date."

Sidney just blinked at me. "Er…okay. That was a whirlwind. Friendship dates are good. Do you want to…tell us more about it?"

~~DATE #3 HOTTIE WITH THE DOUBLE SHOT WHO WAS COOL AS A CUCUMBER~~

Fuckfuckfuck. "Um. I. Um." Could they smell me? I had to reek of nerves and also today was not the day to have tuna for lunch, what the hell had I been thinking? "Um, well, actually I kind of…need advice. About a thing. If that's okay?"

Eyebrows up and over the rims of their glasses. "Sure. I don't know if I can be of help, but I'll certainly try."

I swallowed hard. My mouth was as dry as asphalt in summer. *Please don't reject me live on YouTube. Please don't be mad I did this.* "So there's this, um, this hypothetical situation. Or, like, say I have a friend."

Sidney laughed a little. "I'm with you. You have a friend."

"Right. And my friend has a friend."

They bit their lip to keep from grinning. I mean, I thought that was why. The corners of their mouth seemed to be resisting the tooth-pressure holding them in place.

"My friend has, um…feelings. For this other friend. Right? And um. But see." I paused, frustrated by my own knotty fake scenario. "So the other friend, that my friend has a crush on, doesn't date people? Like, usually." Now I was gnawing on the inside of my cheek, peeking up at them through the not-great shield of my eyelashes.

Their eyes widened and their mouth went a little slack.

"But it's less of a rule and more of a...guideline. The, uh, not-dating." I swallowed again, but my mouth was so dry I kind of choked and started coughing. And because this was my life, I didn't just cough once or twice and recover, I coughed until I couldn't breathe, which made me cough more, and then I was doubled over, hacking, with tears in my eyes.

"Here." A bottle of water was pushed into my hand.

I sipped and managed not to sputter water all over my host. When I could straighten up, eyes still full of tears from coughing, they were leaning all the way over, holding out a little plastic pack of tissues. "'M so sorry," I mumbled.

"I should have offered you water in the beginning. Are you all right?"

"Yeah. Um." I dabbed my eyes with a probably overstated attempt at dignity. *Have mad coughing fit live on YouTube: CHECK.*

"You were saying that you have a friend. Who has feelings for someone. And that someone doesn't usually date?"

"Right, yeah."

"And you're...asking advice. For your friend."

I winced. "Okay, this is dumb. Obviously the advice is for me. Which I get we all know and are playing along, but let's not." I looked into the camera. "I have a crush on someone who doesn't usually date. But I don't want to pressure them. Or disrespect them. I don't want to slobber all over them with my feelings or whatever, but also, if there's any chance they might be interested, I want to let them know that I'm interested. If that makes sense? I guess the question is, what's the most respectful way to express interest in someone if you're not sure, for whatever reason, that they might return it?" I sat back, feeling a little dizzy.

And avoiding Sidney's gaze.

For like five seconds, but then I couldn't help but look up at them.

Today they had on a slick black buttoned shirt with the cuffs rolled halfway up their forearms, which I found...um... weirdly tantalizing. The contrast of black against their pale skin, maybe? Or just, like, them. In general.

Looking at me thoughtfully. So. Not repulsed, I didn't think?

"That's a complicated question," they said slowly.

Oh fuck me. I gnawed hard on the inside of my cheek to keep from taking it all back.

"Not everyone will feel the same way, of course. Speaking for myself, I think it's entirely possible to express your feelings in a way that makes them...non-aggressive."

With a silent apology (or maybe thanks) to Mara, I stole her words. "Yeah, um, I don't want to sound like I'm *entitled* to anything. It seems like kind of a hard balance."

They nodded. "That's exactly the right idea. And I think people can feel it if you're approaching them with a feeling of entitlement, versus when you're not. But yes, speaking strictly for myself, I think I would want to know if a friend of mine had those feelings. Better to have the information than not have the information."

Was my face glowing bright red? It felt like I was lit up Rudolph's nose-style. "Okay. Um. Thank you for your advice. Also, you never told me that your OG fans called you 'Spunk.'"

Now both of us were blushing. "It didn't come up. In fact, that should *never* have come up." They looked at the camera. "People telling tales out of school will be eliminated from the pool of volunteer dates. And I will *so* get you back, Date #3. Revenge will be mine."

I mouthed *Sorry* at our invisible audience, where I hoped Mara was watching, and cheering for me. Or maybe...cheering for *us*.

Sidney cleared their throat. "Okay, I think we'll leave it there for today. Blah blah blah, links, likes, you know the drill. See you next week." They waved and cut the video.

Holy anal beads, Batman. I nearly choked in the act of swallowing my own spit again and grabbed for the bottle of water. Sidney's bottle of water, now that I thought about it. They gave me their bottle of water in my hour of need.

Which I eyed them over as I took a very slow sip.

They were just...sitting there. Staring unseeing at their monitor.

Were they about to politely invite me to never darken their doorstep again? Or tell me off for confronting them on camera? Or...

...continue staring at their monitor as if I wasn't there?

The silence unspooled around us, growing more intense with each passing second. Should I be saying something? Had I said too much? On one hand, I really, like, *needed* them to talk. On the other hand, it was kind of a relief that they weren't demanding anything of me, like answers, or an explanation.

What would Mason do right now? What would Mia do? Or Ronnie? Not Oscar, though. Definitely doing the opposite of whatever Oscar would do.

My mind was flying in all different directions so I ended up doing what Declan would do, which was fumble putting the cap on the water and drop the rest of the bottle in my lap. If only YouTube could see this performance, people would be throwing themselves at their computers trying to date me. Hashtag clumsy dumbass makes fool of self again.

"Sorry," I sputtered. "Sorry, sorry, I drank most of it, at least it didn't land on the keyboard—"

"It's okay. Let me get you a towel." They were calm and competent and didn't look in any way disturbed by either my advice request or my spilling water in my lap. Just another day making YouTube videos, right?

I managed to mop myself up and awkwardly hang the towel over the back of the chair to dry, which left me standing so as not to sit on the chair with the wet towel hanging off it. But Sidney had started to do whatever they usually did at the end of a video, and while last week I'd blithely slipped behind them to get out from the studio area, this week that seemed somehow intrusive, so I just stood there. Hovering.

"Sorry, give me just another minute," they said distractedly. "Do you want to finish off the chocolates?"

I clutched at my stomach. "Oh god no. I'd throw up." Brilliant play, Dec. "Um, but thank you?"

They, like, chuckled. "We don't want that."

"Yeah, if I were going to make myself sick, it'd be better to do it live for views, right?"

"All in all, I'd prefer no throwing up. Not even for views." I cringed. "Sorry, that sounded assholey."

Silence but for some clicking and typing. And then...

"They're all going mad in the comments. If this keeps up hashtag-Sidlan is going to be trending. What goofballs."

Cue: nervous laughter. "Uh. Yeah."

They looked up at me. "I...you took me by surprise. I um. I'm processing? Sorry, I feel like I should be immediately responsive but I think I just need a minute here."

I put up both of my hands. "Totally okay. I get that. Completely. No worries at all. Can I…like…do you need me to leave?"

"Not at all. I mean, I'd invite you to stay for dinner, but I'm pretty sure I don't have any food."

"You must have something. I mean, what would you eat otherwise?"

"My neighbor hates leftovers, so she's always dropping things off. And I eat a lot of stuff out of boxes." They paused, still fiddling around on their desk. "You could look if you wanted? I think you might be more food inclined than I am."

"Okay." This was strange. Was it strange? Yes. Poking around in a new friend's kitchen was strange. I could put together dinner at Mason's or Mia-and-Ronnie's. But usually I was friends with someone for ages before they sent me into the wilds of their pantry.

Sidney didn't have a pantry. Sidney had one cabinet and a set of bookshelves with food in it. The fridge was free of dead produce this week, but also free of anything else resembling a meal. The freezer, though, held a package of frozen broccoli, a half-filled ice tray, and the better part of a pound of coffee. I switched back to the fridge, which did hold (somewhat shockingly) a bulb of lemon juice. And the toaster oven had two mini baking sheets.

I stuck my head up. "How do you feel about broccoli?"

"I have broccoli?"

"In the freezer."

"Oh. Um, good, I guess? I like it as a vegetable. I think that package has only been in there a few weeks. You think you can make broccoli into dinner?"

"Ye of little faith. Though no, not really. But I can…roast broccoli. And we can eat it. If you want." Did they want? They'd invited me, right? I didn't think I'd imagined it.

They smiled, biting their lip again.

I smiled back.

"That sounds nice. Thank you. Do you mind if I'm no help at all? I want to monitor the comments a little while longer."

"No problem. This is not a team-lift cooking situation anyway. You're okay with lemon too?"

"I have a lemon?"

I laughed. "Um. No."

"I didn't think I had a lemon. I like lemon, though."

"Got it. Give me twenty minutes, half an hour at the out-side." I preheated the toaster oven and tossed the still-frozen broccoli with oil, salt, and pepper, hoping that the fact it was still frozen *and* that I was using a toaster oven wouldn't totally screw up roasting it. Fresh lemon would have been better, and garlic would have definitely helped, but what the hell. Roasted broccoli with lemon juice on top was good even with subpar ingredients.

And especially when the point was spending time with someone. Not really eating so much. Which I was at least pretty sure was the point of me making food.

"Can I ask what you're monitoring for?" I asked once the broccoli was in and the timer was set.

"Anything that gets popular attracts a lot of homophobes and misogynists, so I'm flagging anyone who's replying to other comments with poison. If they're just commenting on their own, I don't worry about it. But I do try to at least protect my people."

"That makes sense." Since Sidney was still studiously doing computer things, I went back to a more thorough investigation of their kitchen. They had basically given me carte blanche. And anyway, it was better than like...staring at them. In that shirt. With the rolled-up cuffs. What was it about the rolled-up cuffs? How were rolled up cuffs almost suggestive? But they totally were.

So, the bookshelf pantry. Pasta, more pasta, no sauce, unopened jar of green olives, dusty box of mac and cheese, dusty box of cereal. A bunch of what looked like thrift store appliances, all dusty: rice cooker, toaster, plug-in grill. I considered and rejected the idea of making a *You could run an appliance store out of here* joke. For one: it wasn't that funny. For two: they were busy. For three: I was mostly just trying not to freak out and if I started rambling I might never stop. They'd have to walk me down to my car, still going, and lock me inside, waving with forced cheer from the sidewalk as I drove away, my car full of the sound of my voice going on and on and on and on.

It could happen.

"I have to stop looking at this, they're losing it. My regulars will hold down the fort. Probably." They cleared their throat. "I can't believe you're producing food from my kitchen."

~~It's a tough job, but somebody's got to do it.~~ No.

~~I'm a genie, rub my belly and see what else I produce.~~ Oh my god, *NO*.

"Well, I…yeah…" I squeezed my eyes shut really hard, hoping that time would skip back fifteen seconds and I could rewrite that line.

They cleared their throat again. Closer this time. "So you have a friend who needs advice? Sorry, I know you said we weren't pretending, but I don't know how else to like…start this conversation."

I opened one eye, and yes, they were looking at me. Obviously. On the me side of the desk so they were essentially in the kitchen now. "Um. Well like. Okay. So um." I took a deep, slow breath. "I am totally not trying to in any way invade your space, or your not-dating guidelines, or anything. But it has come to my attention that I'm like…attracted. To you. Errrrrr…so yeah. FYI. I'm open to talking about it. Or not talking about it. Either way, I'm making broccoli with lemon juice."

"Ohhhh, I had a plastic thing of lemon juice, right?" They shook their head. "Sorry, that was in no way a good response to what you just said. Um. Do you want to sit in actual chairs? I feel weird standing here awkwardly."

"Cool. Yes. Let's do that."

Then we were sitting in actual chairs. Both of us looking at our hands. I was looking at my hands in such a way that I could tell they were also looking at their hands.

"I like your shirt," I said.

"Oh. Thanks."

"The, uh, rolled cuffs thing. Is a…thing I like. I guess? I mean, yes, I must, because I do. On you." I covered my face with my hands. "Oh my god, this is ridiculous. Please put me out of my misery."

"I'm sorry. I don't want to do this wrong."

"Wrong how?"

"I don't want to…"

Oh no, they were trying to let me down easily, this was the worst, dammit, I'd messed this up, I should have known I would totally mess this up, why would anyone want to date someone whose claim to fame was leaving their last boyfriend at the altar, oh my *god*—

"…give you the impression I'm creepily preoccupied with you. Because I'm not. I don't think."

Wait. What?

"But it has also come to *my* attention that setting you up with other people is not exactly working in my best interest."

"It's not? I mean, I thought the show was going okay?" I peeked through my fingers.

"Oh, the show is great. I meant to show you the email I got from my contact with the company sponsoring, it's really supportive. And views are up." They seemed to kind of pull back. "But I meant it's not working for my personal interests."

I waited, but they didn't say anything else. "Um. I think I'm going to...need more than that?"

"Sorry." They grimaced. "I keep apologizing. It's a nervous tic I've tried to stop doing, but not that successfully. I'm trying to say—"

The oven timer went off.

"Aw man," I mumbled, getting up.

"Declan, wait." They stood too, so close to me I was worried they'd smell my tuna breath. "I think we should go out. Together. On a date. If you want to."

"Yes. Definitely. I definitely, for sure want to, yes. Please."

They exhaled. "Okay. Good. Sweet."

"Yeah." I couldn't help grinning. "Sweet."

The timer went off again.

And then we ate broccoli.

"You must be a wizard." Sidney shook their head, setting their empty plate on the edge of the desk. (We'd eaten on our laps because: no table.) "I would not have believed anyone could prepare an edible vegetable in my kitchen."

"It's not my best work, but I'm happy with it." Feeling daring, I added, "And anyway, it seemed like the point wasn't so much dinner as hanging out together."

"Very true." With a satisfied breath, they sat back.

I put my plate on top of theirs and did the same. "So um, scale of one to five, how messed up was it that I asked you for advice live on YouTube? I was a little worried that would be messed up."

"Actually, I find that I…am less likely to get into mental tangles when the pressure is on. Some of my best spinstering is done live because I don't have time to think too hard about the answer. So on a scale of one being not messed up and five being very messed up, I'd put it at a one." They shook their head slightly. "That was actually easier than this. I don't know what it says about me that I'm sometimes more comfortable in a livestream than I am in, you know, my life."

"It's probably a good place to be comfortable if you do it a lot. And I don't think that I would be as comfortable on video if you weren't. I for sure feel calmer because you're so at ease."

"Oh." Faint color in their cheeks again. "Thank you."

"This could be a pretty bitchin' episode of The Love Study," I offered. "Whatever happens."

"You think? You realize if we confirm their suspicions, they will be relentless."

I shrugged. "That doesn't bother me. But you have to, you know, work in that space."

"It's more… I've never given them evidence to support any of their theories about me. They know I'm genderqueer, they know I'm somewhere between twenty-five and thirty-five, they know I recently moved from Southern California to Northern California. People who dig into the archives know a little more because I wasn't as guarded when I first started. But that's basically…it."

"That doesn't have to change if you don't want it to. We can keep it completely off-limits." That might be the smartest thing to do. Though then my friends would have to come to me for the details of my dating life instead of getting them on YouTube.

"But doesn't that make me a massive hypocrite? I was willing to throw you to the wolves, but the second I get involved I'm like, *Hey, no way, that's out of bounds.*" Their forehead creased. "And it's not a bad thing to be out and queer and trans and *accessible* when it comes to dating. Maybe that would help us not fall into the same sorts of patterns that don't really seem to be working for everyone else."

I wanted to support them. But I couldn't decide what support would look like, so I defaulted to humor. "I think I volunteered for wolf duty? For sure you don't have to feel guilty on my account." When that didn't make a dent in their distress, I added, "All I know is that I really like you. A lot. And I'm glad you like me. And we should spend more time together. So there."

They looked at me for a long moment. "But do we have physical chemistry?"

Which would have been a seriously bad question to be asked by someone, except by now I could tell when they were teasing. "Five. Straight-up. Do we have intellectual chemistry?"

"Five," they said.

I held up both hands. "Maybe we start with that. We have another week before we have to decide what to tell YouTube."

"They'll be all over me when I post the taped show on Friday, but I can ignore them. One's success on YouTube to a certain extent relies on one's ability to tune out certain frequencies." They held out a hand. "It will be a pleasure to go out on a date with you, sir."

I took it. "See, I kind of wanted to kiss your hand all gentleman-like, but I didn't want that to feel misgendering or something. I would kiss anyone's hand if I were trying to be suave."

"You may kiss my hand," they said, smirking.

So I did. Heart fluttering, worried that my lips were oily,

but not too fast. Kissing Sidney's hand was not something to be rushed. I allowed my lips to press firmly against their skin, inhaling a little, then withdrawing.

The act of doing it, of receiving permission and then taking my time, made me strangely bashful. I couldn't quite look at them after. Though I also didn't drop their hand, which was warm in both of mine.

"Physical chemistry," they said softly. "Indisputably a five."

Yes. "So um...my people will contact your people about our date."

"I look forward to it. Thank you for making broccoli."

"Totally my pleasure. I enjoy cooking."

"Even in a kitchen with pint-sized appliances and no food?"

I polished my nails on my shirt. "Especially! The challenge is fun."

They smiled and I felt weirdly...not possessive, exactly. More like greedy. In a good way. Greedy for more time with them, for more smiles.

Which is when I realized we'd made it to the doorway and I was awkwardly standing there. Staring at them. "This is weird now. I lingered too long and now it's weird."

"It's not that weird. See you soon, Declan."

"Yep, right, see you soon." I waved, backing out, almost losing my footing. "Oops. Probably I should not fall down the stairs."

"That'd be good."

I waved. "Byyyyyye."

They laughed, still standing in their doorway. "Byyyyyye."

I managed to get myself to the car without any further fouls against my own person.

And oh my god. I was going on a date. With Sidney. Yaaaaaaaaaaay.

Chapter Twelve

Sidney texted me on drinks night to say they were staying home this week. I hoped it wasn't because of me, but on the other hand, I knew my friends were going to be ridiculous, so not forcing Sidney to witness that was potentially advantageous to our future. Friendship. Whatever.

I got to the Hole a little late, but through some magic (or just good timing), the Motherfuckers had snagged our first favorite table.

That was an omen, right?

"Three cheers for Mr. Big Shot!" Mason called when he saw me.

To my instant and utter mortification, my terrible, awful, very fucked-up friends cried out three actual choruses of "Hip-hip hooray!"

"You guys are the worst," I muttered, attempting to bury my entire body behind Oscar.

"I've been meaning to ask you," he said, way too innocently. "You're a celebrity now, right? Shouldn't you have on a fake mustache? Aren't you worried about getting recognized?"

I slugged him hard in the arm. At least he had the decency to yelp.

"Okay, okay, let's be civil about this." Ronnie paused. "What's it like, banging a YouTube star? Is it different than banging a normal person, or—"

"Shut up, we aren't, and seriously, shut *up*."

"You're *not*?" She pulled a shocked face. "And if not, why not?"

I pulled myself up to my full seated height. "A gentleman never tells."

Mason pushed a Coke toward me. "So spill, since you're no gentleman."

"I am affronted, I say *affronted* by your manner, sir! Weehawken!"

"At dawn!" the others called.

Which had all of us laughing, both out of habit and from a sense that things were righted. It was always a little odd when one of us acquired a new...person. That they'd seen it kind of happen over YouTube was a little odder than usual. And I hadn't really shared details. But there weren't many to share.

Well. Maybe a few.

"You kissed their hand," Mason said flatly. He turned to Mia. "Did he ever kiss *my* hand the entire time we were together? No, he did not."

She patted his arm—*there, there*—but looked at me. "Aww, Dec, that sounds super romantic."

"I don't know. I thought about doing it and asked if I could and they said yes and...it seemed like the thing to do at the time?"

Ronnie leaned into Mia. "He asked if he could! How freaking sweet is that?"

"Consent is *so* freaking sweet."

"Okay, quit being such big lesbians about it." Mason poked me. "I've actually seen your sweet side and that was an all right show, but it's you making dinner that cinches it for me. Who can resist a man who makes dinner?"

"I threw some broccoli in a toaster oven."

Oscar shook his head. "I find Sidney's living situation depressing. You always see big YouTubers in these gorgeous houses. Not with a kitchenette and a toaster oven."

Mia reached for Ronnie's hand, holding it on top of the table. "They're not that famous or we wouldn't have ever met them. Famous YouTubers don't work the early stocking shift at the store."

The idea that I could have somehow missed meeting Sidney made my whole body contract, like I was physically pulling away from the idea. "I'm so glad I met them. Even if most of our relationship has been conducted in embarrassing YouTube segments."

"Until now, but Mase is right, you made them dinner. That's huge."

"You guys have very low expectations of me. I brought them chocolates the week before."

My friends all goggled around at one another.

"What?"

Mason sucked in a breath, waving one hand around in an *oh no she didn't*. "How many times did this man bring *me* chocolates when we were dating? Once! One time! And he mostly bought them for *himself*!"

"Sweetheart," Ronnie said, leaning across the table. "I think maybe he just wasn't that into you."

"Hey!" both Mason and I yelled at the same time.

Ronnie grinned.

"Also, let it be noted, Mase, that I ate most of Sidney's, too."

He let his head drop into his arms. "What are we going to do with you, man?"

"Um. Buy me chocolates?"

"Naw, you owe me chocolates. Forever."

"This is why they couldn't get married," Oscar said to no one in particular. "Poor communication skills and too much sugar."

Both of us reached out to shake him at the same time.

"Okay, okay, okay! Quit it!"

"Listen." Mia waited until we'd stopped giggling like mad men. "This seems really good, Dec. And I'm happy for you."

Ronnie raised her glass. "Me too."

The others followed and I reluctantly raised my Coke as well.

"To Declan!"

"To Declan!"

"You guysssss…"

Mason reached over to pat me on the back. "All joking aside, I like them, and I like you two together. You got this."

"I really don't."

"We have your back," Ronnie added. "Anything you need."

"Um, no." Oscar looked down his nose at me. "You lucky asshole."

At least two people kicked him simultaneously.

He sighed. "Fine. I have your back too. Even though I don't know why you need anyone to have your back since you've seriously been dating for *five minutes* and already found someone you want to see more than— Ow!"

Ronnie smiled pleasantly. "All he needed to hear was the first part, darling."

After that topics mostly shifted to the usual orders of business—work, wedding stuff, family of origin updates, wedding stuff—and away from me, which was nice. But it left me with too much time to think. Was I really trying to do this? Date someone? Was I really trying to bill myself as a person who could...do that?

I'd barely dated in college. Barely. If this job required experience, I'd be distinctly unqualified. Plus, I'd left my last (literal) engagement at the last (literal) moment without any warning. No, I guess I could have walked up to the altar and then turned and run for it.

But that was why I couldn't get out of the limo. Because if I started walking, that would be it, I'd go through with it, even though in that moment I knew it was a bad idea.

I hadn't known it *until that moment*. And Mase didn't realize that until later. A long time later.

So how was I supposed to go into anything with that kind of track record? This whole thing was made of bubble gum and toothpicks. What was I thinking?

The nice thing about your ex being your best friend is that they don't hold back. That's also the worst thing.

"You got scared so you're trying to justify backing out. Get your shit together, Swick-Smith."

I leaned into him as we walked to our cars. "Remember when we were thinking about hyphenating our names?"

"Declan and Mason Swick-Smith-Ertz-Scott." I could hear the grin in his voice. "Sometimes I wish we'd gotten married just so we could introduce ourselves as the Swick-Smith-Ertz-Scotts."

"And send Christmas cards. 'From the home of the Swick-Smith-Ertz-Scotts.' It'd be us in front of a fire holding up our phones with cute puppy photos."

"Ha, like we wouldn't actually get puppies, we'd just have pictures of puppies? Nice touch."

"I don't think we're responsible enough for puppies, Mase."

"Truth."

It was nice, walking arm in arm with someone. Would Sidney be into that? I'd have to ask.

"Don't get scared," he said more seriously. "Have fun. You obviously have fun together, focus on that."

"Yeah, but…" I wasn't sure how to phrase the thing that kept niggling at me. "But like…what if I fuck it up again?"

He exhaled, breath white in the cold air. "Honey, you didn't fuck it up last time."

"I *left you at the altar*."

"I was there. Yeah, okay, you definitely fucked it up. With regards to the wedding, not the relationship."

"Uh, and the difference is what?"

He patted my arm. "Look, I wanted to be married. A lot. I thought you did too."

"I mean… I thought I did? But then I guess it scared me more than I wanted it." It still made me sad. Some part of me never stopped wishing I'd…wanted to be married as much as Mase had? Or maybe that I'd figured out I didn't sooner? "I still don't know how I could have not fucked that up."

"Well. You could have, you know, told me *before* our families were all assembled and we'd paid for the catering." Arm squeeze. "Before the invitations went out, even. Or, like, in that first conversation when both of us were all 'Should we?' you could have been like 'Maybe not.' Just spitballing here."

"I didn't know at that point, though." It was simultaneously hard to remember that moment and impossible to ever forget it. "I was so excited. And you were excited. And it seemed like we could…do anything, be anything. Our future was this big open door and we just had to climb through."

He smiled as if he was remembering that too. "Yeah. It really did feel that way. But what I worked out later, sometime after I'd stopped fantasizing about kicking your butt and before I casually asked Mia how you were doing like I didn't actually care?"

I bit my lip. Giggling right now would be wrong. But I could so picture that. "I badgered all of them incessantly to tell me if you were okay."

"I wasn't."

"Yeah, then I badgered them about how I could help until Ronnie got super mean and was like 'This is all your fault, leave him alone!' Which, you know, fair."

"I needed some *space*. For sure. But what I realized was that it felt like this big open door, but if we'd actually walked through it the whole thing would have collapsed. And I don't think it would have taken years, either. I think we would have hated each other real damn fast, Dec. If we'd gotten married we probably wouldn't still be friends."

I stopped walking to look at him. "Oh my god, don't even say that."

"It's true. We were twenty-three. And stupid. We wanted to hold a big party and almost ruined our friendship." He shrugged and pulled me against him to continue walking. "Anyway, you're not marrying Sidney."

"I don't want to marry anyone, honestly. No offense to you and the rest of the marriage people."

"We'll try to get over our collective disappointment."

"Oh burn. Hey, I'm quite a catch, I'll have you know! I make broccoli!"

He giggled. "I just imagined you with a magic wand, like transfiguring a pencil into a head of broccoli."

"I always had a problem with the fact that they'd transfigure things into totally different masses. Isn't there some physics rule about matter or something that makes that impossible?"

"*I won't read Harry Potter because: physics* by Declan Swick-Smith."

I elbowed him. "I saw the movies!"

"You are an uncultured travesty."

"GASP."

He laughed. "I most regret our lack of marriage when you speak aloud things normally typed into a messenger window."

"Middle finger emoji. But the black one, you know, I'd want to be culturally sensitive while flipping you off. Wait, hang on, would that be fucked up? Since it wouldn't really be your hand flipping you off? Shit, now I'm super confused."

"Your attempt at sensitivity which is actually worse than not attempting sensitivity is noted and appreciated, o white man," he intoned. "Where would my people be without the dark-skinned emojis so generously granted by your people, the people of the default emoji skin color?"

Both of us giggled.

"I'll want to know pretty much every millisecond of the date, by the way. Take good notes."

"Maybe Sidney will record it for posterity."

Mason's eyes lit up as if that was a real thing.

"No!" I said quickly.

"But—"

"No!"

"For the children!"

"Absolutely not."

He made kissing faces at me. "I bet you'd let them record if they wanted to."

"They *do not* want to record our date."

"You should at least post a date selfie on Instagram."

I rolled my eyes before realizing that might be a thing. "Is that a thing?"

"Do you even *look* at my social media accounts? It's like we're not even friends!"

I let that sit until the echo of his shriek died away, then said, "But seriously."

"You're a terrible human being." He pushed me toward my car. "Take your lack of Instagram hashtag knowledge and go home."

"Hey, is that what those pictures of you looking all 'Smooth Criminal' are?" I called. "Date selfies?"

"Go home, cave man!"

"Aww, you watch my program! Mase, d'you want me to set you up with the conventionally handsome chivalrous guy? I bet I could!"

"You *monster!*" He blew me a kiss. "Love you, text me everything. Real time is acceptable."

"I will be busy!"

"Hell yeah you will!"

We waved one last time before ducking into our cars and driving away.

Chapter Thirteen

Since neither of us were interested in a fancy dinner date, I figured we'd do something different and get breakfast instead. Except I hadn't reckoned on Sidney's work schedule. They worked all early morning shifts stocking, which they said they preferred because for the first half of their shift the store was closed, and after that there weren't too many customers. But it did mean they weren't available on Saturday or Sunday until after noon.

So I proposed lunch instead. Watch me roll with change.

"Oh, going traditional, very daring," they said when I explained.

"What? Not traditional! Hello, traditional is *dinner*. I'm thinking outside the box! Breaking the mold!"

"Breaking the mold, yes, clearly." I could tell they were smiling even though we were on the phone. (Yes, the actual phone again, like it was the fifties or something. Sidney was editing video and said they could talk briefly on the phone, but couldn't really text.) "Lunch sounds good. Do you have a place picked out?"

"Have you been to The Diner in La Vista?"

"Nope."

"Then it's time you went! Should I pick you up or do you want to meet there or what?"

"I'll be just out of work, so either we should meet there or I should pick you up."

"Oh, good point." I calculated distances from the store to my place to the restaurant. "I'm totally not on your way. I'll meet you there."

"Sounds good. See you Saturday afternoon."

That sounded very final. Obviously they were working, so I just said, "Yep, see you then!" and "Bye!"

The second we hung up I was wracked with doubt. Maybe this hadn't been the right thing? Should I have offered to make dinner (or lunch or brunch)? Should I have skipped meals altogether? Despite Sidney knowing a whole lot about me, I felt like I knew virtually nothing about them. Which wasn't totally accurate, but wasn't totally inaccurate either, especially when it came to dating.

All of that could be addressed on our *actual* date, which we were *actually* going on. Saturday afternoon. At The Diner. I ignored the butterflies in my stomach and reminded myself I was being very unconventional because: lunch. No big deal. Right? Right.

I'd forgotten how crowded The Diner could get. We ended up waiting twenty minutes for a tiny table in a corner next to the kitchen, but at least that gave me time to text Mason a super freaked-out-looking date selfie.

Once we sat down I still had trouble relaxing. "Um."

I fiddled with my napkin. "I hope you don't have a lot of anxiety in crowds."

"Only a little. Are *you* okay, though?"

"Um."

They leaned forward. "Do you have a lot of anxiety in crowds?"

"Only a little?" I smiled weakly, my stomach churning. "Sorry, did I screw up our first date? We should have gone somewhere else, right?"

"Do you want to leave? We don't have to stay."

But it had been my idea and we'd already waited for the table and everything. Plus, it wasn't all the people so much as it was all the noise. Conversations happening all around us, pots and pans and voices from the kitchen, the music playing not quite loudly enough to identify, the door opening and closing with its little bell. The whole thing was overstimulating.

I took a deep breath, ready to say maybe it'd be best if we left, but suddenly the server was next to us and I...ordered instead. Like my brain abandoned the idea of leaving and decided to forge ahead without my full and active consent.

Sidney shot me another look before also ordering, as if granting one last moment to change my mind. But I didn't.

I'd expected our first date to be basically easy, at least compared to dates I'd been on with other people. We weren't strangers. We were already friends. So that should have made the conversation flow easily, right?

Well, it didn't. The conversation did not flow. Our friendship did not magically alleviate first date weirdness. I felt sorta cheated.

We talked. Obviously. It's not as if we just sat there staring at each other for the hour it took to get our food and eat it. But I was pushing myself to come up with interesting anecdotes, or interesting questions, and I thought Sidney was doing the same.

Take two people who are into each other, add dating, everything falls apart. What kind of terrible recipe is that? I'd have to call Your Spinster Uncle to figure it out.

The second we got outside The Diner I felt better. The very second the door closed on all that intensity my whole body sort of sighed in relief.

"You all right?" they asked quietly.

I wished they would reach for my arm like they had that one time, when we were eating chocolates. "I'm all right. Sorry. Got overwhelmed or something."

"I have more work I need to do today, but you could… come over. If you wanted?" They frowned. "Sorry, I don't know what you'd do while I was working. That's maybe a terrible idea. Just, I feel like we've barely seen each other yet."

"Me too. Isn't that bizarre?"

They glanced back at the restaurant. "Maybe not that bizarre."

"Yeah. I failed us."

"You did not fail us. But I don't think we should do another lunch date on a weekend at The Diner."

"Agreed. Um, I'm not sure what I'll do if I come over either, but I'd like to. Maybe I'll stop at the store and buy food to make?"

A corner of their lips lifted. "We just ate."

"Maybe we need dessert."

"For lunch?"

I put my hands on my hips. "Are you rejecting my lunch dessert? What kind of monster rejects dessert at any time of day? If you're anti-dessert, you need to tell me right now, that's a total dealbreaker."

"Being anti-dessert, misusing 'literally,' and wearing fashion glasses. Let's remember to discuss this more on Monday." They smiled. "I'm not anti-dessert at all. I'm pro-dessert. I just think it's a little awkward if I've invited you back to my apartment to make me dessert while I work. That seems strange."

"I love making food, it'd be my pleasure. Anyway, I'll be over in a little while, okay? I mean, really, is that okay?"

"Yes. It sounds nice. Not dessert. That too, but I meant seeing you more today." And oh jeez, Sidney flushing and tripping over their words, *hello.*

"Yay." I hesitated. "Um. Kind of... I want to kiss you goodbye? Are we not there yet? Is that a thing?"

"We can make it a thing." They stepped forward. "See you later, Declan."

"Yeah. See you later."

We kissed, with a not-perfunctory lingering that promised good things for the future of kissing. Maybe first kisses were supposed to be the stuff of fireworks, I didn't know. This wasn't that. We didn't thump against the nearest steady object in a haste to get each other's clothes off or anything. We pressed our lips together and leaned in a bit close and shared a moment like that, long enough for me to watch their eyelashes flutter, long enough for me to wonder how many times I'd see their eyelashes flutter in the future. This kiss made me feel warm and happy and excited to see them later.

I could feel warmth on my cheeks, and see the pinkness in theirs. "So yeah," I said. "Uh. See you."

"Yeah."

We waved—back to awkward—and got into our cars.

I kind of wished I'd kissed them again. But it could have turned into an endless loop of kissing goodbye, saying goodbye, kissing goodbye. We'd been in grave danger of spending our whole day standing in front of The Diner, alternately kissing and saying goodbye. It was probably best that I hadn't kissed them again.

Later. I could kiss them again later. At least I hoped to.

Since I didn't think the toaster oven was up to anything complex, I opted for berries and freshly whipped cream, with a little cinnamon on top. A lot of people are kind of impressed by the fresh whipping of cream, as if whipped cream not from a can is magic. Which it totally isn't, since it's literally just cream, sugar, and vanilla beaten to the consistency of your choice.

Or at least it's supposed to be that straightforward. Since I knew I'd seen a rice cooker in Sidney's bookcase, I felt confident they must have a mixing device of some kind. Not a stand mixer—even I didn't have a stand mixer, though I did have stand mixer envy when I used the one in my landlords' house—but a hand mixer or at least a blender. I should be able to whip cream in a blender, I figured. Surely someone on YouTube had given that a whirl. So to speak.

Except I couldn't find a blender. Or a hand mixer.

After maybe ten minutes of me poking around in Sidney's kitchen (after they let me in and we pecked each other hello), I finally gave up on solving the mystery on my own and approached the studio trying to unobtrusively get their attention.

Getting someone's attention requires being obtrusive. Doing it unobtrusively takes mad skill. Make a note.

They slid their headphones down, eyebrows slightly raised. "Everything okay?"

"You don't have a mixer, do you?"

"A…mixer. Um. I don't think so? What does one look like?"

I suppressed a smile. "Okay, do you have a blender?"

"I had one. Then it broke. Sorry, I guess I didn't use it enough to replace it."

"It's totally fine, I just made an assumption. Do you have a whisk?" I almost hoped they'd say no. I could run home for my hand mixer. It'd only take, like, twenty minutes there, twenty minutes back.

"I do have a whisk!" They seemed so delighted to have what I was looking for I didn't have the heart to run off for something better.

The whisk, once produced, was surprisingly awesome sauce. "Oh wow, I've never seen one of these in real life! It's a cage whisk."

They bit their lower lip. "Yeah, I found it sort of…compelling. That the little thingie is, um, trapped inside a small cage, and that in itself is trapped inside a larger cage."

I looked from them to the whisk then back at them. "Huh. Like it's imprisoned inside the whisk, being forced to whip things forever."

"But do you think the ball resents being trapped? Or maybe it feels secure in there, snuggly inside of two cages, safe and protected?" They shook their head. "Er, sorry, that's…weird of me. To come up with a narrative for the ball inside the cage whisk. Anyway, you're free to use anything. Or to ask me. Really, do whatever you want." They ducked their head and slunk back to the studio.

Leaving me contemplating the ball inside the cage whisk and its potential feelings about confinement.

I'm…not against confinement myself. For me. Or for others. Confinement can be kinda…hot. I glanced at Sidney, who was very seriously concentrating on their computer. At least I thought they were until their eyes darted up, met mine, then darted down again.

Add *Discuss non-culinary applications of confinement with Sidney* to my list of things to do.

Right, I had a job. And that job was hand-whipping cream. At least I had the right tool.

I giggled again, plastering my hand over my mouth.

"Oh my god, why are you laughing? Are you laughing at my caged ball theory?"

"No! No. Um. My mind went to...other places with it."

"My mind did too."

"Like...bondagey places?" Because probably this wasn't a thing you wanted to assume. Assuming someone was into restraints would be even worse than assuming they had a hand mixer.

"Er, yes?"

I flapped my hands at them. "Goody, we should talk about that later. But you're editing and I'm making whipped cream."

"You are? What, all by yourself?"

"I don't have a whipped cream minion I keep shackled in my—you know, now everything's going to the bondage place."

"Whipped cream minion," they repeated. "*Shackled* whipped cream minion."

I waggled my eyebrows. "I'll be your shackled whipped cream minion anytime, baby."

"That's *terrible*."

"Thank you, thank you, I'm here all night." Oh shit, that sounded bad. "I mean not all night! I mean as long as you want me to be! I mean—"

They laughed and slid their headphones back into place.

I melodramatically banged my head against the counter a few times, hoping they were still watching and amused.

Then I got to work.

Was this still part of our first date? Because it was way

better than sitting in a loud restaurant trying to have stilted "first date" conversation. I prepped strawberries, raspberries, and peaches while letting the cream chill in the freezer with a medium-sized metal mixing bowl for a few minutes. Then I loaded the fruit into the fridge and busted out the cage whisk.

"It is a pleasure to whisk with you," I whispered. "I look forward to whisking with you in the future." And oh, sweet slutty salamanders, that was some incredible freaking whisking. Hot damn.

Never has hand-whisking cream gone so quickly. Don't get me wrong, I still entered into it with my heart full of doubt (alas, our cultural reliance on mechanisms to do work for us, tsk tsk, insert solemn headshake about the state of the world). I made the cream vanilla-heavy and sugar-light, as my personal preference, but left it soft enough that I could add more sugar if Sidney preferred it sweeter. Which meant I needed them to taste it. I took the bowl (which, okay, I was proud of; even with a cage whisk, hand mixing is not for the faint of heart, though it could be argued I hadn't needed to whip quite so much cream) and a clean spoon and presented them to Sidney with a flourish.

Grinning, they dipped the spoon and lifted it to their lips.

I saw it. The moment they realized what they were tasting and how delicious it was. They started going back in with the spoon, but I snatched it away. "Nope nope nope, no germs. Is that sweet enough for you or should I add more sugar?"

"It's *incredible*. Why don't people make whipped cream if it tastes that good? That's way better than the stuff in the store."

"I have no idea. It's super easy. I mean, it's *terribly hard* and I have *labored endlessly to bring you this bite of heaven*."

They laughed. "I appreciate your labors, my little whipped cream minion. Can I have ten more minutes to finish this segment? Then I'm all yours." Blink. "Er...for dessert. Or, no, that's even more suggestive."

There was something so damn charming about Sidney trying to backtrack out of an accidental innuendo. They frowned, like it was a puzzle they couldn't quite solve. "Anyway, do you mind waiting for ten more minutes?"

"Not at all. The cream will keep. I'll meet you at the armchairs in ten."

"Thank you."

I bowed low over my bowl of whipped cream. "At your service." When I rose out of my bow, they were looking at me. Intently. "Um?"

"Nothing. Sorry. Working now." Headphones on, deliberate turn back to the computer.

Mental note: get Sidney to look at me so intently I feel naked again. That was hot. I shook off the lingering twinges of, well, okay, something like arousal, but *anyway*, I shook it off and went to plate the fruit in preparation for our lunch dessert.

Plated, ready to go, cinnamon shaker standing by. By the time I was done cleaning, ten minutes had passed and a glance toward the studio seemed to indicate Sidney was wrapping up too. The lack of table area was a little stressful, but I made do by putting each bowl in an empty spot at the edge of the desk.

Then I...sat there. In a chair. And waited.

"I'm the worst," they murmured. "Sorry, I'm done. Let me just..."

I hadn't brought a book or anything, but I figured they wouldn't mind if I looked at their books. There was a low bookshelf running under the desk, next to the chairs. (Sidney could give a class in organizing small apartments, it was super impressive how much stuff they managed to fit in their place without it feeling cluttered.)

A few graphic design books, a lot of filming books, a handful of small business books. A tiny corner of mystery novels. I was still poking through when they clicked off their monitor.

"I'm really sorry. I should know that if I think something's going to take ten minutes, it'll probably take twice that. I hope dessert isn't messed up?"

"Nope. The cinnamon's less crisp, but it's kind of a cool look when it gets all saturated and blurry, and it's definitely not going to affect the flavor." I handed them their bowl when they'd sat down. "Do you need time to decompress before, like, talking and stuff?"

They went very still. "Actually...that would be amazing. Is that all right?"

"Totally all right."

"Thank you."

I grabbed one of the books I'd been looking at—about making short films—and paged through it. I didn't want to start eating without them, but I didn't want them to feel a bunch of pressure to be *on*, either. And I sort of love picking up a book on a subject I've never even considered before and learning about it. I'm kind of a nerd for random stuff.

The book had pretty well absorbed my attention by the time Sidney spoke. "That's the first filming book I ever bought myself."

"It's really interesting."

"It is?"

"Hell yes. Like, how lighting influences narrative? I never even considered that."

They smiled. "Yeah, isn't it fascinating? Because it's also about how the brain processes stories, all the things your brain is taking into account without you consciously realizing it."

"Exactly!" I surrendered the book back to its place on the shelf. "I should have read that before planning our faildate this morning and I would have known that The Diner at noon on Saturday was not the right soundtrack for our date."

"We are not calling it a 'faildate.'"

"Oh yes we are." I straightened up. "Excuse me, I am the subject of The Love Study, and I can refer to my dates however I want."

They chewed on that for a moment, an unwilling smile tugging up their lips. "I feel like I should be able to argue with that as the other person on the date, but as the facilitator of The Love Study I have to concede you're right."

"Thank you," I said primly. "Shall we dessert?"

"We certainly shall. I've never thought about how 'breakfast' is the only meal word you can use as a verb. You think that's because it's basically a contraction including a verb?"

"Maybe?" I gave it some thought. "Can you use 'supper' as a verb? I didn't grow up in a 'supper' family so I don't know how it works."

"I think you can 'sup.'"

Ten really dumb jokes tripped on the tip of my tongue. "It's taking a lot of self-control not to make any ridiculous puns right now."

"If I could come up with a good pun about your lack of punning, I'd use it." Their expression got serious. "Declan. You don't have to withhold your puns from me. I accept you no matter how punny you are."

I leaned forward. "I think you're going to regret saying that. Except now I'm punless. What if your acceptance has robbed me of the ability to pun?"

"Mmm, yes." They stroked their, like, five whiskers. "I have heard of such cases. The Pun Cure, it is called. Only those derided for their pun-making can truly embrace their puntastic identity."

We looked at each other like total goofballs for a full ten seconds. Then we laughed.

"I can't believe you've stolen my superpower." I handed them their dessert (again).

"I hope this doesn't hurt your feelings, but I don't think of you as particularly into puns. Have you been holding back?"

"Well, when I was a teenager I thought puns were legit hilarious and clever. It was pointed out to me in college—when I acquired friends who were, you know, honest with me— that my relentless punning wasn't that funny. So I curbed the undesirable behavior. Mostly." I would have kept talking except they had taken a bite of peaches and cream and I could tell they were no longer listening.

"Ohhhhhhh." Was that a moan? I hadn't ever made Sidney moan before (*yet*, anyway), but that sure sounded like a moan. "This is…this is so…" They ate another bite, with a slice of strawberry. "Oh wow. This is…words can't even do it justice."

Technically none of the fruit was even in season, though one of the great things about California was year-round access to edible fruit. I took a bite of my own and yep, pretty dang good. "Yeah, it's adequate."

"Adequate? This is delicious."

"If this was late summer, it'd probably be better."

"Okay, you can make it again for me in late summer and I'll let you know. But for real, this is delicious. And the cream! The cream melts in my mouth." They flushed. "Oh no, now everything's a sex joke. But I don't care, because this is…so…goooooooood…"

That time it was definitely a moan, and definitely on purpose. I shook my head, attempting to not be in any way moved by Sidney moaning over my food, though it made me feel appreciated and a little turned on.

We scraped our bowls clean with our spoons when we were done and Sidney took them up to the sink. "I can't get over how good that was. Fruit and whipped cream. But the cream made all the difference. It's nowhere near that good out of a can."

"I should think not! But no, I know. And it's always sickly sweet and vaguely chemical out of a can. I make it a little less sweet with more vanilla and no can flavor."

"The lack of can flavor is a treat, thank you. Thank you for all of it." They sat back down again, seeming restless. "I feel like you took me out for lunch and then I asked you to come back to my place to make me more food and sit around while I edited video."

"We split lunch! And I guess you sort of did? But I don't know." I thought about the whole day, from my pained date selfie until now. "This has been the best part of our date for me. It was for sure not lunch."

"Are you sure? I'm sorry I had a bee in my bonnet about editing. I had it in my head that I was going to do it today and didn't revise my plan in time to realize I probably could have done it tomorrow."

"Don't you work tomorrow too?"

"Yeah. Through Wednesday."

I shrugged. "I guess you can feel bad if you want, but I had fun today. I like making you food. And talking to you. And not-talking to you but knowing you're here. Um. So yeah. Anyway."

They pushed their glasses up on their nose. "I really liked having you here while I edited, if that's not too weird a thing to say. Most of the time I can't have other people around while I'm working, it's too distracting. But I don't know. It was nice knowing you were here. That you'd be here when I was done."

"Me too." ~~Also maybe we should have sex right now.~~ No. *Maybe we should kiss.*

I opened my mouth to propose it when they said, "Can I kiss you again?"

"Omigod, yes. All the yes. I was about to say the same thing."

Being kissed by Sidney was a bit like homemade whipped cream—a little sweet, a little velvety, a lot melty. I edged forward on my chair and they cupped their hand around my neck, a move I almost always loved, which I especially loved in this moment, with them, because their hand was so warm, like their lips.

We parted just enough to breathe, but their hand kept me in place, looking at their eyes through two sets of lenses.

"Thank you for dessert," they whispered.

"Pretty sure this is the real dessert. Damn. I think I could have done a cherry on top pun there somehow."

They smiled, but it was a soft smile, almost gentle. "I really like you."

"I super duper like you too. You're kinda terrific, Sidney, FYI."

"Thanks." Their voice was a little husky now.

"Um. I can't decide if this is where we have sex or say goodbye?"

"I have a counter offer."

I grinned. "Lay it on me."

"What if we kiss some more and then say goodnight? I have to wake up at three a.m. I don't want to be worried about how many hours of sleep I'm getting before work the first time we have sex."

"Very reasonable." I nodded. And nodded again. And again.

They squeezed my neck (which, hello, I also quite liked). "Did you break a hinge or something?"

"Ha, no. I'm nodding in agreement with your logic. Which is logical."

"I'm good at logical. Most of the time. So do you accept my terms?"

"I am all about your terms. Punch me in the nuts the next time I skip over kissing before saying goodbye."

"I don't think I'll be punching you in the nuts, Declan. Not my kink." But they would kiss me, and they did.

We eventually scooted the armchairs closer together and got a little limb-tangled with the kissing. It was slightly awkward, but somehow that added to the charm of it. I wouldn't kiss just anyone slightly awkwardly between two armchairs, but for Sidney? Yes. There was no couch or futon, the desk chairs would have been worse, and the bed seemed like tempting fate.

Armchair making out it was, and it was good.

Our goodbyes were punctuated by a few more kisses, with me brushing their hair back and them with their hands on my shoulders. My lips were tingling when I got in my car, in a good way. A promising way.

I couldn't wait to see them again.

Chapter Fourteen

I was nervous for The Love Study. Mara had texted me to say sorry she was so busy, she still wanted to do coffee and knitting, and oh, hey, since we're here, how was the date with Spunk? Which made me laugh and I sent back a bunch of heart eyes and told her she had to tune into the show to find out more.

Except by the time we sat down to stream, I was gnawing on my lips and fiddling with the wrapper on the bottle of water Sidney already had waiting for me when I arrived (just in time, but not late).

"Are we doing this?" I asked in a small voice. We hadn't really discussed what we'd say about our date to our—or their—audience.

"I think so. Unless you don't want to?" I thought I detected a little bit of hope that maybe I'd be the one to call it off.

"I…" Usually I wanted nothing more than to proclaim

something I enjoyed to the world. I loved talking, and I loved talking about myself, and I loved talking about things I lo—liked doing, and right now being with Sidney ticked all those boxes, but for some reason it didn't feel quite the same. Aside from sending my friends a few excited puppy GIFs and telling them that Sidney liked my (literal) whipped cream, I hadn't much gone into it.

Which was a little weird for me. But it was new. That was probably why. Anyway, this was the show, and I'd signed up for it. "It's not that I *don't* want to talk about it…"

"Then we will. Just pretend the date wasn't with me. Right? Talk about it the way you would any other date."

"Right. I mean…" I frowned at them, searching for words. "This is weird for me. Usually when I feel like this about someone I'm all Paul Revere-ing it from the rooftops."

"This is YouTube. It might be different."

"Maybe? But I don't know if that's the thing. Um. What… what do you think? Like. I guess since there's a sponsor, we should probably do it?"

"No. I mean yes, but no, I'm not…holding you, or, uh, *this* hostage to YouTube, sponsor or not." They took a visible breath, in and out. "I feel pretty exposed right now, to be honest. But I don't think that's necessarily a bad thing. It's new. Like you said."

"Yeah." I paused. "So…you think we should do it or not do it? I don't want you to feel exposed. I mean, you know, unless that's our goal. Is that our goal?"

"Maybe it is. At least, I knew you were opening yourself up to that when I asked you to come on the show."

I reached out, a little tentatively, and touched their arm. "If you don't want to do this, then we'll just say there was no date this week."

"The show…" They shook their head and looked up at

me over the top of their glasses. "Thank you. I think maybe it would be good to go through with it, as long as you're okay with that."

"Good for you or good for the show?"

"Both? Good for me because it's a challenge and it's a little uncomfortable. Good for the show because we had a valid date experience."

"You mean faildate," I teased.

"I do not mean faildate *at all*."

We smiled at each other for an extended moment. Then I kind of moved forward, and they kind of moved forward, and we kissed. We pulled back, both of us still smiling.

"Okay, then," they said. "Should we do this?" The mouse hovered over the record button.

"Um. Yes. Let's do this."

They nodded. And clicked.

Roller coaster car: at zenith. *Hold on to your keys and cell phones, kids, we're about to go downnNNNNNN…*

"Welcome to another episode of The Love Study, the series about love, dating, and the pursuit of queer companionship in a bleak and hopeless world. I'm your spinster uncle Sidney, and this is my co-host, Declan." They turned to me. "Hi."

I couldn't help grinning like a fool. "Hi."

"So."

"Yeah."

"Date #4."

"Yep."

Now both of us were grinning with a sort of giddy recklessness, like we were together at the top of the roller coaster.

DATE #4 HOT-AS-FUCK GQ WITH RED GLASSES WHO'S EXCELLENT AT KISSING

"That *is not* what we're calling me."

"Hey, when you go out with you, you can decide on your stock photo description. But since *I* went out with you, I get to decide."

"So that means I decide on your stock photo description?"

I hesitated. "I'm the subject of the study. I don't have a stock photo description."

Their eyes narrowed. "That's definitely not the rule."

"Moving right along," I said quickly, turning to the camera because looking at Sidney was distracting. "You guys—sorry, I mean that gender neutrally—you all, this date started out as a massive fail. It was a faildate. I accept full responsibility for initiating said faildate."

Sidney raised a hand. "For the record, I object to the terminology being used to describe this date, but I acknowledge that Declan has the right to classify dates however he chooses, as he is the subject of the study."

"Thank you. Ahem." I realized I was looking at them instead of the camera and tried to focus. "Our faildate began at lunch on Saturday at The Diner in La Vista. Any of you who've ever been to lunch on Saturday at The Diner in La Vista will probably realize why it's not a great first date location."

They leaned forward confidentially. "Most of the people watching have no idea where La Vista even is. It's an international audience. Because: the internet."

"Wait, we're on *the internet* right now? I am shocked!" I stuck my tongue out at them and went back to the camera. "Anyway, as I was saying, think classic American diner, lunch on a weekend. The place was packed, and loud, and we had to wait forever for a table, then forever for our food, and to be honest, I went into serious sensory overwhelm and kind of couldn't deal."

"It was really loud," Sidney agreed. "Hard-to-hear-your-self-think levels of constant noise."

"And then we got outside and it was such a relief I had to take a minute. And Date #4 was so nice about it, y'all, like so *so* nice about it. Because I went into anxiety mode and they didn't act like I was a freak."

"You're not a freak. Though you might have some internalized ableism about anxiety. Anyway, I would not have classified that as a faildate, even though it was a…fraught date."

"A seriously fraught date. Which Sid—um—Date #4 then fixed by demanding I make them dessert."

Sidney gasped and hit my arm. "I did not!"

I smirked at them. "That's how I remember it."

"All lies."

"Okay," I said to the camera. "It wasn't a demand, and I'm the one who basically forced lunch dessert on them. But to whatever degree making your date dessert after initiating faildate can fix things, I think this did? Or spending more time together fixed it? I'm not sure."

"I reject the notion that our date was broken, *but* I concede the point: it improved after I invited Declan over to sit here while I edited and ignored him for like two hours." They turned to me. "I wanted to say thank you, again, for giving me a few minutes after I finished working to just be silent before we started talking."

I shrugged. "Sure thing."

"What made you think to do that?"

"Um." I thought about it, conscious that I was dead air on YouTube, but not willing to brush it off. "I guess because I was projecting a little? Back when my anxiety was…worse than it is now, sometimes transitions were hard for me. I'd leave work and just sit in my car without starting it to decompress from work mode and get into not-work mode. I thought that might be helpful to you too?"

"It really was. And I don't think to do that when there's not a physical change—like driving or walking home from work—so I appreciated the reminder." They smiled at me and I had the distinct impression that if we weren't on You-Tube right now they might have kissed me. The smile had a potential-for-kissing aura to it.

Smile auras are totally a thing.

"So I, um, didn't do our, like, Love Study rating thing."

"You don't have to if—"

"Fives across the board," I cut them off. "Physical chemistry: five. Intellectual chemistry: five. Would absolutely date again. I mean, if Date #4 wanted to."

"Fives for me too."

I held out my hand for a fist bump. "Not too bad for a faildate."

"It wasn't a faildate," they growled.

I waggled my eyebrows at the camera. "They just growled at me. You heard that, right? Everyone heard it? Comment if you heard Date #4 growl, because I'm almost certain I—"

Sidney plastered a hand across my mouth, which was weirdly hot, and looked dead into my eyes. "Behave yourself."

"Omhg," I mumbled, fanning myself.

"Declan."

I attempted to compose my face into a Serious Expression. They sighed and unmuzzled me. "So you had a good date."

"I had a *great* date. The second half, anyway. I mean it."

"Can you—without joking—try to pick apart what separates a great date from a less successful one? I think that would be helpful for people."

"Um. Okay. I'll try." I took a deep, cleansing breath, but

they were looking at me with such deep suspicion that I immediately started giggling. "Sorry! Sorry. Okay. I think part of it is the chemistry? Like, if you have a ton of chemistry with someone, I do think it's easier to…smooth over the inevitable bumps. And there were bumps. The whole lunch was a massive bump."

"Maybe define what you mean by 'bumps.'"

"Um, like, awkward moments? Awkward stretches? Of mutual awkwardness?" I paused, hoping I wasn't going to accidentally hurt them, but they were nodding.

"I agree. I'm pretty awkward in general. No date with me will ever be without awkward moments. Or bumps."

"Yeah, me too. And also, regardless of one's personal awkward level, first dates are rife with naturally occurring awkwardness."

They grinned. "I dig that." They looked at the camera. "You heard it here, officially, on The Love Study: first dates are rife with naturally occurring awkwardness, even when you like each other a lot, even when you're having a great time."

I leaned forward and lowered my voice. "Um, does that mean…you had a great time too?"

"Obviously."

"Yay!" I resumed my first-date-analysis posture. "So yeah, chemistry can help with awkwardness. And willingness to do something different. If we'd just had lunch and then gone our separate ways, I don't think I would have spent, like, all of yesterday bouncing around my apartment singing Disney songs."

"You did?"

"Um." Oops. "…maybe?"

"Aww. That's good. I'm glad. I mean, that you were okay coming over. Which I still feel weird about."

"It was a risk, I think. In terms of…" What was I trying to say? I knew I had a point. I considered the camera and our invisible watchers. "Okay, say you go out with someone to a bar or something and it doesn't work out. You cut your losses, right? If it's not going all that well but you feel something with that person and you totally switch it up and propose a different thing, that's a risk." I turned to Sidney. "Thank you for taking that risk. I really loved hanging out making food while you worked."

They bit their lip for a moment, then said, "You're welcome."

Neither of us said anything, just kept staring at each other.

Sidney turned to the camera and transitioned into the sponsor ad read, which maybe only felt abrupt to me because I was super excited to hang out with them post-video. I was practically holding my breath by the time they said, "Thanks for watching and I will spinster at you more next time." And: click.

I sat all the way back in my chair and exhaled. "Wow. That was kind of a rush."

They also sat back. "I'm exhausted now."

"For real."

"I need to—" Hand wave to indicate all the stuff they needed to do.

"Yeah."

They minutely shifted the position of their keyboard. "Will you stay for a little while?"

I'd stayed after the last three videos, but I sort of got why they were asking specifically. We'd gone from casual friendship to…something else. Different permissions were required. "I'd love to."

They nodded and applied themself to Spinster Uncle admin and logistics.

Since I could now watch them with impunity, I did. The rainbow suspenders were back, this time over a high V-neck blue T-shirt. They also had on a rainbow bracelet and a Hello Kitty hair clip holding a braid back from getting in their face. I licked my lips, thinking about kissing them. And about whether they'd think it was awesome if I unclipped their hair sometime. I might have a hair thing. Not as in fetish. Just that it seems sort of intimate to be allowed to take someone's hair out of a style. Like you need to be close for that, it's not an offhand thing.

"Do you want me to tell you what I'm doing?"

I blinked.

"You're staring at me. I thought you might be curious."

"Oh. No. I just…like looking at you. Is why I'm staring. Sorry, I can stop." I performed an elaborate stretch and managed to knock over my water bottle, which was thankfully still capped. But good idea, accidental clumsiness. I drank some water. Stretched again. Drank again.

"Oh my god, go back to staring at me if you want, your fidgeting is making it hard to concentrate."

I moved my chair a little closer. "Okay."

They opened their mouth, then shut it. Then tried again. "Feeling awkward. I should have gotten us food or something. I did eat some salads this week, but now I'm down to shredded carrots and sunflower seeds. Which I think even you can't make into a meal. And I ate the rest of the whipped cream yesterday. Mrs. MacLeod will probably bring over leftovers later, but I can't guarantee it."

"We could order in. Or go out. Or go back to my place. The Jenkinses—my landlords—aren't home so we could use the main house." I checked my watch. Still early. More than enough time to go somewhere if they wanted to.

"I have bread. We could make peanut butter and jelly?"

"Sold! PB&J it is. Can I bust out your toaster? PB&J is more fancy when you lightly toast the bread first."

They laughed. "Of course it is. That sounds nice."

"Sweet."

We feasted on lightly toasted PB&J and then huddled around their computer, laughing at the commenters on Your Spinster Uncle, who were apparently in ecstasy over our "couple quotient."

"They're feral," Sidney said.

I pointed to YourSpinsterOwl, who'd commented, *You two are the physical manifestation of the heart-eyes emoji* with a heart. "Aww, your brother is seriously adorable."

"He's the best."

"I always wanted a sibling, but it's only me in my family."

They nodded. "It was just me and my mom for years when I was a kid. We moved all the time, had very little money, and I changed schools a ton, which is supposed to make you adaptable and good at friend-making, but I guess I never figured that out, so I was alone a lot. Then she hooked up with Arman's dad when I was fourteen and Arman was born a little while after that, which was a huge shock, but probably the best thing that ever happened to me."

"Wow, really?" Oh my god, how much did I love listening to them talk about themself? So, so much. "That's amazing."

"It was. Until then I don't think I understood how to like...*be* with people. I guess that sounds weird." They paused, fingers lightly tapping the edge of the keyboard. "I'd always thought of myself as alone, but Arman made me... real, in a way. He needed me, loved me, made me want to be around for him. I'd always assumed I'd go back east for college, or England, Ireland. Somewhere far away. But I stayed a lot closer because I didn't want him to forget about me."

There's only so sad you can be on someone else's behalf,

and I didn't think Sidney would appreciate me getting all weepy over their, like, teenage self. But that sounded so damn lonely. "It seems like it worked out? I mean for Arman. He got this totally extraordinary older sibling he can watch twice a week on YouTube."

They kind of laughed. "Yeah. I don't know about extraordinary, but I feel confident we aren't going to lose touch."

"Not with him commenting on every video." I risked touching their arm, just lightly, the way I liked it when they touched mine. If Mara was right, they didn't share much, which made this…even more special than it already felt. "Thank you for telling me. About your brother."

"Thank you for listening. I don't want to bore anyone, but I think my little owlet is pretty awesome."

"I think so too. And you're a really good role model. Like, you're doing a great service and illustrating your relationship principles in real time, for your brother, for your fans, for whoever stumbles upon these videos. Though I totally wish we had a cooler ship name."

"Now we know: date only based on the coolness of your ship name with that person." Sidney's voice regained some solidity. "I think this puts Your Spinster Uncle out of a job, actually. The number one priority of all relationships is ship name."

I shouldered into their shoulder. "You should write a self-help book. That's how you'll make your millions, solving all dating problems once and for all."

"There could be an app too. 'Forget all those dating sites with their complex algorithms based on how much you might like another human being! Try our app, which uses an arbitrary algorithm taking into consideration only your first names!'"

"Honestly?" I thought about my friends and their adventures in online dating. "I think people would install that just for fun. It might work. Like, you'd have a self-selected dating pool based on people thinking that was entertaining."

"And we wouldn't let them even choose genders or race or height or whatever. It'd be the purest form of dating: based only on your names fitting in a catchy way."

"Alas, we would never have gotten together." I rested my head against their arm and sighed.

After a brief hesitation, they put their arm around my shoulders. "There, there. We've already gotten together. No app can keep us apart now."

I readied my best *Braveheart* voice. "No app can keep us apart now!"

Both of us giggled.

"We are ridiculous," they said.

"Yeah. It's rad, right?"

"Pretty much."

We sat close in our chairs and enjoyed the show in the comments until I went home.

Chapter Fifteen

The day of The Big Fitting—i.e. Oscar, Mason, and I getting fitted for our wedding rental suits—dawned on a Wednesday in the first week of February. I got to work early so I could get out early and was a little shocked that Jack was already in the fish bowl. Since most of my event planning time was at odd hours, I didn't usually get to the fish bowl right away, but I had a few things I could knock out with emails to vendors. And it'd give me an opportunity to get ahead on proofreading the "Fling bricks" (the packets we'd hand out to everyone in attendance).

"Oh. Hey, Jack. Um." I was so taken aback I just stood in the doorway for a few seconds staring at him. He looked terrible. Like he hadn't slept. His sleeves were rolled up, but where on Sidney it looked intentional and sexy, on Jack it just looked messy. His hair was half-combed, and a comb was sitting on the table next to him.

As if he noticed it at the same time, he grabbed it and shoved it into his gym bag. "Why are you here this early?"

"Trying to get some hours in so I can leave early for an appointment later." Should I have checked with Jack before doing that? I was his supervisor. Did that mean I could do whatever I wanted or had a greater responsibility to make sure he knew where I was? I couldn't decide. I didn't want him to think I was skiving off work, so I added, "Deb lets me flex a little when I need to."

He waved a hand. "That makes sense. I'll be out of your hair soon. I like working here because it's so quiet in the morning. No one gets to this floor until nine."

"Yeah, same." I put my stuff down at the other end of the table and went about my usual setting-up routine, booting up my laptop, glancing over my lists for the last few days to make sure I had a plan for everything I'd meant to get done and crossed off everything I'd gotten done. The shared spreadsheet made it clear that Jack had done…a lot. At this rate we might not need full-time hours for the next two weeks.

I also checked the voice mail box for the other job I was covering, took a few notes, made a new list for that job, and a new list for the Fling.

By then the coffee maker thing was heated up, so I went back to the coffee/tea room to make a cup. (In what I considered to be one of the more genius inventions, the coffee/tea rooms were converted closets with sinks, pod coffee makers, and hot water dispensers for tea, which meant that you could stay caffeinated all day long without going too far away from your area, and it wasn't a full-on kitchen which meant no one could corner you there with two hours of small talk.)

After a moment of thought I made another cup and pocketed some creamers and sugars. There was always the possibility Jack would throw it back in my face—literally or, more likely, figuratively—but the guy looked grim so it was worth a shot.

I set the cup down near him and the cream and sugar beside it. "Thought you might want some."

He laughed harshly. "I look that bad, huh?"

"It's seven a.m. Who *doesn't* look bad at this time of day?"

He glanced up. "You don't look bad, Declan." He winced. "Shit, I don't mean that in a harassment way, I'm not hitting on you. I just mean it looks like you took a shower this morning."

Yikes. I mean, technically I was his supervisor? But he was definitely older than me. I would for sure have felt creeped out if I thought he was seriously trying to pick me up.

"I'm sorry if I made you uncomfortable," he said stiffly. "I didn't mean to. I'm not humaning well today."

"It's early, you have time to regain your humaning abilities. And I totally did not think you were hitting on me, it's fine. I brought you coffee, though, if that helps." Only now it seemed kind of weird. "Um, I'm…also not hitting on you."

He offered a wan smile as he pulled the coffee toward him and dumped two creamers and two sugars into it. "Understood. We are officially not sexually harassing each other."

"Yep." I hopped out of my chair. "Uh, sorry, forgot a stir stick, I'll be right back."

"I got it." He picked up a ball point pen and used the non-writing side to stir.

It was a weirdly unrefined thing to watch him do. Jack always seemed so put together, ready for any new challenge. To see him stirring his coffee with a cheap blue pen was incongruent with my idea of him.

Then again, he still had only half of his hair combed. And his laptop screen was dark, as if he'd been staring at it for long enough to go to standby.

"Um. Everything...okay?"

"Not even a little bit. No. But you don't need to hear about my problems. I hope your appointment today is a positive thing instead of a negative thing."

"Sure, I mean, more a check-it-off-get-it-done thing. Two of my best friends are getting married, so the rest of us are going to get our suits fitted today."

"Ah. Marriage." He nodded, absently running a hand through the side of his hair that had, until then, been neat. "I wish them the best of luck." He said it so darkly that I wasn't sure how to respond.

After a too-long pause I went with, "Thank you?"

"Jesus. Sorry." This time he went at his hair with both hands, took a gulp of coffee, and stood up. "I'll be right back." Out he went, down the hall toward the nearest bathroom.

My guess was confirmed when he came back seven minutes later (I wasn't tracking the time for any reason other than I thought I might have to go make sure he was okay if he... never came back). His hair was damp and roughly styled, his cheeks were fresher like maybe he'd splashed water on them, and he'd unrolled his cuffs to his wrists. All around he looked more awake. And more Jack.

"I apologize for being a basket case," he said as he snapped his laptop shut and shuffled his papers together. "I have a personal thing, but that's no excuse."

"I think it is an excuse, though? I mean, for looking tired." The thing was, we'd been mostly on-the-chilly-side-of-civil to each other, which made it hard for me to sound sincere in offering sympathy. But I found, somewhat to my surprise, that I was honestly sympathetic. "Sorry you have a personal thing."

"Thanks. I've only got a few more calls to make later today

and then I'll be ready to start assembling the Fling bricks and goody bags. And thanks for the coffee." He raised the mug, shouldered his gym bag, briefcase, and left.

I sat alone in the fish bowl and stared after him.

My evil plan (which was to say the one my boss knew about and thus wasn't evil at all) worked and I got out of there with enough time to get to the fitting before the appointment. I parked and wiped imaginary sweat from my brow.

Mase was already inside waiting on his suit to be brought out. "Hey, Dec." He kissed my cheek. "Please tell me you stayed after the show and had such amazing sex with Sidney that you completely forgot to tell me about it."

"Oh my god."

He waggled his eyebrows. "Spill. You owe me all the vicarious details."

"We did not—" I lowered my voice "—have sex after the show. But when we do, I'm pretty sure it'll be amazing."

"Details, cupcake. At least tell me about the making out. I know there was making out."

I'd always been this guy, the guy who delighted in sharing all the details. Not in a gross way, in a celebratory way. Which made it weird that this thing I felt so celebratory about…also made me kind of want to keep them to myself.

This wasn't the same as hooking up with a cute guitar player at a party in college and going back to my friends full of stories. This felt…more real. More soft, almost, like I didn't want to risk leaving indentations from talking about it with other people. "Um. I think… I think it's private?" I made a face. "That's bizarre, right? Me feeling private?"

He smiled and brushed his lips over my cheek again. "Aww, baby, I'm super happy for you. That's so sweet." He might have said more, but we were interrupted.

"Mason?" A crisp young Latinx man gestured to a fitting room and hung Mase's suit. "This is you."

"Thanks." He straightened his shoulders and headed in.

"And you are?" the guy said to me.

"Declan Swick-Smith."

"Same party?"

"Yep."

He nodded and disappeared to the back, leaving me scuffing my sneakers on the floor and wondering if I could find the shoe polish I knew I'd bought at some point. Maybe? I'd kept it on the floor of the closet in my last apartment, and then I'd moved. I didn't remember packing it or unpacking it. Then again, I didn't remember throwing it away.

"Declan."

I followed the guy and thanked him. "Mase?" I called over the half-wall. "How're you looking?"

"Irresistible. You?"

"Half naked, will update."

He laughed. "I like you half naked, Dec, but I don't think Mia's parents would be thrilled with that as a ceremony look."

"I'll have to rethink." I sighed loudly. "Weddings are *so* inconvenient."

"Hopefully Mia and Ronnie go through with theirs. The Motherfuckers are oh-for-one right now."

Ouch. I wasn't sure how to respond to that, but thankfully Oscar's voice giving his name—presumably to the fitting dude—provided a distraction. "Hey, Oscar!" I called.

"Must you speak to me through a dressing room door?"

"Um, yes?" I pictured the disgruntled expression on his face and grinned, alone, to myself, in my dressing room. "How was your day? How's work? Anything exciting happen?"

"You're a terrible person," he muttered as Fitting Attendant Dude got him settled next to me.

"I know! Too bad you love me in all my terribleness!"

"Y'all," Mason said from my other side. "Ronnie did right by us. I look *fly*."

Fly, omg. "I'm gonna report you to the Department of Outdated Terminology for that. Also, I wanna see!"

"Get your ass out here, then."

"Yeah, yeah." I turned sideways and surveyed my appearance. I had to agree. We were in cream colored suits with lush lavender ties to pick up the lavender the brides were wearing. My suit looked damn good on me and the fit was perfect.

I emerged from the dressing room about to say *I* looked fly except the words died on my lips.

Mason looked absolutely magnificent, and I suddenly remembered getting fitted for our own wedding—the excitement, and joy and abandon of it, of letting ourselves become wrapped up in the whole thing.

"You look great," he said, holding a hand out to me. "C'mere."

I let him pull me into a hug, shocked by how moved I was seeing him in a suit, wearing one myself. "Jesus, I just had the strongest memory."

"Me too. I think we've aged well, don't you?"

We turned to the mirror, still one-arm-hugging. We both looked freaking hot.

"I know everything went to hell, but it was…really nice thinking I was gonna marry you, Mase."

His reflection smiled. "Yeah, it was wild, wasn't it? It feels like two lifetimes ago."

And it did. Usually. When we weren't in wedding suits. Or when I wasn't contemplating a relationship with someone. "Yeah, but also like maybe it was last week. God."

"Don't tell me you're having regrets, Dec. No offense or anything, but I've sort of moved on."

I elbowed him. "Shush. I'm not having regrets, I'm having *a moment*. If you don't mind." A moment of…doubt, maybe. A moment of reliving the worst thing I'd ever done and having no idea if I could promise I wouldn't do it again.

He kissed my cheek. "You look super hot. You know. In your *moment*. You have to let me take a picture for Sidney. I feel certain they'd want to see you in this suit, Dec."

"I'm not sure that's—"

"It is, shut up." He stepped back and made me shift until he liked whatever was behind me. "There. Done. And sent."

I rolled my eyes as if I was annoyed when I kind of wanted Sidney to see me all dressed up.

"Too bad about your hair though," he said.

I fake-karate-chopped him to the gut and he humored me by doubling over. "You're such a jerkface."

"Poor you."

Oscar's voice came from the dressing room. "I look like a marshmallow."

Mase and I exchanged glances. "Not even possible," I said. "You're not sweet enough to be a marshmallow." Mason punched me and made a face. "I mean, I'm sure you don't."

"Why cream? I look better in black."

"Just come out!" Mase called.

"But I look like a *marshmallow*." Still, the door pushed slowly open.

"Oh my god, you look fantastic, dummy." I went up to where he was lingering out of range of the three available full-length mirrors and straightened his tie.

"No, you guys look fantastic. I look like I've never been to the gym and eat too many donuts."

We used to try to convince him he looked good. Now we skip that step. I got all up close behind him and Mase shimmied against him face-to-face, both of us feeling him up. "Mmm, daddy, you're so sexy," I whispered.

"You turn me onnnnnnn," Mason whispered in his other ear.

Oscar held out for maybe seven seconds before laughing and shoving us away. "Go to hell, both of you."

"Ahem." A discreet throat-clearing drew our attention to Fitting Attendant Dude.

"Please excuse my friends," Oscar said, blushing dark.

FAD was obviously used to ignoring the antics of his customers. "Are any further alterations necessary?"

Mase ran both hands up his torso. "Not here, honey."

I had the distinct impression FAD wanted to sigh. He turned to me and I decided to let him off the hook. "My suit fits perfectly, thank you. Oscar?"

He grimaced at his reflection, turning to the side. "Do you have some magical way to make me look less like a marshmallow?"

FAD stepped forward, assessing the situation with a professional eye. "Will the groom be wearing a cummerbund or vest?"

"No groom," I said.

"Two brides," Oscar added.

"Ah." Pause. "Are either of them wearing a suit?"

"No."

He nodded. "Would they object to a cummerbund in their groomsmen? That may help some, if I understand your...dissatisfaction correctly."

"Wouldn't that just draw attention to—" Oscar gestured at his midsection.

"No, sir. The cummerbund, when worn correctly—and I will show you how—makes one look taller. Longer."

He didn't say *thinner* but we were all thinking it. I'd never considered the tight rope you'd walk at a place like this, trying to address people's insecurities without confirming them.

Oscar turned to Mason and I. "Am I being stupid?"

Mase reached for his hands. "You don't look like a marshmallow. But if wearing a cummerbund will make you feel better, then let's do it."

"You don't mind?"

"Sweetheart, I *know* you don't think a cummerbund can detract from my personal charisma."

Smiling weakly, Oscar looked at me. "You don't mind, Dec?"

"Hell no. Cummerbunds are kinda sexy in a weird way."

FAD nodded. "I'll be back shortly."

We only waited a little while. More measurements were taken and we made another appointment for the following Friday to pick everything up, including cummerbunds in the same shade of lavender (who knew?).

Before we left Mase held out his phone open to a message from Sidney. To his picture of me in a suit, they'd replied with a *Golden Girls* GIF of Blanche Devereaux spritzing herself with water as if something was too hot to handle.

I tried not to blush but it's hard to fool old friends.

"That is so stinkin' cute." He kissed my cheek. "You still look damn good in a suit, babe."

I should have said *Thank you* or something equally innocuous. Instead I said, "You look better than you used to."

He kissed my other cheek. "See you."

"Yeah, see you."

Watching Mason walk away hurt me somehow, a deep ache that went all the way into my marrow. There had been a time in our lives when I'd loved him more than life, and yet I'd left him standing in front of everyone we cared about, left him to make all the apologies while he was still devastated, confused, angry.

How could I even think about doing this again? Another relationship, another thing that would spin out of control when I wasn't looking, which I would destroy like I had before. If I'd done it to someone I'd known and loved for years, who could tell what damage I'd do with someone I'd only met recently?

I realized FAD was eyeing me through the window of the shop and started walking to my car. A cummerbund might help with self-confidence, but I doubted FAD had anything that would help with massive commitment issues and a tendency toward abandonment. *Sigh.*

Chapter Sixteen

Halfway through the day on Thursday I got a text from Sidney that read, *So, how does sex tonight sound to you?* Followed almost immediately by a text that read, *I wrote and deleted like twenty-three more subtle proposals until I decided that we're both grown-ups and direct might make the most sense.*

Commitment issues? What commitment issues? *Hiiiiiiiii, I WILL BE THERE WITH BELLS ON. MY DICK. BELLS ON MY DICK. (Not really. Unless you were into that.)*

I do not think bells will be required, Sidney sent back.

We achieved some logistical understandings—we'd order takeout, I'd go home by midnightish so they could not totally screw up their sleep schedule—and I went back to work with a veritable spring in my step.

And texted Mason a jumping up and down GIF.

He texted back, *I'm having wine for dinner and taking my-*

self to a lousy Netflix rom-com in my living room. HAVE FUN. Softened by the kissy-face selfie he sent along with it.

I sent him a whole line of hearts and pretended to work for the rest of my shift. Actually worked? Actual work was done. While my mind was on other things.

Like Sidney. And how I'd have to stop by my apartment and shower and dress for the occasion. The occasion of sex with Sidney, hello, one must look one's best.

Skinny jeans that made my ass look good, black T-shirt, silver choker. Not quite right yet. I texted Mase (this date selfie thing was legit) and he told me to try a scarf with the ensemble. I added a gray scarf shot through with shimmery threads and sent him another picture.

I got back *You so sexy*, which seemed solid, and a row of hearts which made me feel good. Before I left I laid out the clothes for the morning and pre-made a lunch, because everything needed to go smoothly.

I…may have also grabbed a little tinkling bell still out from Mia and Ronnie's Christmas gift. Just in case. Not for my dick. But I thought it might make Sidney laugh, and I liked making them laugh.

We were both nervous. That was the first thing I noticed. They let me in and we stood there awkwardly for a minute.

"Sorry, was this weird? I think this was probably weird, right?" They bit their lip.

"Nah. Well. I didn't think so until right now? Um, hi. Can I kiss you hello?"

"Yes please."

That was less weird. Kissing. Lingering. Stepping a little closer until both of us had our hands on each other, until our bodies shared heat.

"Less weird?" I murmured.

"Yeah. Um, I have to keep reminding my brain that it's okay to go for it. Because we've actually planned on sex."

"Usually you tell your brain something else?"

They flushed. "Well, if we're about to shoot a video, or if I know you're planning to go home soon, then yeah."

"We could do up a sandwich board for YouTube: *Gone fuckin'*."

"We *are not* putting a sandwich board on YouTube that says *Gone fuckin'*."

I pouted. "Aw, c'mon, Sidney! It'd be funny!"

They kissed me. "Granted, it would be. Only instead of a fishing pole it'd be what, a bottle of lube?"

"A bottle of lube and a set of fur-lined handcuffs?" I said hopefully.

"Those cheap fur-lined cuffs are impractical. I have better restraints than that."

I pulled myself against them, clutching their arms. "Oh, swoon. What else do you have in your bag of tricks? Please tell me you have a literal bag of tricks."

"It's more of a...box."

After much begging, I was permitted to see the box of tricks, which did not disappoint. "Oooh, butt plugs and vibrators and magic wands, oh my!"

"The magic wand is really loud, but it's the first thing I bought when I moved into my own apartment. I still worry that the neighbors think I'm jackhammering or something."

I giggled. "Jackhammering *yourself*."

They shoved me. "Oh my god."

"What?"

"That is not how one uses a magic wand! Unless one has the correct attachments."

I looked into the box again. Maybe...

"Sorry."

"Alas." I draped myself across the bed. "Visions of jack-hammering danced in my head. Then died."

"Well." They held up a sleek looking dildo. "Not entirely."

"Oh boy. Oh damn. Oh yes. So, um, sex?"

Sidney grinned. "Is this where you offer to be my jack-hammer?"

"I was thinking maybe this was where you showed me what you like. I mean, either way. I'm open to anything. Up for anything even. Wait, do you have a strap-on?"

"Dude. Of course. Why? Are you in need of a jackham-mering?"

"You know I am." I did a seductive eyebrow waggle that in no way made it look like I'd lost my eyebrow remote at an inopportune time. "Also—" I produced the bell with a flourish from my pocket. "Just in case."

They laughed.

Sometime—some *hours*—later we stood in the kitchen eating Thai food out of takeout containers. Sidney and I had gotten different types of curry, and while I was a big communal food person, they were very much an eyes-on-your-own-plate person. They did offer a bite of theirs and, after a brief hesitation, accept a bite of mine, but then we settled into eating our own curry.

Standing in the kitchen because we were hungry, and also, at least on my part, because I was hoping we'd return to the bed afterward. Which somehow seemed less likely if we settled in on the armchairs.

"We're going to need a decoy date," I said when I'd eaten enough to not be starving.

"Ohhh. Yes. You mean because the alternative is sharing the details of our sex life with YouTube?"

Wait, maybe I was being strange. "Am I being strange?

I'm not usually all that reserved when it comes to sex? But this feels... I don't know." I didn't want to be all *This feels super special and I don't want to share* even though that was sort of how it felt.

"I don't think you're being strange. To be honest, I'm kind of relieved. Not that I would have balked if you'd wanted to be more open, but being less open, at least about this, suits me."

"Good. Okay. Decided. So we'll need a decoy date."

They nodded. "I concur. Can you do Saturday afternoon again?"

"Sure. The Jenkinses will be gone if you want to come over to my place. We'll have the run of the main house because I dog-sit when they're traveling."

"That sounds good. To be clear, I would have proposed getting together again even if we didn't need a decoy date for The Love Study. We don't really. We could just tell them, 'Things are good.' And then have people call in or something." They pushed their glasses back with a knuckle. "I guess I'm just saying that my interest in seeing you again this week has nothing to do with YouTube."

"Ditto."

"Good."

We ate the rest of our food and cleaned up what little mess we'd made. I filled them in on my work project and Dire Jack. They filled me in on a few more memorable characters at the grocery store (all of whom I already had in my internal cast list from talking to Mia). Just as I was getting ready to propose sex (again), they said, "How is the wedding planning going? I hope that Ronnie's sister is still coming?"

For this horrible extended moment I was picturing Mason in his suit, and then his face when I couldn't get out of the limo. It wasn't a complete flashback, but it was definitely an emotional glitch where I could feel all those feelings as if it was happening again, like the word "wedding," which I'd heard and said a lot lately, was this sudden *portkey* to the past and I had no choice but to be sucked into it.

It only lasted a few seconds and I tried to cover it up by enthusiastically recounting our fitting room event, but Sidney wasn't fooled. They played along, letting me overact my anecdote until I kind of fell silent and waited for them to call me out.

My friends would have called me out. Gently. But persistently.

Sidney took my hand and led me back to the bed. We kissed and lay against each other and I closed my eyes when they wrapped their arms around me. Being held made it safe enough to speak. "Sorry. Mase made this joke the other day about the wedding, about how hopefully Mia and Ronnie go through with it because we—like, our friends—are oh-for-one. And I know he didn't mean it to be cruel at all, but I think it got under my skin."

"You still feel guilty?"

That was only the most obvious part of it. "I probably always will, you know? But I guess part of me still thinks if I'd been…stronger or something, we could have had that life we expected to have."

"Hmm." Their fingers trailed up and down my arm in this wildly soothing way and I tried to just feel it, every centimeter, every shifted arm hair, every goose bump from every shiver. "Do you wish you'd forced yourself to go through with it? I…didn't get the impression Mason wished that."

"No. He doesn't. And realistically neither do I? But there are way better ways to break off a wedding than flipping out on the actual day of the wedding. I wish I'd figured it out sooner. Or maybe that I'd never thought it was a good idea in the first place."

"Was it the idea of being married? Or the…what you said before? The life you expected to have?"

"I think that appealed to me." I tried to sort it out in my head while they kept touching my arm. "Or just the idea that I'd have something other people recognized, you know? My parents paid for a lot of my college, and it's not as if I grew up and became a doctor or a lawyer or something. I grew up and became a temporary office worker."

"Which you like."

"Which I like *a lot*, but it's not what they expected from me. I'm queer, and they're fine with it, but it wasn't what they expected. They *love* Mason. They would honestly get us back together in a second. Us getting married was something they understood. We loved each other, we were committed to each other, of course we should get married."

Sidney nodded, the movement brushing against my head. "It's difficult to be always outside of that model. Any model, really. But that's a potent fantasy for a lot of people, and not just for themselves."

"Exactly." I sighed. "That's exactly right. I broke Mase's heart. But in a way I feel like I broke my parents' hearts, and even my friends'. Like we had this great thing that everyone celebrated and I screwed it up. Threw it away."

"And you…said you go to therapy?"

"Ha. I went to therapy for a while. You think the wedding's triggering me?"

"It would make sense if it was."

"Even though it was six years ago?"

"I don't think triggers come with expiration dates."

"Yeah. True. Anyway, I'm sorry I'm all over the place." I

kissed their neck, which was the skin I could easily reach. I wasn't quite ready to lift my head and look them in the eye.

"I'm sorry I asked about the wedding. I'll leave it to you to bring it up if you want."

"It's going really well. Ronnie's sister is still going to be the maid of honor or whatever, which is great. And they're getting down to the wire since it's Valentine's Day." That was enough change of subject. Probably? I lifted my head. "Are we still on for V-Day Eve next week?"

"*V-Day?* I'm not going to *The Vagina Monologues* with you, Declan."

I blinked. "Wait. Is that a *Vagina Monologues* thing? Oh shit. I've been seriously saying that for years like an asshole! I meant Valentine's Day!"

They were looking at me with a mixture of sympathy and laughter. "Maybe people took you as a crusader to end violence against women?"

"I am! I'm a crusader! I don't like violence against women!" I collapsed over their chest and buried my face. "I can't believe this. Where were you when I was in college and thought I was being cool?"

"I was probably in college going to *The Vagina Monologues* every Valentine's Day and trying to sort out my complex responses to it."

"Oh my god, right? Me tooooooo. I can't even deal with this. My friends are going to laugh really hard at me."

"It's a reasonable mistake, I think. But to answer your question: yes. Unless you want to bring me to a theatrical production, in which case I might be washing my hair."

"Noted." I reached out to play with their hair, lying on the pillow. I hadn't quite had the courage to ask if I could take out their clips earlier—it felt too soon for that; hair intimacy is different than sex intimacy—but I had asked if it was okay if I touched and they'd said yes. "The wedding is the day after our Valentine's Date."

"Then we should do something low-key, right? They're not having a bachelorette party?"

"We're doing a sleepover tomorrow night. Ronnie said she's too old for a bachelorette party."

"Aww. That sounds nice."

"Yeah." Sidney's hair was light brown, nearly blond at the ends. I finger-combed it out over their pillow. "So um… sex again? Unless you're unwilling to have sex with someone who's seriously spent the last nine years using the phrase 'V-Day' like a dope."

"You are not a dope." They shifted, sliding down until our faces were on the same level. "I totally planned on more sex, but we don't have to. Cuddling is also nice."

"I think we have enough time for both."

They smiled. "Me too."

Chapter Seventeen

Ronnie and Mia lived in a legit house. It was a small house, and the neighborhood wasn't high-end or anything, but it was cute, and it was an actual house, and they even had a guest room.

Not that any of us were using the guest room.

Oscar brought his own air mattress (it made him feel better to have control over his sleeping arrangements, and it had gotten to the point where I felt better just seeing his familiar nest whenever we stayed somewhere). Mase and I were on couches—or would be, later.

We'd descended on the house shortly after work, dropping our stuff in a pile by the door, taking off our shoes, and taking over the kitchen. Mia hadn't gotten home from a meeting at the store and since Ronnie hated to cook, I was in charge.

I started taking stuff out of bags and waited for them to figure out what we were doing.

"Salad!" Ronnie called. "No, there's cheese."

"You can put cheese on salad," Oscar said, sounding unimpressed with what he saw so far.

"Not mozzarella," she shot back. "Oooh, sun dried tomatoes, yum."

Mason poked at one of the remaining bags before I could stop him. "Cauliflower rice. Huh."

"Cauliflower rice," Oscar repeated. "Are we fucking hipsters now?"

Ronnie gasped. "How dare you! I'll never forgive hipsters for adopting TERF bangs and screwing up my ability to effectively pre-judge people."

"Amen, sister." Mason shook his head. "I'm not getting this. Omelets with cauliflower? What are the eggs for? Some kind of scramble?"

I filed that away because cauliflower rice would probably make for a delicious scramble. "We…are making…"

Longgggggggg pause. Until Mason hit me.

"…pizza."

They gaped.

Ronnie sorted through the ingredients again. "What, like, deconstructed pizza? Since when did we put cauliflower in any form on pizza?"

"No." Oscar set his expression on *disgruntled*. "Not doing it. You can shove your vegan-ass, gluten-free-range bullshit right up your—"

"Oh yum!" Mase said. "Cauliflower crust. Someone was just talking about that."

"It's obviously not vegan," Ronnie told Oscar. "There's mozzarella. And eggs."

He shook his head. "Don't care. Not eating pizza made out of vegetables."

"Honey, you love veggie pizza."

He continued to shake his head.

"Don't worry," I said to Ronnie. "I'll win him over. I made this the other night and it was delicious."

"Ooooh, for Sidney?" She kind of sang their name.

"Shut up, no, for myself." Sure, okay, I'd thought of it as "testing" the recipe for when I could make it for Sidney, but whatever.

"Awww." Mase pinched my cheek. "Blushy McBlusherson over here has an enbyfriend."

"Oh my *god*, shut up, don't call them that. Unless they like it, which I don't know, because it hasn't come up."

He whipped out his phone. "Maybe we should—"

I dove for it, he pulled it away, we tussled, I tried to corner him and get his phone but he dodged and ran right into Mia just coming in the door. Mason slipped behind her, shouting, "Block him!"

Mia's withering glare landed on me. "Explain."

"Um..."

"Don't mind them, love." Ronnie saved me by taking Mia's purse and jacket. "Mason's just torturing Dec about Sidney."

The glare disappeared. "Oh. Well, that's okay, then." She kissed her fiancée hello. "I thought it was something bad."

"It *is* something bad!" I ducked between them and managed to get to Mase, but only after he held his phone up in triumph.

"Ha ha! Message *sent*!"

I groaned and converted my tackle into banging my head on his shoulder. "You're a monster."

"I just have a question. Sidney doesn't mind questions. Also, look at you not even challenging the premise."

"What premise?" I whined, still banging. Banging my

head on Mase's shoulder was much more satisfying than banging it on my steering wheel.

"The premise that you two are doing a thing that could actually use a word."

"It's great," Mia said from behind me.

"I agree," Ronnie added.

Oscar made a strangled sound. "I find the whole thing offensive and I'm viciously jealous."

"Aww." Mase hugged me. "He says the sweetest things." His phone dinged. "Hey, I wonder if that's—"

My phone dinged. I groaned. "What have you *done*."

"Sidney said they don't identify as enby, so probably not," Mason reported.

I looked at my phone. Squinted at it. With one eye completely closed.

We haven't discussed titles, but we could if you want. Maybe "datemate"? It's not great, but it's...something.

"They think maybe 'datemate'," I said slowly, typing, *Or we could just use each other's names. We don't NEED titles.*

My friends started discussing titles and pet names in the background as we all shifted back into the kitchen proper.

I will give it more thought. It feels...slightly appealing to me to use titles. But we don't have to if you don't want to.

Ack. That wasn't what I meant at all. I furiously typed out another reply voicing my support for titles unless *they* didn't want them.

"I love 'bae,'" Ronnie was saying, "but at this point I think maybe white people should stop appropriating black culture. You know, as an experiment."

Mase laughed. "Hey, at least white folks aren't starting a billion dollar industry off 'bae.' But yeah. 'Partner' is good, but not casual. Do people use 'significant other'?"

"I tried," Mia said. "But it doesn't exactly roll off the tongue." She sidled closer to Ronnie. "I like 'lover' myself."

Oscar made gagging noises.

My phone dinged.

I've talked about this on the show, but it was always general. I'm weirdly unprepared to think about it personally. I think…for something serious… I'd dig the term "companion," like "long-term companion." Sort of reclaiming something once used to diminish queer relationships. But "datemate" or "datefriend" or just "date" would probably make the most sense right now.

Oh wow. "Companion." Um. The word shot glitter-sparks all down my spine. I bit my tongue. *I agree. Variations on "date" for now (for both of us, please). "Companion" as a more, uh, settled thing. If relevant. Um. So. Yeah.*

Mase poked me. "What'd they say?"

"We're using 'date' or 'datefriend' or 'datemate.' Right now. While things are…casual."

He pretended to swoon. "Your date, Sidney. God, that's adorable. Sidney's date. Awww."

Ronnie and Mia added their *awww*s to the chorus.

I would have told all of them to shut up again but my phone dinged.

It's a pleasure to be your datefriend, Declan.

I way-more-than-pretend-swooned. "I, um, really like them," I said to my friends, and sent back, *I am at your service, my date.* Which was probably too much, but I…really, really liked them.

"Are they good at fucking, though?" Oscar said. "Because that's important."

Mase held up both hands. "That is *private* and we're leaving Dec to it."

Another round of *awww*s from the brides-to-be. Ronnie reached out to squeeze my shoulder. "That is super sweet."

"I don't know about that—"

"No, it really is," Mason agreed. "But now the sweet part is over, get in there and make us dinner."

I hid in the bathroom just long enough to text Sidney to tell them I'd made our sex life off-limits to spectators and I wasn't sure why but it felt right. Plus a blushing emoji.

They sent back, *That feels right to me too.* Plus a blushing emoji.

Then I went and made dinner.

Everyone loved cauliflower crust pizza. Even Oscar.

The theme of the sleepover was "terrible wedding movies." *Our Family Wedding* was the kind of terrible that you couldn't stop watching, even as you were cringing at the "It's okay I'm making a racist joke because I, too, am a person of color" punchlines. And also counted as rehearsal because that was so gonna be Mia's dad in a week, making alllll the jokes and being like, "Look, I'm Korean, it's okay." We totally loved Mia's dad, but wrangling him in company was going to be a whole *thing*.

Our second movie was *27 Dresses*, which was a massive waste of Katherine Heigl, who everyone in the room except Oscar would so bang. Or like…have coffee with. Because she seemed awesome. And third wedding movie was actually breaking the theme, because *The Perfect Wedding* was a cute feel-good gay-boys-in-love story that had all of us *awww*ing by the end of it.

We took a break for dessert, which was chocolate fondue in white, milk, and peanut butter varieties, with a bunch of stuff to dip in it. Oscar and I had collaborated on the chocolates and Mase had brought the dipping stuff.

"You guys are the best," Ronnie said happily, feeding Mia a white-chocolate-covered strawberry.

"We really are." Mason made a big show of dipping a marshmallow, swirling it around somehow lasciviously. "Dec, should I cram this in your face like the two lovebirds?"

I stuck out my tongue at him. "Not unless you want me to bite your fingers."

"Ooh la la, he plays *mean*. I'm into it!"

Oscar dipped three pretzel sticks, one in each chocolate, then ate them all at once. "White chocolate and peanut butter don't really go together," he concluded.

Mia leaned toward Ronnie and whispered, "I'm trying to make that into a race thing but I can't make it work."

"You can be my peanut butter anytime, baby," Ronnie whispered back.

I booed. "Quit it, you'll make me sick before the chocolate does."

The fiancées exchanged suspicious glances. "So, um." Ronnie frowned.

"Yeah, we…" Mia refilled her wine glass. "We just wanted you guys to know you mean the world to us."

"Oh god." Oscar appealed to Mase and I. "They're about to get fucking sappy. Make it stop."

"Don't make me muzzle you," Mase said. Then, to the ladies, "Go ahead, lovebirds."

"We've been thinking a lot, you know, with all the stuff about my sister, and whether my parents will even show up, and how awful they'll be if they do, and…" Ronnie wiped her eyes. "And anyway, it's really important to me that all four of you know that you're my family, and I appreciate it so much. And I'm so, so glad that I happened to luck into having you as a roommate freshman year, Oscar."

"Oh Jesus fucking Christ, come here." Oscar sighed heavily and gave Ronnie a huge hug. "Like you could ever get rid of me. You've been stuck with me since that day you called in sick to Latin when I was super hungover and nursed me back to health."

I nudged Mason. "Hey, remember that day I was super hungover and you stood beside my bed and taunted me with burritos that made me want to puke? That was real sweet too, Mase."

"I'm pretty much the best."

We grinned at each other.

Mia, now also teary, sniffed. "Also we thought this would be a good time to say you guys are collectively in charge of my parents, so make sure they don't do anything embarrassing."

Mase shook his head. "I can't tell your dad to stop cracking Korean jokes. He loves making people uncomfortable."

"I asked Mom to medicate him or something, but she refused."

"It'd be such a good wedding gift, though!" I said. I guess it violated some kind of medical oath or something for her mom to lightly sedate him in time for the ceremony. Plus, probably whatever her dad ended up doing would make for funny stories. Later. Way later.

"Is the sappy shit over yet?" Oscar asked. "I want more chocolate. Maybe with a spoon."

"Absolutely not," I said. "Germs. We cannot all get sick right before the wedding."

Ronnie shoved Oscar as he was going for the chocolate. "Did you hear what Declan just said? *We are not getting sick before my wedding, mister.*"

Mason tilted his head to lean against mine. "Wasn't it nice a minute ago when they were all cute and remembering their beautiful friendship?"

I laughed. "Yeah, thank god that's over. What're we watching next?"

We stayed up past midnight, despite all of us bitching that we were way too old to stay up that late. When we'd lived in the dorms I thought sleepovers couldn't get better than sleeping bags and a twenty-four pack of whatever beer we could afford. I'm really happy I was wrong. Adulthood sleepovers rock.

Chapter Eighteen

Since our Saturday date was a decoy date, it felt like the pressure was off. I put together a good salad for lunch and Sidney came over a while after they got off work. I'd already been watching a documentary, so I caught them up a little on Viking travels and we settled in.

The Jenkinses had been back briefly, then gone away again. I didn't know that much about my landlords except that they were married (or at least used the same name), they traveled a lot, and they loved their dog. Toby's an Australian shepherd. That's all I know about his pedigree. He's also a total cuddle monster, and he really does need company. He's sad when I leave for work in the morning and I always turn on Animal Planet as per my instructions.

I vaguely had the impression that Mrs. Jenkins was an expert in...something medical? And that Mr. Jenkins did... computer-based work?

And they were really nice to me. When they assured me I could use the downstairs of the main house, they meant it. They had a cleaner come once a week whether they were there or not.

We took Toby for a walk after lunch. It was…weirdly normal-seeming to have Sidney there for regular things like feeding the dog and taking him for his walk. I kept thinking I wasn't being a very good host, but it just…didn't feel strange to have them in my space. (Or to pick up dog poop with a plastic bag while they stood by, continuing to talk about an archaeology podcast they'd recently heard, which we'd started discussing when watching the Viking show and kept going back to.)

I showed them my little apartment in the backyard after we got back from our walk. Which…took some time. I gave a very thorough tour. Of my tiny room. And, uh, my bed. And also there was the shower.

When we were dressed and available for dog company again, I made a pot of decaf in the main house (because Sidney still had to go home and go to bed at a decent hour so they could get up at three in the morning for work). We ended up on the couch with our legs pleasantly tangled, and Toby snoring contentedly at our feet.

"I've been thinking about The Love Study," Sidney said.

"Okay."

"I think we might consider ending it. Officially."

I blinked. "Oh. Wow, I hadn't even thought about that. But what about your sponsor?"

They did one of their understanding nods. "I considered that. The money has been nice, for sure. Or being able to count on it has been nice. But I think…the show has done what we designed it to do. A microcosm of the dating world, an example of a few potential outcomes." Their thumb rubbed rhythmically up and down the side of the mug. "And selfishly I kind of want us dating to be for us. Not for the channel. Not for the money, or the views, or the shares, though all those things have been nice. But this, you, being with you is...more important."

I swallowed. "It's really important to me too. Like, usually I tell my friends everything, but this feels...specialer. More special. You know what I mean."

Their eyes met mine and I knew they were going to kiss me in the moment before they did, had that anticipatory thrill right before their lips touched mine and I closed my eyes, needing something from it, maybe an acknowledgment that this was special for them too.

"I really, really enjoy you," they murmured. We kissed for another minute before they pulled away, but not far. "Um. Do you think we should end the show?"

Part of me was relieved by the idea. Part of me was almost sad. I'd gotten used to talking to that faceless audience, to putting my thoughts in order so other people could understand them, which kind of helped me put them in order for myself. "Not gonna lie, I'll probably miss it a little."

"Oh, no, I don't want to end it just for me. If you want to keep going on dates with other people and coming on—"

I kissed them. "Please don't make me keep going on dates with other people."

"I don't really have an exclusivity thing. But I don't intend to date other people than you right now."

"Ditto, ditto, ditto. I mean, partly because dating is *hard*, but mostly because I just...um...because I think you and I..." I ran down in a puff of unspoken words.

"The statistical likelihood of finding someone else with whom I share this level of both physical and intellectual chemistry seems low," Sidney said, nodding super seriously.

And then almost immediately cracking a smile. "It makes sense to conserve my energy."

"Um, exactly. Also, I like you so, so much, oh my god." I buried my face against their shoulder, which took some flexibility given the way we were sitting with our legs between us. To cover up my words, I said quickly, "Speaking of energy, do you want to go home soon? I'm hyper-conscious of the time."

"I can stay awhile longer."

"Yay!" I picked my head up. "In that case, should we forage for dinner?"

They grinned. "I've spent my entire life thinking of food as a form of fuel I had an obligation to consume in order for the machine to run. You've turned it into an adventure."

"Oh hell yes." I grabbed their hand. "Come adventure with me into the depths of the Jenkinses' refrigerator. Only the gods know what we might find there."

"That sounds exciting and a little bit dangerous."

I performed an eyebrow waggle. "Much like myself."

"Indeed."

We decided we'd do one last episode of The Love Study the following week and take questions. I wasn't as intimidated as I had been before by the thought of people calling in or writing in to ask stuff. And it seemed only right to give the folks some warning.

I definitely wasn't prepared for the uproar our announcement about ending the show would cause.

"Y'all are acting like Declan is dying," Sidney said finally, amused and exasperated. "He's perfectly fine. He can visit the show whenever he likes."

"Wait, I can?"

They shot me a quick smile. "I'm not excommunicating

you or anything. You've been a guest now. You'll be welcome again."

"Whoa. Far out." I realized I was just staring at them and turned toward the camera. "So yeah, I'm not going to poof out of existence or something. Though that'd be cool. Do you ever sit around wishing magic was real and that was a thing you could, like, learn to do?"

"Poof out of existence?" Sidney asked. "I feel certain I've never wished I could do that. No, I take that back. I may have wished that. Not in a happy way."

"Uh, true. I didn't catch that until I'd already said it. I meant it in a happy way now. Like *poof* suddenly I appear. Then when you're sick of me, *poof*, I'm gone again."

They raised their eyebrows, arching over their glasses. "How likely do you think it is I'll get sick of you?"

I leaned forward and lowered my voice. "You might. I once left someone at the altar, you know. I may be insufferable."

"Declan, I think that means *I* should be afraid of you deciding you're sick of *me*, right?"

I mock-gasped. "Never! I would never. Perish the thought." I did a dramatic partial swoon.

"Okay, okay." They addressed the camera after barely pausing to appreciate my swoon. "More seriously, I wanted to thank all of you for your support the last six weeks. This has been a lot of fun, and it's been a nice change of pace from the usual Spinster Uncle shows. I know it's easy to get used to a format and then to want that consistently, so I really appreciate your willingness to allow me to play with the channel a bit."

"Lobby in the comments if you want Spunk—" I smirked at them "—to do this again. I have some friends who might be willing to give The Love Study a try since it's been so successful, though they're out of luck because I totally just snagged the most amazing single person in town. Possibly in the state."

Sidney seemed momentarily at a loss for words. "I..."

"So yeah, shout it up in the comments," I said again, kind of covering for them, kind of hoping I could get Mase to agree to do The Love Study. Mostly because Sidney was good at setting people up and also because I thought it might revitalize him on the whole dating front.

Of course, I'd have to convince him, but I thought I might be able to. Maybe.

"I think there might be more comments on this video than any livestream I've ever done." Sidney scrolled. And scrolled. And scrolled. "Um, sorry, everyone. I try not to look unless I'm specifically asking for something but wow, you really like The Love Study."

"Maybe there will be a season two!" I put in hopefully. I looked directly into the camera. "Some of you out there could use it. You know who you are."

They shoved me, making me giggle, and rolled into the ad read and outro, adding, "Next week's episode, the last of The Love Study, will be a Q and A, so please feel free to send your questions by email, Instagram tag, Instagram DM, or voice message. You can also comment or call in with your questions next week. I think that's it, thank you for watching, and I will spinster at you more next time."

I waved as they cut the recording.

Both of us exhaled. I leaned back and Sidney leaned forward to continue scrolling.

"Is it batshit?" I asked with some trepidation.

"They are losing their collective mind. I don't understand why. Do you think they expected us to date for their entertainment forever?"

I put my hand on their arm. "Sidney. That's *exactly* what they thought. Isn't it?"

"Now that we're saying it aloud...probably. Yes."

"Jeez, that's...creepily voyeuristic."

"Also pretty predictable. This is the age of reality shows and daily vloggers. That viewers expect to witness the ins and outs of strangers' lives might not be that odd." They shook their head. "But I'm glad you aren't tempted to do that. I think I'd have a hard time dating a daily vlogger."

I only had a passing idea of what a daily vlogger was, but I thought Mason followed some people who posted videos all the time. I kind of understood the inclination to watch, but I couldn't really imagine being the star of my own constant YouTube channel.

"You're safe with me. I have no desire to, um, vlog daily."

"It's the editing I don't get. Editing one video a week is exhausting to me. I can't imagine doing it every day." They shook their head again. "This is a little...invasive at times. Well intentioned? But it's as if they are...rather overinvested in our relationship right now. Hmm...this is an...unforeseen side effect."

I knew I should care about what they were saying, but really I was just watching them, all focused on the computer, sort of musing under their breath about the commenters. I caught "...report you..." and "...that's um...no..." but mostly I watched them, the furrow in their forehead, the glint of the monitor on their glasses, the angle of their wrist as they navigated their little red mouse.

"Sorry," they murmured. "Almost done. Probably."

"Do you want Thai again?"

"Umm...that sounds delicious. Do you mind ordering? Get me any of the curries."

"Got it."

By the time the food showed up Sidney was turning off their monitor and I'd put waters on the desk next to the armchairs. They insisted on paying (because: guilt at apparently abandoning me while they worked again, though I just went back to that same film book and read about sound effects). I hadn't even been meaning to stay for dinner, but it seemed like it made the most sense to order in while they finished up.

In deference to Sidney's early shift we were very virtuous and only kissed a little before I went home.

An Ripati

204

Chapter Nineteen

Deb surveyed the ~~disaster~~ progress we'd made with the Fling bricks and took a deep breath. "I didn't realize we still had a binding machine."

"Um. I...thought that's...what you wanted? You did say the bricks should be bound. And I found it in one of the store rooms." I gulped. She *had* said that. Hadn't she? I'd written it down! I glanced at Jack, who was no help. "Was that not what you wanted?"

"I did say they should be bound, Declan. I clearly should have been more specific."

Oh shit. I'd fucked up. Massively, if the way she was staring in bemusement at the pile of rejected prototype bricks was anything to go by.

I tried to apologize, but my throat was too dry to speak.

"I figured you'd have them bound at the printer's." She picked up one of the spiral-bound booklets. "You did this with that old machine? It looks like it's from the bronze age. Or the fifties."

It wasn't *that* old. I'd googled it because we couldn't find a manual or anything. It did look clunky. It definitely hadn't been designed to sell based on sexiness; no one would stay all night in line at the Apple store for this baby. (Look, Ronnie and I only did that once, and I haven't bought an iPhone since, I swear. It's like a rite of passage or something, spending way too much money on an iPhone the second it's released. I had to get it out of my system and now I've moved on.)

"So you're saying…" Jack paused delicately. "That we could have simply paid someone else to do this?" He didn't look at me. I couldn't help looking at him.

"In theory. This is very nice, though." She flipped through. "I almost can't believe you got that thing to produce something this decent."

At least there was…that? "Sorry. I didn't know. I went poking around and found this and just…assumed it's how we were supposed to do it."

"Maybe we could still give the job to someone else." Now Jack sounded hopeful, the traitor.

"We've got almost half of them done," I countered. As long as you used a loose definition for "almost" and "done." To my surprise, Jack didn't even correct me.

"Oh, I like these. What would you say the total cost was for the supplies you had to buy in order to bind them?"

I knew down to the cent. The facts and figures were all meticulously recorded in a spreadsheet. "Thirty dollars. Ish."

She turned toward me. "Thirty dollars."

I gulped again. "Um. Yes?"

"For how many?"

"A hundred."

"In theory," Jack added.

"Well, yeah. But we didn't need all one hundred, so it's okay that we had a few...practice runs."

A smile took over Deb's face. "We usually pay twelve dollars *per copy*. You two have just saved us a great deal of money on this project."

I sank down into my chair, which I'd forgotten existed during the period of abject dread following Deb's arrival. "Oh."

"To be fair," Jack said, as if the words were causing him pain, "it was all Declan's doing. I would have hired out the binding job in a second if I'd known that was a possibility."

Deb looked at me again.

I shrugged. "We worked together. There's no way I'd have gotten as many done if Jack hadn't been working on it during his shifts." Even though he'd whined at first. It wasn't necessary to mention that. Probably.

"I didn't expect you to have started on the bricks in earnest yet. We have a few final edits for the annual report."

A thump as Jack also sat down. "The report we've already had printed."

"The very same." Her smile widened. "The good news is it's just a few changes on just a few pages. No need to have the whole thing reprinted."

Both of us surveyed our conference table of piles in various stages of punching and binding. "What...does that mean?" I asked faintly.

"I think all you'll need to do is have these five or so pages reprinted, and then swap them out for the current version." Now the smile resembled that of an alligator toying with its prey. (I didn't know if that was something alligators did, but it seemed in character for them.) "No big deal for a couple of guys who can bind things by themselves, right?" She held up the report she'd grabbed and kind of shook it before placing it carefully back on the pile it had been in. "Good work. I'm *very pleased* with the results. I'll check in tomorrow."

In the silence after she left the room I tried to decide if Jack was pissed at me, or in general, or something else entirely.

Then, abruptly, a sound I'd never heard before emerged from his mouth. It took me a few seconds to work it out. He was *laughing*.

"I can't even believe we did this. Not only did we make a ridiculous amount of work for ourselves, we now have to do it all over again."

"I'm sorry." I meant it too. Deb had seemed happy about the money, but she'd also seemed sort of dumbstruck by the whole fiasco. Which didn't exactly bode well for either of us. "I honestly had no idea we could just...order them printed and bound. I mean, obviously I knew that was a thing, but I figured it was expensive and frowned upon. Once I found the bookbinding machine I thought that's how they must do it."

He waved a hand. "I probably would have thought the same thing. If I'd really considered it, I would have realized that a place like this wouldn't do their own report binding. Hell, Declan."

"Yeah. Sorry."

"It's funny. Honestly. And Deb loves to save money, she meant that."

"Oh. Good, then. I guess?"

"Twelve dollars per book. We're in the wrong line of work."

"Seriously." I sipped some water, trying to soothe the stress-ache in my throat. "What's the over-under on me being fired by end of business?" I tried to make it a joke, but it felt a little too real, the screw-up a little too fresh.

"Not a chance." He paused. "They'd wait until after the event."

I almost forgot he was a coworker and threw something at him.

He laughed again. "Sorry. Look, it was an honest mistake, it resulted in a money savings for the company—"

"Not necessarily. They're paying our labor where they wouldn't have had to otherwise."

"Yeah, but this time was budgeted for the Fling already, and we've used it in a way that maximized savings in other areas. I swear, it's fine."

I slumped. "I'm such a tool."

"You're not. You could even argue—and if you ever tell anyone I said this, I'll deny it—that Deb should have made it clearer what she expected. Though with her this sort of thing is more of a strategy than an error."

"What do you mean?"

He stood and began uncoiling the reports we'd already coiled, in anticipation of, you know, *plugging in five new final pages oh my god what had I done*. I tried to get my breathing under control and focused on what Jack was saying.

"...to know Deb through her wife, who was one of my professors and pulled me in like a little waif. Anne's the same way. She'd leave an assignment open-ended just to see what people would come up with. I know it seems a little backwards, but this will endear you to Deb more than producing the same thing she expected you to produce. Of course, that's only if we pull the rest of the Fling off."

The notion of Jack as a "waif" derailed my internal mortification train. "So you've known them for a long time?"

He glanced at me. "How old do you think I am?"

"Not...that old. But if you went to undergrad out of high school, then you've known your old professor for a while."

Seeming to decide I wasn't insulting him (if that was a

perk of me making a fool of myself with a book binding machine, I'd take it), he shrugged. "A while."

"Is that why you're working here?"

"I applied for my job just like everyone else." Not as defensive as he would have been a few weeks before, but a little touchy all the same.

"Uh, yeah, it really had not occurred to me that Deb hired you to be nice. Like, for a long time I thought she only kept me around because she liked me, but that's obviously dumb. She's not that kind of boss."

"True." He paused. It felt like a pause. Not a terminal point.

So I waited.

And sipped my now cold coffee.

And watched him uncoil reports. Which was soothing except for the guilty voice in the back of my head that kept prodding me to help.

"My grandparents are having trouble living independently," he said finally. "They raised me, and despite the problems we've had in the past, I care a lot about them. It's hard to see them struggle. I'd had a relatively high-pressure job before this and I couldn't keep up with the strain of it while also trying to watch over them when I wasn't at work, so I...quit. And started working here."

Whoa. Dire Jack had a semi-tragic backstory. Not that I should have been surprised, but in a way I was. "I'm really sorry about your grandparents. That sounds super hard." *Super hard* probably didn't scratch the surface of it, but it was the best I could come up with on the spot.

"It's difficult to convince independently minded people they need more help than they can get on their own."

"Yeah, I bet."

He began stacking the uncoiled completed reports in alternating vertical and horizontal sections. "Do you want to pull up the new final five pages? Should we send them to the printer or print them ourselves?"

"Maybe the printer? They should match."

"That's true. Some of the printers here are high quality, though if there are images we might want to have them professionally done. We could print a few test pages and see if it's a noticeable difference."

"Good call. It'd be faster to print them now and get them swapped out for the bad pages immediately. Also, I think that might help with my sense of mortification; if I have to do that tomorrow, I'll feel bad all over again."

He waved a hand, elegantly dismissing my ennui. "This is all just details we're learning for next time we do this. Like demand a *finalized* report by a certain date. And price check having the reports bound, especially if they're longer than this. We can't comfortably punch more than twenty pages, which is manageable at this length, but for longer it probably wouldn't be worth the labor."

I started gathering up the coils to bundle them back into the little compartment on the binding machine. "Yeah, imagine trying to do this many 500-page reports. Shudder."

He shook his head. "Hard no."

"Agreed."

The phrase *the next time we do this* kept bouncing around in my head. I would have said the last thing I wanted to do—besides becoming a permanent employee—was work with Jack again. But now? I wasn't as sure. Suddenly it felt like we were in it together...and all it had taken was him having a minor breakdown before coffee and me initiating a bunch of mutually wasted time.

"Oh god, I'm really sorry," I mumbled.

"If this is the worst thing you've ever done, Declan, you've lived a charmed life."

I nearly didn't say it. After all, I didn't have to. Jack would never meet my friends, would never hear their handy little tagline for me. But on the other hand, it sort of felt like a dismissal, like he really thought it *was* the worst thing I'd ever done.

"I left my last boyfriend at the altar."

He looked over. "Shit. Sorry. But..."

"I know. It's horrible. He's still friends with me and stuff. It's not like he hates me or anything. Now, I mean. He was pretty pissed at the time. For obvious reasons." *Shut up, Dec.*

Jack stared at me for a very long moment. "If my failed experience at marriage is anything to go by, you might have saved him a whole lot of heartbreak."

Jumping jackrabbits.

"Anyway, I didn't actually think making use of company supplies for company business and inadvertently saving the company a huge chunk of money was the worst thing you'd ever done. On most lists, it would qualify as a *good* thing. If you're networked to the printer by the bathrooms, I think that's our best bet for quality."

So...topic closed, apparently. I sent the finalized five pages to the printer by the bathroom and went to refresh my coffee while waiting for it to print. When I asked if he wanted a cup, he said yes. Which, while earlier in our work relationship I would have taken as an affront, as if I was serving him, now almost felt like camaraderie.

If this was how you won friends and influenced people, I should pile extra work on my colleagues more often.

Chapter Twenty

Pre-wedding drinks at the Hole were being held at our second favorite table, a booth along the windows, but thankfully nothing seemed to be fazing the brides-to-be.

"Our last drinks as single people!" Mia said, kissing Ronnie.

"Which means drinks in two weeks will be so much more relaxed!"

"Cheers!"

By merit of respective arrival times, Sidney was against the window with Mason between me and them, and Oscar was blocked in by the two cuddling fiancées, a situation that lasted about ten minutes before he commanded them to get out of the way so he could have the outside booth seat across from me.

Still somewhat glarey, he said, "Shouldn't you be sitting with Sidney?"

"Um." I glanced around Mase. It *would* be nice to sit with them. I mean, I'd considered that when I sat down, but I didn't want to make a big deal out of it even though Mase would probably have no issue switching.

Sidney shrugged. "I think we can date from this remove. Right, Declan?"

At which point I had no choice but to agree. "Yeah. Sure."

Their eyebrows dipped below their red frames, but the conversation moved on and both of us let it.

"About our honeymoon," Ronnie said, grinning.

"Veronica, if you start with that one more time—" Mason shook his fist at her. "I swear I will hurt you."

"What? I have no idea what you're talking about! Look at how innocent my face is right now." She turned to Mia and whispered, "Do I look innocent?"

"Not really," Mia whispered back.

"Does everyone have their assignments?" Ronnie asked, in no way innocently.

Since honeymoons are hella expensive and Ronnie and Mia had spent a lot on their wedding (deliberately; they'd decided it was a big enough priority that it made sense to go a little wild), we'd offered to facilitate a staycation honeymoon. Which meant that we had a roster of food deliveries split between Mase, Oscar, and me. We'd gotten some other stuff to deliver, too, like hilarious sex toys, but mostly it was food. Okay. Some of it was *suggestive* food. The message thread where we'd brainstormed it was rife with explicit-use-of-vegetables GIFs.

Too bad there's not a great way to scrapbook message threads. That would be a really funny wedding gift. *Here's how we planned to troll you on your honeymoon using only food, enjoy!*

"We have our assignments." I put my hand over Mase's, which were balling up a napkin to throw across the table. "I can't believe this time next week you'll be honeymooning, that's batshit."

"It's super exciting!" Mia bobbed up and down in her seat a little. "Also, we've been planning it forever and I'm nervous."

"Are you most excited for the wedding itself or the being-married part that comes after?" Sidney asked (in what I privately thought of as their Spinster Uncle voice).

"Oh, our lives together, definitely. I mean, I'm hugely excited for the wedding, but it's been so much work, and it's so stressful. Once we're settled down afterward I think..." She glanced at Ronnie, who kissed her cheek. "I think it will be really fulfilling. Just to be married. I don't know, is that Disney and trite?"

Sidney shook their head. "Not at all. Actually, I hear from a lot of people on my show who find marriage feels *more* meaningful to them than they thought it would. Queer people especially."

"That honestly makes me feel better. I don't want to be taken in by dumb narratives, but I love that we can do this. That we have the right. It's all just timing, you know? We happen to be alive in this moment when not only can we live freely, but we can get married, too." Mia looked down at the table. "Oh my god, soapbox, sorry. I just get kind of verklempt when I think about it."

Ronnie kissed her cheek again. "It's true, though. I'm grateful in a totally non-Thanksgiving way that we're getting married."

"Y'all are gonna make me cry." Mason dabbed his eyes. "I'm happy you're getting married too. And I remember being that excited."

I felt like I should probably chime in, but if I'd been that excited, I could no longer recall it. Now all I remembered was the sensation of impending doom, which had seemed to creep up from the ground whenever I stood still longer than a few minutes. Mostly I'd kept myself busy so I wouldn't deal with it.

"Does it feel like a political act?" Sidney asked. "Sorry, are my questions weird? I have a lot of questions, but you don't have to answer them if you just want to enjoy this moment."

Mia smiled. "I'm enjoying this moment of drinks! I'm pro-questions. It definitely feels like a political act to me."

"It's so serious, yeah." Ronnie tapped a fingernail on her wine glass, contemplatively more than nervously. "It's this weird mix of political and personal, private and public. I don't think we'll understand it all until years from now."

Sidney nodded. "That makes sense to me."

"Hey!" Mia bounced a little higher in her seat. "We could go on your show! And talk about the awesomeness of marriage! And answer all the questions!"

Mase nudged me. "Damn, you aren't even officially off yet and Mia's trying to take your spot."

"I'm not! I meant if you wanted someone—a couple— a married couple—" She scrunched up her nose. "Now it sounds dumb, Mase, jeez."

"I would really like it if you came on the show to talk about the kind of relationship you have, the ways you're compatible, the things you have to negotiate. Since people want different things from relationships, it's really helpful articulating different models of how that can look."

I settled my chin in my hand and gazed adoringly past my ex directly at my current. "You are so sexy."

Mason laughed and hit me, Oscar groaned, and Mia and Ronnie applauded.

Sidney blushed. So, so sexy.

They texted later, when I was curled up in bed with ~~yet another Netflix documentary about unhealthy food~~ a celebrated work of literature.

Do you want to phone with me for a few minutes?

And like, *yes*. I didn't consider myself a phone call person, but I liked to hear their voice in my ear, not just in my head when I read their words.

I paused the...celebrated work of literature...and dialed their number.

"Hey, datefriend." That's how they answered. *Hey, datefriend.*

Heat spread beneath my skin. "Hey. Nice to hear you. Again. Even though I already heard you earlier."

They laughed softly. I wondered if they were lying in bed, like I was. Or maybe in an armchair, legs all tucked under, book on their lap. I was still a little lost in thinking about where they were, how they looked, when they spoke again. It took me a second to replay it.

"You had a question about what?" I asked. When in doubt, echo back what someone's just said.

"Earlier, when Oscar asked if we should be sitting together...did you want to say yes? I felt like I'd sort of stomped on whatever you were about to say there."

"Oh, no, it's fine." Sidney noticed too much was the problem. They shouldn't have been able to tell I'd had that flash of disappointment.

"Well." They seemed to hesitate. "I think it's fine either way? Ultimately, I mean. But I guess it's important to me that we're doing something that works for both of us. And I really enjoy sitting next to you, so I didn't feel totally ambivalent, but I also didn't want to disrupt the whole table at that moment."

"Sure, me neither."

Silence for a long moment.

"Declan?"

"Yeah?" I swallowed.

"I need to be able to trust that you'd tell me if you wanted to do things differently."

Their voice hadn't gone full Spinster Uncle, but had acquired a level of detachment. Semi Spinster Uncle, maybe. Decaf Spinster Uncle.

"I like how we're doing things," I said, trying to keep a high, defensive pitch out of my tone. "Don't you like how we're doing things?"

"I do. I really do. I like that I feel comfortable on the phone with you, and that I can think clearly when you're in my space, that your presence doesn't distract my brain until I'm just coping."

I nodded, even though they couldn't see it. "Yeah. It was really nice having you at drinks, even not sitting next to each other. Nice to hear you talk, and laugh."

"And we've avoided the Drinks Curse since I've been a few times now."

"Omigod. We *have*! I'll have to text Mase later. Wow, go us. It's different, though. I mean, from situations where the Curse was in effect."

"In what way?"

"Um…" I stretched out, cradling the phone between my ear and my pillow. "First, will you tell me where you are? Just so I can try to picture you?"

"Oh. I'm in my bed. That sounds more, um, salacious than I intended. And before you ask what I'm wearing, an old pair of sweats and a Sia T-shirt."

I grinned. "That still sounds pretty hot."

"It's cozy. What're you wearing?"

"Boxers and a thermal shirt. The in-law unit isn't all that well insulated. Also in bed, by the way."

"Yay for beds. Tell me how I'm different from other victims of the Drinks Curse?"

"Maybe that you didn't come to drinks as a significant other? You started coming as a, like, friend. Communally. Wait, that sounds a little weird."

They giggled in my ear. "I don't think I've ever been a communal friend before, but it sounds fun. Are blindfolds involved?"

"Not at the Hole! That's a fine, upstanding establishment. Communal sharing of friends is only permitted in the private back room."

"I'm trying really hard not to make any of the obvious jokes right now," they said after a pause.

"I admire your self-control."

A huff of laughter.

"Anyway," I continued, "you know what I mean. You weren't there as *my date*. You were there because you go to drinks now. You would, even if you and I weren't dating. Right?"

"True. So you think that protects me from the Curse?"

"It sure seems to be. We haven't incorporated a new permanent member to the Motherfuckers...ever. We've had some people come and go, and a lot of people drifted away in the months after graduating from college, but the five of us have been together since we were, like, twenty. Huh."

"That's really cool. I don't have friendships that have been that consistently close for so long. Definitely not in person."

"Yeah, I'm glad none of us moved away. Oscar talks about it sometimes, and Mia and Ronnie might when they decide to have kids, but it hasn't happened yet." I cleared my throat, daring myself to tell them that I would have booted Mason out of his seat in a heartbeat if I'd thought they wanted to sit next to me as much as I'd wanted to sit next to them. But in the end, I couldn't say it. Didn't know how to say it without sounding needy and weird. And it seemed like they'd forgotten they asked, which was probably a win. I promised myself I'd be honest—or at least try to be honest—if they brought it up again. "So um...you don't have a lot of close friends?"

"Not the way you do. The way a lot of queer people do. It's like some queer superpower that completely missed me. I'm not very good at keeping people around."

"Except Arman?"

"Because he's stuck with me, I guess." They paused and I wished I could see their face. Was it doing the same slightly yearning thing it had done the first time we'd gone to drinks and Mase and I had been goofing around? "I was so used to being alone that it became the thing that felt...safest, I guess? It always made me a little sad, that I didn't have this amazing chosen family. But I also wasn't sure how to...do that. How to find those people. How to be close to them if I did find them."

"Huh, yeah. I think I just got super lucky? If I hadn't been roomed with Mase, I seriously don't know what would have happened." What a horrible thought. I tugged the covers in tighter around my shoulders.

"I've been thinking about his concern, how hard it would be to bring someone new around, but even now that we're dating, you guys seem comfortable having me at drinks. I don't pick up any...aggressive vibes from anyone. Or jealousy."

"No way. I think he's been attracted to some real assholes is the problem."

"Present company excluded."

"Dude. I left the man at the altar. And he looked *good* in that suit too."

"I'm sure he did. But since he doesn't consider you an asshat, I think you insisting on it reeks of unhelpful guilt-flailing, not productive accountability."

"Oh my god. Um." I swallowed, glad for once we were in separate rooms so I could pull the blankets over my head. Ouch. And also valid. Which was the worst kind of ouch.

"Er, sorry. I just spinstered at you accidentally. I try to only do that with consent." They cleared their throat. "I mean, I can't take it back. I meant it. But I shouldn't have said it. Anyway, I've only had good experiences at drinks with the Motherfuckers."

I didn't quite dare to come out of my blanket cave, but I did take the subject change. Or subject return. "The problem is that Mase brings around people who are jealous *of us*, then wonders why we don't get along with them."

"Ah. I hope it's all right with you that I don't really get jealous?"

Seriously, no one had ever said that to me before. "Is it not okay with other people that you don't get jealous?"

"For some people jealousy serves as proof of commitment."

"Oh. No. Yuck. I definitely do not want you to get jealous. And I'm not jealous of your legion of adoring fans." They made an inarticulate sound into the phone and I laughed. It still felt a little awkward, but I decided to run with it. "Your public, your devotees, your—"

"I'm going to remember this and get you back. Later. In the future. Creatively. By means you would never expect."

I legit shivered in anticipation. "That sounds pretty awesome. I look forward to it."

Sidney growled.

"You realize it turns me on when you get all big and scary on me. Bring it on. Spunk."

This time both of us laughed. We talked a little while longer then went to bed.

Despite having ended the conversation in a good place, I was still stuck on what they'd said. I was accountable for what happened with Mase. Wasn't I? I mean, he'd been super pissed about it for a long time, even after we started talking again, even after Mia came up with drinks and we all met up once a week. It's not like he immediately forgave me— we had to fight and cry and have angry break-up sex before we'd really worked it out.

Well, Mase had worked it out. I still felt shitty pretty much all the time. Which was fitting, right? I'd done a horrible thing. That...*was* accountability. Wasn't it?

Chapter Twenty-One

I picked up my suit on the way home from work Friday night, hanging it against my closet door since the closet itself was packed with all the things and I for sure couldn't squish my suit in there.

Then I stared at it.

I was super happy for my friends getting married. And also? Part of me? Couldn't wait until it was over. Which seemed fair because part of *them* couldn't wait for it to be over either, and weddings were known to be stressful as fuck and all that. But I did kind of wonder if maybe Sidney wasn't that far off, when they suggested I might be triggered by the whole thing.

I didn't want to be. I definitely didn't want to make Ronnie and Mia's awesome wedding about, like, *me*. But I couldn't avoid the suit and it was looming in a corner of my unit like a big dark storm cloud, taking up way more space in my brain than it was taking up in real life, until I actually curled up in bed and faced away from the suit as if it was threatening me.

Okay. I might have been a little...affected by the whole thing.

It was this huge, glaring reminder that I couldn't be that guy, the guy in the beautiful suit, marrying the other guy in the beautiful suit. I couldn't make that work, and I thought I'd come to terms with it, but suddenly it was all in the forefront again, like my brain was composing a list of my personal failings.

DECLAN'S PERSONAL FAILINGS

• Attempted to be a real person in a romantic relationship. FAILED.

• Attempted to get married. FAILED.

• Attempted to be a good friend to people getting married and not make it all about him. FAILED.

• Attempted to look good in wedding suit... Okay, being honest, I looked damn good in my wedding suit. So, like, SUCCEEDED. At this one thing. Which is me looking good in a suit.

I pulled a pillow over my head but it didn't make me feel better.

It wasn't like I didn't want to be that guy. I did! At least sort of. I wanted to be...happy the way getting married made Mia and Ronnie. Happy the way it would someday make Mason. But maybe that wasn't a thing I could ever do, or ever be. Maybe it would just be this painful, festering sore in me where other people had wedding bells and china patterns.

It wasn't that I couldn't *feel* it. That was the worst part. When I thought of Sidney, I felt all warm and fluttery, excited and melty and full, like I was totally inside myself with them. If I could just not feel, if leaving Mason at the altar had broken my ability to feel like this, that would be one thing. It might suck, but at least it wouldn't get all over other people.

Instead I was left with all the feeling and wanting but none of the ability to actually execute the thing I wanted. Which was…which was…

I had no idea. Which was why I'd given up on romance in the first place: How do you pursue something if you don't know what it is?

Get through the wedding. Just deal with it. Suck it up. Put on a suit, stand with Mase and Oscar and Ronnie's sister, be a decent person long enough to get through the wedding.

One more day. And it was our Valentine's Date, which we'd designed to be super casual and low-key and comforting. Maybe Sidney would be down for just, like, cuddling on the couch and making out a little. Because seriously that sounded so good, like it could build me up enough to survive the entire next day.

Which I was going to do. I wouldn't no-show the wedding, even if that suit was freaking me the fuck out. Once it was on, I wouldn't have to look at it. I'd be fine.

Except then I'd be looking at my friends and they'd all be looking beautiful, just like they had on the day of *my* wedding—

I tugged the pillow down harder around my head, squeezing my eyes shut against that vision of Mason looking so damn movie star handsome, so damn hopeful. He'd forgiven me, and he meant it. I knew that. But thinking about his expression always hurt.

He'd trusted me and I'd totally blown his trust. It didn't matter that I hadn't meant to, or that the therapist I'd seen after had told me that I couldn't control having a panic attack.

Like, okay, maybe not? But I should have done pretty much anything but run away and leave him to clean up the mess.

A few tears seeped into my pillow, which was not the mindset I wanted to have right now.

My phone dinged and I contemplated not looking at it, but I felt so crappy, I thought whatever it was surely couldn't make matters worse.

Sidney. My heart gave a little leap at their name on my screen. *I came up with this idea for our date tomorrow. I think you'll really dig it.*

I just stared at the message. An…idea? I wondered what kind of idea. How could I ask in such a way that it wouldn't seem like I was against it already? I wasn't against it already. I didn't think. Except that our original idea was about the only thing that sounded good to me at all.

Another ding. *Still at your place if you're willing. I'm not proposing either theater or fancy restaurants.* And a smiley face.

Relief tugged at my feelings. No fancy restaurants, no fork decisions, good. Right? Right. It'd be fine.

I sent back, *Oh yay, I'm excited.* And another smiley face. Because I was excited… I thought. Probably? I was definitely happy to see them. That was true and accurate. And if they'd had an idea about our date I didn't want to disappoint them by being all like *Sorry, can't do it, would rather have a boring night of doing nothing instead.*

Plus, they knew me really well and it would probably be the perfect thing even if it wasn't what I was expecting. That seemed logical. Based on past experience.

Ding. *I'm excited too and also a little nervous.*

Ding. *How was your day?*

I took a slow breath and elected not to mention that I was hiding under my covers because my wedding suit was a threatening presence in the corner of my apartment. *Pretty good. Event planning is going well. Dire Jack is actually less dire after I screwed up, which is nice.*

Ding. *People are strange sometimes.*

Seriously.

I flailed with the pressure of acting normal like this was any other day when in fact I was freaking out. *How was your day?*

Ding. *Good. Productive. Posted the usual Friday video. Shot a video for next week. Assembled some questions for our live Q and A on Monday.*

Wow, I'd managed to forget we were doing that. The end of The Love Study. *I'm a little sad to see the show end. What will I do on Mondays now?*

Ding. *I figured you'd be happy to have them to yourself again.*

Which I wasn't. Even though the pressure of racing to Sidney's apartment would be off. *I think I'll miss it.*

Ding. *You can always come just to hang out, on camera or off. I think I said that before, but in case I didn't.*

That would be weird, though. Me just sitting there. *I wouldn't want to bother you.*

Ding. *I wouldn't have offered if you bothered me. But obviously I don't expect you to come over after work on Mondays just, you know, to come over.*

Except I had been doing that. What were they really saying? That they didn't want me to? That they did? I banged my head into the pillow a few times, which was more dissatisfying than failing at banging it into my steering wheel. They didn't…expect me to come over. Dammit. Was that code for I should? Or I shouldn't?

Ding. *Sorry, I think I made this weird. Anyway, I was thinking about maybe asking Mara if she'd want to come on a new series of TLS. I'm 89% sure she'd run away in horror, but I might ask, anyway.*

Ooooooh, that would be amazing. And I liked Mara so much the one time we'd managed to hang out. I sent back, *Yes! Do! And she's partially responsible for me having the guts to talk to you, so I sort of feel like we owe her whatever help we can give. (Or that she's interested in.)*

Ding. *I didn't know that! I forgive her for spilling my old show nickname then.* With a winking emoji and immediate follow-up message: *That winking thing looks way creepier than I thought it did, I officially take it back.*

I smiled at my phone, which was admirably lighting up my duvet cave, though the screen was beginning to fog up from me breathing on it. *Oh no, you've emoji-winked at me, no takebacks.* I sent back five creepy winking faces and one tongue-out because I felt that best expressed my feelings on the matter.

Had they giggled when they saw that message? I hoped they'd giggled.

Ding. *No takebacks on emojis does seem like a fair deal. I suppose...*

EMOJIS ARE FOREVER

Ding. *Literally lol. I look forward to seeing you tomorrow.*

Me too. You, not me. I look forward to me seeing you. Not the other way around. And before I even knew I was doing it, I added a heart eyes and hit send.

Sidney sent back a heart eyes.

I buried my head in my bed again.

Tomorrow would bring a chill, calm evening with my date. Huh, that didn't sound as good to me when we weren't together. A chill, calm evening with Sidney. Now *that* I could totally get behind. And on top of. And underneath. And against. And—

I braved the suit in order to eat some pasta with a pesto sauce I'd made. Too bad I didn't have enough for our Valentine's Date. I could make more. Or a different sauce. Maybe I'd play with ingredients in the morning. Just in case. Sidney had said they had an idea for our date, which might mean food, but with Sidney it was just as likely to totally not mean food, so making a sauce was good prep work. And if they'd already planned on food, no problem, I'd have leftovers for a few days.

If it wasn't food, then what was their idea? But they said we'd still do it at my place, so it had to be pretty low-key, right? I hoped, anyway. That's what I needed: a no-pressure date with my Sidney. My date. Sidney, my date. My date Sidney. Not *my* Sidney, that was weird.

Also, the suit was looking at me again.

I washed my face and brushed my teeth and climbed in bed to watch a documentary on art restoration, carefully facing away from the damn suit. Eventually I fell asleep with visions of cuddling dancing in my head. And no damn wedding suits.

Chapter Twenty-Two

In preparation for Valentine's Date I cleaned my apartment and the big open kitchen/dining room/living room of the main house. Toby followed me around, lying in his bed in each space at an angle from which he could watch me clean. Then I made a sauce. A *just in case* sauce. Because you never know when you're going to want to serve your datefriend pasta with a delicious homemade sauce (and it was delicious).

Fifteen minutes before our date was supposed to happen I remembered I hadn't cleaned the half bath in the main house and ran over to do that, imagining myself in mid-toilet-scrub when the doorbell rang. But nope, avoided that by being mid-actual-peeing when the doorbell rang.

At least Toby understood me. He was a nervous pee-er too.

I didn't know why I was suddenly nervous. Suit hangover? Wedding dread? That sounded bad. I shouldn't be dreading the wedding. Or rhyming. I shouldn't be plying rhymes about dreading weddings.

The doorbell rang again.

I banished Toby to the back yard and went to answer.

Sidney. Looked. *Amazeballs.* Dark gray shirt pinstriped a very subtle shade of violet, black brocade vest over that, and a flowy skirt. With clunky combat boots.

"You...you look fucking awesome." I gestured to my own old-jeans-and-ratty-T-shirt combo. "I had no idea we were dressing up, I'm so sorry. I mean, I thought about dressing up, but then I thought maybe that would be strange, so I didn't, but now I wish I had."

They smiled and kissed me hello. "You always look good to me."

Which definitely should have felt nice, but instead just compounded my crimes. "I'm really sorry. I hope this doesn't mess up our Valentine's Date." A voice in the back of my head was moaning, *This was supposed to be casual, what happened to casual?*

"How could it?" They held up the grocery bags they were carrying. "Kitchen?"

I led them through to the back of the house. "I've been on the edge of my seat to find out what we're doing."

They set the bags on the counter and turned toward me. They'd done a thing with their hair where it swooped to one side with a braid that started above their right eye and ended over their left ear.

"I like your hair," I said, feeling weirdly shy.

They touched it. "Thanks. Um. Okay. This might be a silly idea? But I brought over stuff to bake cookies. Because you said you preferred that to a fancy dinner date, which is traditional for Valentine's Day. But if that doesn't sound good, we can always acquire actual food instead. We can do whatever. I'm not devoted to the cookie idea."

Oh god, they'd tailored the date to, like...me. And I'd shown up in ratty clothes internally whining about wanting things to be casual. "Oh my god, that sounds *amazing*. Let's make and then eat a whole bunch of cookies." I waved my hands around. "Go on, what'd you bring?"

They exhaled. "I was into this a few days ago, but then when I packed it all up to come over I started thinking I had guessed wrong. This dating thing is not for the faint of heart, Declan."

"You're telling me. Now let me see what you got." They stepped aside so I could look at all the goodies. "Oh boy, are we making sugar cookies? And, like, decorating them?" I shoved my glasses up as if to better see what I was unpacking. "Oh my god, are these *dinosaur cookie cutters*?"

"You have to be a little careful with the T. rex's arms. Sometimes they crack off. But for the most part, they work really well. I mean, I haven't used them that much, but I can make a small batch of cookies in my toaster oven."

I jumped up and down, partially in genuine delight, partially in residual nerves and overcompensation. "Sidney. This is the best. When do we get started?"

"Now, I think?"

"Yaaaaaay!" I might have been overdoing the enthusiasm a little judging by the uncertain look they shot me. "Do you want something to drink? I have sparkling water in legit glass bottles, also I have the makings for hot cocoa, which we can have now while baking, later while eating, or both. Because we're grown-ups and we can have as much hot cocoa and cookies as we want."

They hesitated. "Do you have marshmallows?"

"I have *two different kinds* of marshmallows. I was totally in the mood, but I couldn't decide whether to go with ginormous white ones or multicolored little ones, so I bought both."

Sidney nodded approval. "I find the small ones are more visually appealing in a cup of cocoa."

"I agree. And they melt faster. But sometimes you need a really big marshmallow in your life." I held their gaze with a ridiculous smile on my face.

"That sentence wants to be innuendo but I can't make it work," they said after a second.

"I know! I tried, though." I rubbed my hands together and surveyed our ingredients. "So, mixing bowls. Mixing bowls, mixing bowls, must find the mixing bowls."

There should be a scientific formula for how much cookie dough gets eaten before the cookies go into the oven. You'd have to take into consideration the number of bakers and the length of time since each of them last ate, plus tolerance for the risk of salmonella poisoning.

Sidney and I apparently both had a high tolerance for potential food poisoning, though they told me it was the flour you really had to watch out for.

Sugar cookie batter, while not as satisfying to eat as chocolate chip cookie dough, was still pretty tasty, and once we had all of our dinosaurs in the oven we did a fair amount of "cleaning" up the bits that were left over by, you know, eating them in between sips of cocoa.

"I considered getting the pre-made icing," Sidney said, running a damp cloth over the counter while I washed the dishes we'd already used. "But then I realized that it might be nice to have something to fill the time with. It was weird. I already know we're comfortable just sitting here watching

TV, so I don't know why I felt all this pressure to come up with things for us to do."

Which would have been an acceptable place for me to admit I was a little jittery too, but I didn't know how that would help, so I didn't. "What kind of icing are we making?"

They rinsed off their hands and started drying mixing bowls. "It's just powdered sugar and lemon juice, but I brought colors and actual brushes to use."

I nudged them. "Brushes? We're going to *paint* our dinosaurs?"

A pink flush stole over their cheeks. "I, um, saw it on YouTube."

"Did you do...research for this date?"

"Look, I don't date, it's Valentine's Day, which I know has some meaning to you, and I really wanted you to have a good time—"

"Teasing, teasing, sorry." I nudged them again. "No matter what, it's bound to be a much better date than us sitting in a fancy restaurant having to choose between multiple forks."

"I get off on using the wrong fork for things. Sometimes it's not obvious, but sometimes it is. Or spoons. Using a soup spoon to stir coffee really makes people uncomfortable."

I giggled. "You are so sadistic."

"I consider it my job to unsettle people. Or less my job and more my calling." They glanced over, one eyebrow slightly raised, Very Serious Expression. "I didn't ask for this calling, Declan, but it is my grave responsibility to give back to the world that has given so much to me."

"So much, uh, being-unsettled?"

"Ha. Actually, yeah. I never seemed to make sense in any context I was put into, so now I bring my not-sense-making right to other people's doorsteps. Or computer screens, whichever."

"I like it. Your way of not making sense. It makes a lot more sense to me than other people's way of making sense. If that *makes sense*."

They groaned. "Too far. You took it too far."

"Just far enough." I shut off the water. "Okay, what's next?"

By the time the cookies were cool (the ones that survived the initial, uh, human meteor strike of us "tasting" them, anyway), we had four bowls of very brightly colored icing: hot pink, neon green, electric blue, and lemon yellow.

"I love this food coloring," I said in satisfaction.

"Livens things up a little. Should we divide them between us?"

I counted. "We have odd numbers of T. rexes and pterodactyls."

"I'll take an extra pterodactyl, you can have the extra T. rex."

"Well, okay, but I think Team T. Rex can kick Team Pterodactyl's ass."

"I'm pretty sure there are birds alive today that descend from pterodactyls."

"Oh-ho-ho, common myth, my friend, common myth. Though I think birds might actually be dinosaurs, they do not descend from pterodactyls." I took a bow. "Thank you, I watch a lot of weird documentaries."

They stared at me. "No. Really?"

"Yep yep."

"But...but... I liked the idea of dangerous looking pterobirds flying around somewhere." They looked totally crestfallen.

"Um. I feel like I just told you Santa's not real."

"That is *exactly* what you did." They grabbed my upper

arm, shaking me a little. "Why can't you let me have my illusions of pterodactyls, Declan?"

"If I'd known how much it meant to you…no, I probably would have told you, anyway. But I would have been more gentle about it!"

"I'm sad now. I'm in mourning."

I hid my smile.

"I'm in mourning for the pterodactyls I will never see in real life." Their voice began to rise dramatically. "All these years I have fantasized about taking a trip somewhere—a rain forest, maybe—and seeing birds that shared DNA with pterodactyls, but now, in one fell swoop, you have destroyed this dream."

"I am a monster," I agreed solemnly.

"Truly. You are a thief of dreams."

I lost it. "Oh my god, *a thief of dreams*." My maniacal cackling set Sidney off and then both of us were losing it a little, maybe because we were anxious about the date, maybe because the idea of a *thief of dreams* was legit funny. Probably more the former than the latter.

Sometimes the brain triggers a burst of absurd amusement when it registers a high level of emotional tension. I didn't see that in a documentary or anything. I made it up. But it's totally accurate. Science should find a way to do a study. Or no, we could! After The Love Study we could find other stuff to study! I'd propose it to Sidney maybe, but later, when I was better able to decide how bad an idea it was.

Decorating cookies went well, and I managed to make a pterodactyl with a hot-pink-with-electric-blue-rim Santa hat on it for them. "Sorry I ruined Pterodactyl Claus for you," I said, presenting it with a flourish.

"I'll recover. I made you a rainbowish brontosaurus."

"Aww, you did?" It was super cute, with rows of pink-yellow-green-blue stripes all down its long body and a green head with yellow eyes. "Thank you! I shall call him Stripey. And spare him as long as I can afford to do so." I paused reverently. "And then I shall eat him with all due respect."

They grinned. "That's how you show your respect to a cookie, I think: you eat it."

"Good point. Speaking of, let's finish this and then do some eating."

"I didn't bring any non-cookie food, sorry."

I waved at the fridge. "It'll only take me fifteen minutes to make pasta, no worries." *Yes.* The sauce was ready. Go, past me. Way to pre-make sauce. I wanted to jump up and down with joy at my foresight, but thought it best to act casual.

My business card should read: Declan Swick-Smith: not good at casual.

"I-made-a-sauce," I mumbled.

"You what?"

"Made a sauce. I hope you like garlic." Wow, it's like I went out of my way to be unkissable. "Upon reflection, maybe garlic wasn't the best choice. I was trying to show off. The sauce is really good, though. It's cheesy and garlicky and has a little bit of a pepper kick."

"That sounds delicious."

I barely restrained myself from pouting. "I mean, I love the sauce? But also I am looking forward to making out later? Then I made a very freaking garlicky sauce. Like a jackass."

Sidney swallowed, very possibly looking at my lips. "We have some time in our schedules now, if you want to…make use of it. Um. With kissing."

"Yes! I mean, yes, very calm, very measured yes."

"While the icing…sets. I think that's a thing."

"Icing setting, of course. Sure. All the cookbooks talk about using your, uh, icing-setting time wisely."

"Like kissing."

"I'm sure I read that in Julia Child."

They smiled. "I really like you, Declan."

"I really like you too."

Their lips were soft and citrusy, sweet with icing. In a way it felt almost first-kissish, maybe because of the aforementioned emotional tension. I focused on the small area of our skin touching, trying to keep myself in the moment.

Sidney leaned in, taking it deeper—

Clack.

—until our glasses bumped and both of us drew back.

"Oh god, sorry." They turned away.

"No biggie, and I think it's a shared responsibility. I'm sorry too." Cue awkwardness. "So um…do you think the icing's set?"

"Definitely."

"Should I put on water for pasta while we quality inspect our dinosaurs?"

"Sounds good."

The dinosaurs tasted good (which we already knew, since we'd sampled both the cookies and the icing as we worked). And the pasta sauce was freaking *exceptional*. If I do say so myself.

We had cookies and more cocoa on the couch later. I'd put on a baking show and turned down the volume, just to have something going in case conversation fizzled out. A precautionary measure. This was the thing I'd wanted all night and maybe I'd built it up too much in my head, or maybe I was too self-conscious after feeling like I was date-failing an amazing date, but I was glad the TV was on in the background.

Sidney seemed to be in a weird mood too, or else I was

projecting. I'd asked about something mundane, but we'd wandered into talking about their past dating history, which, given the nature of our relationship and YouTubeness, I knew almost nothing about.

"I figured you had a traumatic dating experience and swore off it or something." I leaned my head on the back of the Jenkinses' couch where we were facing each other, both of us clutching hot cocoa with tiny marshmallows.

"No, not at all. I had a lot of mediocre experiences, a few okay ones, a few lousy ones. And I just got tired of it."

"Because of all those Valentine's Day fights?" Gosh, their eyes were dark in the low light, dark like the deepest part of a lake, like I could dive all the way into them.

"Because I didn't know what the point was. For me, I mean. I understood what the point was for a lot of people, but I didn't share their goals." They stirred a few more marshmallows into their cocoa, seeming mesmerized. "My whole life I've felt… Have you ever let a drop of soap hit water that has something on the surface?"

"Um. Probably?"

"You know how everything pulls away from the drop of soap like it's repelling? Like nothing can stand being anywhere near the soap?"

"Sure."

"That was always me. I always felt like I was that drop of soap. As if my very presence made people move in the opposite direction, everyone except my brother. It was nice once he was born, though I was sixteen by then so I guess I was still more comfortable being on my own."

I swallowed, caught up in the image of Sidney alone surrounded by empty space. I wanted to reach for their hand or pat their knee or something, but I didn't think they needed comfort half as much as I needed to provide it, so I sipped my cocoa instead. Self-soothing through chocolate. Kind of a theme in my life. "That sounds really lonely," I said, since I couldn't think of anything else to say.

"I had friends, casual friends. I don't mean to give you the idea I was that isolated. Just mostly I didn't quite fit in places other people expected me to fit, and I wasn't good at doing the work to keep friendships strong, so they eventually faded." Sidney kept stirring, still staring down into their mug. "Anyway, I made the executive decision to stop trying to find common ground with people who had very different priorities."

"And that was...like...everyone?"

They glanced up. "It seemed like it at the time. But that's why the show was so important. Or I guess why it came to be so important to me. It was a way of establishing common ground and connections, and I know there are a lot of people who feel like face-to-face is the only way to have friendships or community, but that hasn't been my experience. I answer comments most days. I talk to people like Mara, people who've been consistently present for a while, all the time. Those relationships matter to me. When I barely spoke to anyone in the house where I was renting a room, I was exchanging emails with and having conversations with a lot of people I knew from YouTube." They shook their head. "Sorry, I'm rambling. I guess the point was that I gave up on finding common ground with people in my life at the exact moment I was putting a lot of energy into actually doing that? And I didn't even realize it until—well, until now. Until The Love Study."

"Really?" That felt...good. Maybe I was part of something bigger, something positive for them, the way they'd been part of that for me.

"I think...watching you figure out dating, and asking

you questions, has clarified for me some of my...um, what I might potentially want. In that context."

"Oh wow, it's like the show legitimately worked."

They smiled. "Yeah. Right? I didn't think it would have that effect on *me*, but if it has, then maybe it's also working for other people."

"Totally. So like. Um. What...do you want? I mean, I'm asking purely out of curiosity. Not at all self-interest." I gave them my best innocent face.

"Certainly not," they agreed. "No self-interest here on either side."

"I'm glad we understand each other."

Both of us smirked a little.

"I haven't put it all into words yet. I want to be able to go deep with someone, and also have the freedom to be on my own without them taking it personally, like I need a sense of intimacy to co-exist with a sense of space. Mutual growth, mutual change. And I want...dimension. I want the way I relate to other people to expand in more than one direction."

"That sounds really beautiful." It wasn't quite the right way to put what I meant, but it was as close as I could get.

"Thanks. I mean, it's all theoretical, obviously. But I think those would be nice qualities for a theoretical romantic relationship."

"Along with physical and intellectual chemistry?"

They smiled. "Yep."

"I think your theoretical romantic relationship sounds pretty excellent." And I did. What I didn't know was what they meant by *"theoretical."*

"That's good to know."

In the background someone's soufflé was falling. Suddenly I felt unnervingly vulnerable sitting there looking at Sidney. Being looked at by Sidney. What did they see? Someone who was worthy of a theoretical romantic relationship? Or were they more saying that in some fantasy world they'd want those things, but in this one, they were willing to settle for me?

It was hard to avoid the reality of the situation. They might really like me. (And I knew I really liked them.) But sooner or later, I was going to screw this up. History repeats and all that.

I reached for the remote. "I love the judging part. I try to anticipate what the judges are going to say before they say it."

Sidney shifted a little closer, and even though I didn't think I deserved it, I couldn't help pressing my arm against theirs as they sipped their cocoa. "I can't believe I've waited so long to watch this show. Though I bet it's more fun with company."

"Definitely."

They went home at the end of the episode, leaving me the last of the cookies, which I mindlessly ate sitting in front of the TV with Toby the Australian Shepherd curled up beside me, his head in my lap.

Chapter Twenty-Three

The brides looked beautiful, all sun-dappled and luminous. I'd seen them in their dresses before, but I don't know, on the actual afternoon of their actual wedding they looked... more beautiful. Apply all happy bride clichés here—they glowed, they radiated—but it was true.

Every time they looked at each other it was honestly like the glow intensified, their smiles got wider, their eyes got brighter. The breeze picked up at one point, blowing Ronnie's hair into Mia's eyes in the middle of the ceremony, and both of them laughed. Not nervously, and not with the rest of us, but just...as if they were in a bubble only the two of them shared. It was kind of sublime, watching them like that, all euphoric together. After months of stressing about the wedding, when it finally arrived, they spent most of the day holding hands and dancing and laughing, which was perfect.

Mia's dad didn't tell too many Korean jokes (that's jokes

about Koreans, not jokes in Korean, though if we could convince him to joke in a language most people present didn't understand, that would probably make Mia really happy). Ronnie's parents didn't show up, as expected, but her sister made a wonderful toast that had pretty much everyone in tears.

Then there was the dancing. You find out how many queer people are present at a gathering when the dancing starts. I don't want to act like queers are better dancers than non-queers (though statistically speaking, *we are*), but get enough of us together and we can turn anything into a club. Even a local park with three separate playgrounds in sight. (Why does the park need three separate playgrounds? Is that a thing?)

By nine p.m. I was ready to drop. Mason and I had shown up at the bridal residence at eleven that morning to do some decorating and make the bed with sexy sheets (that would probably fall apart the first time they were washed, but whatever). We'd also stocked the fridge with a mix of real food and some, uh, vulva-esque food carvings that had been Oscar's contribution to the honeymoon suite's mini-bar-and-complimentary-snacks-buffet.

My resolve not to get drunk was hanging on by a thread as I made my way back to the small table the three of us had taken over once the party had really gotten going. The loving and adorable brides had just said their goodbyes, after which I'd taken a minute in the bathroom to remind myself that I still didn't want to consume an entire bottle of wine (even though I kind of did).

I slumped down in between Mase and Oscar, propping my head in my hands. "Is it bedtime yet?"

Mason patted my shoulder. "There, there, sugar plum."

"There there what, though?"

"Sugar plum."

"But there there *what*?"

"I was calling you sugar plum. As a joke."

"I realize that, I meant—"

He giggled.

"You asshole." I slugged him in the arm. "Stop messing with me, I'm exhausted. Doesn't it feel like this morning was literally weeks ago?"

"Seriously."

Oscar pulled the last of the wine toward him and dumped it in his glass. "We can leave now, right? We don't have to stay longer now that the newlyweds are gone?"

"Come over to my place," Mase said. "I have a decent bottle of wine and a bunch of junk food I bought last week."

"Sloppy seconds from The Stoner, count me out."

I looked in between them. "Wait, you had The Stoner over again? And you didn't tell me?"

"Dude, you've been a little *busy*. Plus, it's not like we're friends, we're just fucking."

"You bought snacks."

Mase shrugged. "He's always hungry. For obvious reasons. The last thing I want is for him to get the munchies in the middle of sex, so I feed him first."

The line must have repeated in his head at the same time it did mine. Both of us started laughing.

"This is what it's come to," Oscar moaned. "Those two get married, Dec finds true love, Mason starts keeping a stoned sex monkey as a pet, and I die alone. I always knew it would end this way." It looked like he was going to actually pull off the elaborate sad face routine he was attempting...until it all fell apart and he barked laughter. "Oh, fuck us, you guys."

"Nah. Come help me eat monkey feed." Mase clapped a hand to both of our backs and we obediently followed him out.

"Shouldn't we say something to Mia's parents?" I whispered.

"We sat with them all night, they'll be fine."

True. Probably. Anyway, we were out of the tent and passing one of the playgrounds on our way to the cars. The rest of the wedding would have to fend for itself.

"Here's the thing," I started, then lost my nerve.

We were back at Mason's apartment. I was sprawled on one side of the couch with Mase while Oscar was in an armchair with his feet propped on the coffee table. We'd killed two bags of chips and a box of chocolates that somewhat belied Mason's claim that he'd had The Stoner (AKA the last guy he was with for longer than a week) over as a booty call.

Oscar sighed. "Just say it."

Mason only looked at me.

"Here's the thing…"

Oscar rolled his eyes.

"…I'm really happy for Ronnie and Mia." I was. I knew that for sure. Super happy.

"Obviously." The total irritation in Oscar's voice—familiar, heartfelt irritation—made it easier for me to talk.

"Is it fucked up that today also kind of made me…sad?" I didn't want to look at them as I said it, but I couldn't not-look at them either.

"Me too," Mase said quietly. "I feel really shitty about it. And I'm also so happy for them, like ridiculously happy that they have each other, and that they're finally getting married when they've wanted to for so long. It seems like that should…outweigh my, um…envy. But it doesn't."

I didn't envy them exactly. But it was a little hard to watch them all wrapped up in each other without sincerely doubting I could ever be that guy. The guy who gets to be all wrapped up in someone else, and deserves to have them all wrapped up in him.

The truth was that I was a compromise position, like Mase had said at drinks. And it didn't seem fair to ask someone to do that. Even without a wedding, it was a pretty shitty thing to do, knowing you were not good enough for someone and trying to be with them anyway.

"Dying alone," Oscar announced. "My new life goal. Get laid, go home, go to sleep, go to work, rinse, repeat." He brushed his hands against each other with finality. "Decision made."

"You forgot drinks," Mason said dryly.

"If I can fit drinks in to my busy schedule of getting laid and sleeping, I will. But since I'm not having sex with you assholes, I make no promises."

Mase flopped a hand in his direction. "Been there, honey."

"You *bitch*."

I giggled, roused out of self-pity by the memory. Their very short-lived thing was over before Mase and I hooked up. Distant history. Really entertaining now, though. "Remember when you guys—"

"*No,*" both of them said at once.

"Well, I remember, and it's hilarious. Anyway, tell me I'm not a horrible person for having like...complex feelings about the wedding? I mean, not about the wedding. Just about... weddings. And things." *Relationships. Humans in general. One incredibly awesome YouTuber who obviously deserves better than me in particular.*

Oscar rolled his eyes again. "What does it matter if you're a horrible person? Your feelings are your feelings."

"Yeah, but all the same I'd rather feel things that didn't make me a horrible person."

"I don't think it makes us horrible people." Mason reached

for the chocolates box, settling it on his chest so he could pick through the wrappers for stragglers. "I'm really glad we didn't get married, Dec, but man. Sometimes that idea I had for our future feels so close I can almost taste it, you know?"

"Me too." I slouched lower on my side of the couch. "You don't think we could have pulled it off? Not even if we worked really hard at it?"

I expected a quick answer—I expected a *Hell no*—but he continued his in-depth search of the chocolate wrappers and didn't speak for a long moment.

"I'm not sure. Most of the time I know there's no way. We would have drained each other and fought and eventually divorced in a fireball that destroyed the Motherfuckers and maybe ourselves. But sometimes?" He shook his head, at me or at the chocolates-less box, I wasn't sure. "I don't know. Sometimes I think maybe we could have made it work. I think we always would have ended up more friends than deeply in love, but maybe that wouldn't be so bad. Best friends, hot sex, you'd cook, I'd clean. I guess it probably wouldn't have worked out that way in real life."

That *probably* lingered, echoed in my mind. Would we have done that? I couldn't deny the appeal of it. Not having to worry about the rest of it, the romantic stuff, feeling the right things at the right time, dressing up (or not), trying to come up with dates and dinners and topics of conversation. But he was also right that we were better as friends than we'd ever been as fiancés or even boyfriends, and I wasn't sure either of us really wanted a long-term committed friendship. Or, in a way, that's…what we had now.

Mason definitely wanted the transcendent love affair, to be swept off his feet by someone. I didn't know what I wanted. I thought about Sidney, all dressed up, having planned the most perfect date on earth…and how even with all that I still wasn't able to completely feel it. How could I like them so much and fail so spectacularly at my own perfect date?

"To dying alone," I said, and raised my glass of water.

"Dying alone!" my friends chorused.

We dragged Mase's mattress out into the living room and crashed, the two of us on the mattress and Oscar reluctantly on the couch, having not packed his air mattress. It was a glum sort of sleepover that didn't feel any better in the morning.

Six years ago I'd thought I wanted a wedding and a lifetime in bed with Mason. I could still remember imagining that, but for some reason, lying there listening to him snore, it was almost impossible to picture.

The problem was, when I tried to picture something else... my mind went blank. Like I had no future at all.

Chapter Twenty-Four

Sunday was a blur. We eventually got up. We eventually ate food. We eventually parted ways. I took a long, exhausting nap, the kind of nap you wake up from feeling groggy and heavy, as if the minutes you spent fitfully sleeping had formed a scaly layer on your skin.

I took a shower. I couldn't honestly remember if I'd taken one after getting back from Mason's or not, but I figured it couldn't hurt.

It also didn't help.

My phone had died sometime the day before, between videos and pictures and Instagramming and texting the mean things we couldn't say out loud. (It was nice Mia was still friends with like *all* of her exes, but did she have to invite them to the wedding? Because as her friends, we were definitely *not* still friends with her exes.) When I finally plugged it in and turned it on, Sidney had messaged to say they hoped we were having fun.

Just seeing their name made my chest go tight like a boa constrictor had wrapped itself around me and was squeezing, little by little, until I started to break. I couldn't keep doing this. Or I could, just like last time, and while it wouldn't end the same way (I'd never leave Sidney at the altar because they didn't actually want to stand at one), it would end badly, and I'd spend years wishing I'd gotten out sooner.

The choice was really obvious, but that didn't make it easy. How did I phrase *I am incompetent at relationships and you deserve better and if we keep trying to do this I'll just fuck it up again since that's 100% of my track record and also I'm sorry I ever thought I could do this because I can't.* And I couldn't. I knew that now. They'd planned the perfect date and I'd felt crappy the whole time. The wedding had basically been one long exposure therapy session and I'd responded to it by first hiding in the bathroom, and then running away.

Sidney wanted intimacy and growth and change and all I could offer was, like, whipped cream and sex jokes. It was hopeless.

I looked at their perfectly normal, innocuous text again. *Hope everyone is having fun!* There was a smiley face.

I went back to bed.

Due to my epically fucked sleep schedule, getting up for work on Monday was dire. Less than a week until the Fling. Time was short. The fish bowl was…not exactly a hive of activity, but now that Jack and I were semi-friendly it was at least a pretty decent place to spend a work shift.

I was in early, with coffee. I'd brought enough emergency chocolate to share.

Jack didn't show.

Around ten, when I was kind of starting to worry, Deb came in and closed the door. "Jack will be out today and possibly tomorrow. Do you need additional staff to cover his work?"

I just blinked at her. "Um."

"I can reassign someone if you need me to."

"Um." My mind started running down our list. Until I realized this was what I had tools for and opened the spreadsheet. "Will he be back by Wednesday? I'd definitely need help for the set-up and clean-up stuff. I think the rest of this is manageable?" I ran my eye over it again. "I should be able to fit it all in as long as he comes back. At least, that makes more sense than me spending time trying to catch someone up for a day."

She nodded. "Good. And I expect him back Wednesday at the latest."

For an event on Friday, yikes. Still, I didn't want to train anyone. "Okay. Is he... I mean, I know you're not supposed to tell me anything, but is he all right?"

Small, not entirely reassuring smile. "He's dealing with some outside issues. He has support, though."

Oh right, because she knew him in the real world, not just the work world. "Well, if you talk to him, tell him..." Tell him what? We'd spent weeks being barely civil to each other. "Tell him if he doesn't come back I'm making all the name cards Comic Sans."

She smiled like she understood that level of punishment. "I will. Thanks, Declan. And thank you for all the work you've put in on this, it has not gone unnoticed."

I had no idea what to say to that, which was fine, because she waved and left the room while I was still sitting there trying to figure it out. The last thing I wanted at my job was to be *noticed*. Sheesh. What's a guy gotta do to be treated like a cog in the machine around here?

When things were tense, I'd looked forward to being alone in the fish bowl. But today the day just seemed to stretch... and stretch...and stretch while I took care of tedious tasks and list items with no one to snark at.

And through it all the final episode of The Love Study loomed over me like a gathering storm. I tried not to think about it, but I couldn't help it. How was I going to tell Sidney that their trust in me was unfounded? And how the hell was I going to make it through a Q and A episode of the show without completely falling apart?

I ate Jack's share of the emergency chocolate and made another cup of coffee. I needed it.

I almost couldn't get out of my car at Sidney's. My friends weren't watching this time—Ronnie and Mia were honeymooning, Mase was going on a date and said he'd catch it later, and since Oscar was planning to die alone he didn't think it was relevant. Knowing they wouldn't be out there had a strange effect on me, almost as if it took away a sense of security I'd felt during the other episodes.

Now it was just me and Sidney and all of YouTube. Without anyone to catch me if I fell. A small voice inside my head advocated for telling Sidney all of my fears because they'd probably try to understand, but that was how I got drawn in before, by listening to parts of myself that were wildly misinformed. For instance, the parts that said, *You and Mase love each other, of course you should get married!* Or *Maybe you're not the worst person on earth, of course you should try dating again!*

Forcing my arms and legs to move, I made it up to the apartment. Sidney answered the door and stared at me, which

I knew, even though I could only raise my eyes as high as their hands.

I really liked their hands. Which made me want to cry.

"Declan?" Voice low, like they were worried they'd startle me.

"I can't. I'm sorry. I thought I could, but I can't."

"You can't do the show?"

I wanted to say yes, take the out. But that would be knowingly misleading them. It was more than just the show.

They reached out, fingertips grazing my cheek. "Are you okay?"

"I'm fine." I did a laugh-sob thing. "I'm just tired. From the wedding."

"Yeah, I bet."

We stood there and this feeling inside me, this certainty that I couldn't make it work, that I'd hurt them if I didn't leave *right now*, grew until I couldn't deny it. I would fuck it up. If not tonight, then tomorrow. Or the next day. Or the next time they planned a wonderful, romantic cookie date, and no matter what I did I couldn't feel it, I couldn't be deserving of it.

No.

If you love something, set it free, right? And I did. I thought I did. What a supremely stupid time to realize I loved them. But at least it clarified things: I would not hurt Sidney like I'd hurt Mason. I was older, and wiser, and knew just how badly I could fuck something up this time. "I'm so sorry. I'm so, so sorry, I didn't mean to do this—"

"I can cancel the show tonight," they said, backing into the room. "It's no big deal."

"You can't."

"Sure I can. I'm your spinster uncle, and sometimes your

spinster uncle has more important things to do than spinster at people."

Oh, god, that made it so much worse.

"No, you can't." My eyes overflowed. "You can't cancel the show. It's your job, and people need you. And I can't do this. I wanted to, I wanted to so much, but I can't. I'm not made for it or something, I don't know how. And I should have known I couldn't handle this, but for a while it seemed like I could, and I just…wanted to so much." I rubbed tears out of my eyes. "I'm sorry but it's better to end it now than… than keep going until it's so much worse. Believe me, it hurts so much worse when you wait."

Sidney had stopped moving. Maybe stopped breathing. "No. Please don't—"

But if I didn't leave immediately, I'd let them talk me into staying, and I couldn't.

Rip the Band-Aid off fast. Not slow.

I turned, still crying, and ran. They called my name but I didn't stop, just ran to my car and sat there, tears pouring down my face, heart pounding, gasping for breath like air had become water and I was drowning.

You'd think it would be enough to understand you're having a panic attack and you're not really going to die, but every time I think this one's going to kill me.

It didn't. When I could breathe again I drove home.

Chapter Twenty-Five

In between crying and sleeping and hating myself, I was drinking way too much caffeine to stay awake at work. I'd even bought a pack of energy drinks, which Jack (now back from his unexplained absence) side-eyed like it was speed.

Which... I guess in a way it was. But legal. And probably not that addicting. I'd just have to suffer through a few days of come-down after this week, but first I needed to get through this week.

Sidney had left one message on my phone, sounding teary and miserable, only saying that they were thinking about me and that they didn't want to invade my space so they'd leave it to me to contact them, and they really, really hoped I would. After which there was a long pause, a waiting, expectant pause. But they only said, "I'd like to sit down and talk to you. I think we can figure this out." And hung up.

Sure they did, because they lived in the safe, contained

world of Your Spinster Uncle, where questions were asked, answers given, and hearts were only broken in words on a screen, after which good advice was enough to fix everything.

Where you didn't have to see someone's smile wilt on their face when they realized you could never be what they wanted you to be. That wasn't going to happen again. I'd gotten on the roller coaster and run it straight into the ground and now it was over. End of story. Good try, bad fail, finis.

I needed to stay busy, so I cleaned my unit from top to bottom. I gave Toby the Australian Shepherd a bath and groomed him until he was fluffy and preening. The Jenkinses were due back Friday, so on Thursday I made a stir-fry, decided I didn't like it, threw it out and started over. Twice. Nothing tasted that good, but I ate the third one anyway because by then I was tired of cooking.

I deep cleaned the entire kitchen. When I was finally done it was one o'clock in the morning, and I needed to be at the hotel at seven to start setting up for the Fling.

Just enough time to get a few hours of fitful sleep, take a morose shower, and cry. A lot. I cried so much—in the shower, getting dressed, driving—that the second Jack saw me he pulled me out of the conference room and frog marched me to the onsite Starbucks.

"Don't we have a million things to do?" I mumbled.

"Don't take this the wrong way, Declan, but I don't think you're going to be much use to us until you stop—" He waved a hand at my face.

"Oh god is it that obvious?" I scrubbed ineffectually with my sleeves. "Dammit. I keep trying to get my shit together and then…" And then I'd think of the way they pushed up their glasses, or their soft laugh, or the way they sometimes tugged their hair when they were thinking hard and I'd get all weepy again.

"You want to tell me what happened?"

"No. I mean it's stupid. I mean... I'm useless at dating and I really liked the person I was seeing but there's no point in me trying to be better than I am because I'll only fuck it all up again."

He shot me an unimpressed look. "That sounded like a lot of words that spell 'I got scared and sabotaged my relationship.'"

"That's not what happened."

He grunted a non-response and turned to order our coffees. I pulled out my wallet but he smacked my hand away like he was offended, and I was too tired to insist. I'd just have to owe Jack a coffee. Then I'd get him one and he'd get me one and—

Actually, today was probably the last day we would work together. He was still hoping Deb would offer him a permanent position, and I'd probably have to go back to the temp pool at some point, so maybe circumstances would intervene and I'd never end up paying off my coffee debt.

What a terrible thought. I hated owing people stuff. And I'd gotten used to Jack.

He handed me my coffee. I thanked him. We returned to the conference room, but sat down instead of continuing to work while our coffees got cold, as we usually did.

"My grandfather fell asleep in his chair in the living room with a lit cigarette in his hand on Sunday afternoon," he said abruptly.

"Omigod." *Oh my god.*

"They're okay. The house suffered some damage, but nothing too terrible." He sniffed at his shirt. "At least, I think I managed to get most of the smoke smell out of my work clothes."

"That's horrible, Jack, I'm so sorry. It sounds terrifying."

"It was. It was. But, clichéd as it is, it was also, in a way, the thing that was going to happen eventually, and I'm grateful that it wasn't worse than it was. It could have been… I'd been worried that they might…" He shook his head, sipping his coffee. "Anyway, I'd done a lot of research and I already had plenty of contacts so I managed to get them a temporary space in a building where they're on a waiting list for an apartment."

"That's good. I mean, obviously it's also really hard, but I'm glad they're safe at least."

"Me too. And it means I'll probably need to go back to a more lucrative, shall we say, form of employment. But at least I won't spend my sixteen-hour days worried they're going to burn the house down while I'm at work."

"Oh." Jack was leaving. This was it no matter what. God, why was that so sad? We'd only been able to tolerate each other for the last few weeks! I was not going to cry over Jack leaving the company I didn't even work for. Dammit.

He grabbed a couple of high-quality napkins and passed them to me.

"Sorry, sorry, it's not you, it's everything."

"I wasn't under the impression my departure was the thing breaking your heart."

"I'm sorry." I blew my nose and dabbed at my eyes. "But it is kind of sad. I got used to working with you."

"I got used to working with you too. Kid." He smiled.

"You were such a jerk."

"Yeah, I'm sorry. The job felt like charity and instead of handling it with grace, I was a total dick. But you ended up being a pretty good supervisor. Though I've needed to ask you since we met—what's up with the spreadsheet?"

"What? It's a good spreadsheet!"

"Yeah, but most people use apps or email or something."

"I don't have the time to learn all that stuff when my list works really well. Don't talk shit about my spreadsheet, man."

He raised his coffee cup. "To your spreadsheet, the seed of all we see before us."

"To my spreadsheet." I clunked cardboard with him. "We should probably get going."

"Yeah."

"Thanks for the coffee."

"It's only what you once did for me."

So in Jack's mind, this was repayment for a coffee already offered in a moment of need. Maybe that meant it wasn't a debt. Or maybe it didn't matter.

We got to work, carefully crafting the best, most seamless and professional Spring Fling experience the board had ever seen. The food and drinks were on point, the goody bags were perfectly arranged (or sorry, the *complimentary gift bags* of branded junk because apparently if you're on the board of a big company you're too cheap to buy your own pens and USB sticks), the chairs were squared off to the table.

And, most importantly, the Fling bricks were in place. The symbols of so much strife, yet here they were, neatly positioned to the side of each seat, ready to be tossed into various garbage cans, filing cabinets, and piles of miscellaneous paperwork. A destiny hardly fitting to things we'd worked so hard on, but it was their fate.

Jack and I worked the next few hours making sure everything was going smoothly, and overall, everything had. We were just packing up when Deb walked into the conference room.

"You aren't supposed to be here," Jack said to her as he erased the freestanding whiteboard we'd borrowed from the hotel.

"I have a thing. Can you two take a ten-minute not-break or will you be over hours for the day?"

I looked at my phone while Jack looked at his watch. "We only took half an hour for lunch," I said.

"And we probably only have another twenty minutes here, so we can take ten if you want."

She gestured to the table. "Have a seat."

"Oh boy." I looked at him. "I feel like we're about to get in trouble."

"Deny everything."

Deb smiled at both of us. "I've heard rave reviews about the event all day from people not inclined to issue compliments where none are warranted. You reflected well on the company, and within the company you reflected well on me. So thank you, personally, for making me look like a genius for throwing together a couple of temporary employees on an important job."

Jack shook his head. "Why *did* you do that? You said you'd tell me if we pulled it off."

"I was proving a point to my boss, who fears change, and isn't comfortable when 'underlings'—" air quotes "—take initiative. He told me he'd believe it if a couple of newcomers could take on the Fling and not crash and burn."

"And you..." I stared at her, horror filling my veins. "You gave that job to *us*? Oh my god. We could have fucked it up! Like really easily! The bookbinding thing worked out, but what if it hadn't, oh my god, I can't breathe."

"You were great."

Jack reached out to awkwardly pat my shoulder. "Declan's having kind of a day. You should hire him, by the way. As a supervisor. I can vouch for his organization skills, big picture thinking, and compassion."

I chewed on the inside of my cheek, not looking at either of them.

"Oh, I've tried. Three times. But Declan will not be had."

"Try, try again. Especially since you can't have me."

"So you decided."

I found myself sad all over again that Jack would no longer be working for...the company I didn't technically work for.

"It makes the most sense. I want the grandparents to be comfortable, in the best place I can afford. And I can afford a lot more when I'm doing other things."

Deb nodded and held out her hand, which he shook. "We figured this would only be a stopgap for you, but I'm glad to have had you even for a short time."

"Me too," I said. "Like, not at first, but now I might even miss you."

He laughed. "Don't go too far out of your way to compliment me, it might go to my head."

"You know what I mean."

"Yeah."

Deb held her hand out to me too. "You excelled, as I was sure you would."

"Thanks. I thought you were pretty much nuts to give me this assignment, FYI."

"Maybe I was. The risk paid off, though."

We needed to get back to packing up. Deb probably needed to get back to her real job.

I looked up at her, stomach feeling weirdly hollow. "Do you still want to hire me?"

"In a hot second."

"For what?"

"I've thought about that a lot, but I think your job duties

would be as vague as I could make them, that way I could still send you around to do whatever needed doing. One of your gifts is quickly getting to know the people you're working with, which makes your past experience filling positions in multiple departments invaluable." She sat back, never breaking eye contact. "I have employees who are so localized to their department that they never even meet the people working next door. You bridge that, and you do it with style. I'd like to train more roving contact people, Declan. You could help."

I swallowed. It sounded...kind of amazing. I wouldn't be locked down to a desk doing one thing every day forever. And I'd get to keep working with Deb. Maybe I'd get to lobby for space in the fish bowl, which I'd grown fond of.

"You can take the weekend to think about it."

"I'm in. If you want me."

Jack clapped. "Good answer. I mean, you're no me, but you'll do."

I rolled my eyes at him. "Thanks a lot."

"You're *very* welcome."

Deb seemed genuinely thrilled. "Now, that was unexpected. I'm pleased. Can I send the paperwork to the temp agency on Monday?"

Ugh, had I really thought about this? Was it really what I wanted? But what the hell did I know about what I wanted, anyway? If I hated it, I could always quit and go back to temping. And there was even a chance that I'd...like it. That being employed full-time in one job might, like, suit me. I was still a little freaked out. But also a little excited.

"Monday, okay. That sounds good. Um. Now, we should probably get back to cleaning up or we'll be in OT."

"That's the attitude I want in my staff," she teased. "I'm really happy you're taking the job."

"I... I think I am too."

She took my hand, not to shake it this time, exactly. But to squeeze it. "If you start getting restless, talk to me before you make any big decisions. There are a lot of different ways you can fit in here, and we might not nail the right one on the first try, okay?"

"Yeah, okay. Thanks, Deb."

"Oh, thank you. This is the cherry on top of a damn good workday. I'll see you next week."

We waved as she went out.

Jack turned to me, watching as I went back to carelessly shoving goody bags in a box.

"What?" I demanded after a full minute.

"Oh nothing. Only you did something that scared you just then. So that's interesting."

"I'm not scared." Obviously I was, but I wasn't going to admit it to Smug Jack.

"Keep telling yourself that, junior."

I pointed at him. "I am your supervisor, and you will treat me with the respect I deserve." Then, because it sounded hilarious coming from me, I giggled. "Oh wow, I should talk like that all the time. Insta-mood lifter."

"Yeah, I'm not so sure you pulled that off, better luck next time."

We bickered for fun until we finished everything, which I packed into my car to take back Monday morning since we'd run out of time. Before we said goodbye we exchanged phone numbers. I had no idea if I'd ever actually text Jack, and I was pretty sure he wouldn't text me, but still, I was glad we could if we wanted to.

Then I went home. Alone. To my tiny little unit. I let Toby come in and sit on my bed with me while I entered into a Netflix fugue. One of us finished off a bag of Ruffles,

I can't say for certain who it was. I did make sure he didn't eat any of the pint of ice cream I'd picked up on the way home, though. Dairy isn't good for Toby.

A tub of ice cream and a bag of potato chips isn't all that good for me, but I told myself it was probably better than nothing.

Chapter Twenty-Six

The thing I wanted to happen: secure in the knowledge that I'd done the right thing, I would feel very sad for a few days, then moderately sad for maybe a week, then satisfied that the worst was past, after which I wouldn't have to feel sad at all.

The thing that happened in reality: the sadness of missing Sidney—of having hurt them and then not being able to talk to them about it—deepened over time until it became something closer to despondency. I didn't want to do anything. I could hole up in my in-law unit for a little while, but Mason kept texting, then the girls, then Oscar, with Mason never really letting up.

I said I was sick. I said I had the flu. I said maybe I was getting better but I was still rundown and needed to rest. I skipped drinks. Twice.

I couldn't face them. Not after they'd been so happy for me. For us. Not after I'd screwed up so spectacularly when trying not to screw up worse. Had Sidney needed to cancel the show? The more I replayed it all in my head, the less sense it made. Why had I run? Sidney was logical. If I'd just explained that I couldn't do this, that it wasn't in me, they would have understood. Probably.

Except whenever I started thinking about that, I remembered how I'd barely been able to breathe by the time I got to my car, and I'd cried all the way home, and for most of that night, and...

But I didn't want to think about all that, so I tried not to.

I cleaned up the fish bowl, coiling the cords for the laptops Jack and I had used, making neat piles of things that should probably be carted away, like the trash can and the file cabinet. When Deb found me doing all that she told me to set it back up again; the fish bowl would be my base of operations until she decided where to put me.

She'd lowered her voice and added that since no one used the fish bowl, no one technically knew I was there, which might come in useful "down the line."

I had no real idea what that meant, but one side effect of misery was that I didn't really care. I liked the fish bowl. I felt comfortable there. I plugged my laptop back in and rearranged things so I had a sort of desk area facing the window.

In better days I would have taken a picture and posted it on Instagram with a trending hashtag about my new office. Instead I thought about doing that and realized it was way too much work.

For stretches here and there I wasn't thinking about it. Us. Sidney and me. I got through Monday, then Tuesday, reporting to Deb in the morning, doing whatever she assigned me to do. I reorganized a storage room for all of Wednesday and most of Thursday. On Friday I covered a desk for someone who'd gone home sick in Deb's department, which meant she got to show me a lot of stuff I wouldn't have normally seen about her job.

When I accused her of grooming me to be her second in command she only winked and I acknowledged to myself that if I could feel happy, this would have made me feel happy.

Mostly I just felt tired. And still sad. I didn't know why I couldn't shake the sadness. It didn't seem like Sidney and I had known each other long enough for me to be this sad. And we'd only been officially dating for a couple of weeks. Hardly any time at all, right? We'd barely scratched the surface of friendship, of…of love.

God, it was just…really sad, though. Seen from any angle, seen in a microscope, seen from space…really, really sad.

I thought my weak flu excuse had held up pretty well until Mia and Mason showed up at my house Saturday morning, calling my phone over and over from the driveway so I'd come let them into the yard.

"You look like shit." Mason's first words to me.

"Honey." Mia paused. "He's right. You look terrible."

"Wow, thanks for coming over. You can go home now." They barged right in.

Mia made a press of coffee and poked through my cabinets while Mason disgustedly began shoving my dirty clothes (now making up an archaeological record of depression on my floor) into a hamper.

And I sat. On my bed. Watching them. And, after a few minutes, crying again. It was the kind of ugly crying that came with a sort of vague sense of relief, like popping a massive pimple. It was gross and it was messy, but it also felt inevitable and now, finally, it was happening.

"I fucked up," I babbled through my tears. "I fucked up so so much."

They came to sit with me, one of them on each side, coffee and laundry forgotten.

"Baby, you're wrecked." Mase brushed back my hair, his touch familiar and comforting. "What the hell happened? One minute you were happy and the next you aren't on The Love Study and Sidney looks shell-shocked and neither of you show up for drinks."

"Everything seemed fine at the wedding," Mia offered. "Actually, I have no idea. I'm sorry. I wasn't paying attention."

I leaned into her. "It was your wedding, that's all you were supposed to be doing."

Her arm wrapped around me. "So everything wasn't fine? I know it's not fine now because Sidney looks—well, better than you do, but not great."

"You've seen them? I mean obviously you've seen them. Are they okay? How are they?" I did not demand to know if they'd asked about me because they wouldn't have. Boundaries and stuff.

Mia gave me a shoulder squeeze. "They're not great, like I said. But how are *you*?"

"I don't know. I thought I was fine, but then I started feeling bad, and I kept thinking about how I can't do romance, everyone knows I can't, and how Sidney did the sweetest thing for Valentine's, they set up my perfect date, and I couldn't get into it at all, and it felt so empty, but they were into it, and maybe the problem was me like Mase said, and—"

"Hold up, hold up. When did I say what now?"

"How I'm not romantic and Sidney obviously is and I was fucking it up all over again except this time I ended it faster so I couldn't hurt them." I tried to get words out between sobs, but it was hard. "I hurt you so much, I'm sorry, I'm so sorry, and I didn't want to hurt anyone like that ever again."

"You broke up with Sidney because...you and I aren't romantically compatible? Sister, you were right. You fucked up."

"I tried to fix it—"

"No, not that." He grabbed both of my hands, squeezing them. "I didn't say you weren't romantic, Dec. You're plenty romantic. You just do it in a different way than I do, and that would have hurt both of us if we'd tried to stay together."

I hiccupped. More tears eked out of my eyes. "I'm not romantic. You said that."

"No, I said you weren't into bringing me flowers. That's, like, one possible way to be romantic." He squeezed again. "You made Sidney food. You kissed their hand. Tell me that's not romantic."

"And you brought them chocolates," Mia added.

I sniffed. "They were on sale. The chocolates. And Sidney had been listening to a podcast about chocolate, so I thought..." Oh god. I missed hearing about the podcasts they were listening to, telling them about my wacky documentaries. I tried to stay strong this time, but I wanted to curl in on myself until everything went away.

"But that *is* romantic." Mia stroked my temple as I leaned against her. "Dec, romance is...paying attention. You know? It's listening and sharing and enjoying each other."

"And being thoughtful. You never brought me flowers, but you used to do little things that I didn't see as romantic at the time, but totally were." Mase ducked his head to catch my eye. "Remember when you got me that electric toothbrush after I got cavities?"

I groaned. "I'm the worst, oh my god."

"Nah, it was sweet. You saw a thing that upset me and you

tried to help me fix it. Or when you got me that subscription fruit basket for my birthday when I said I was going vegan?"

Mia laughed. "Okay, that was hilarious and also very sweet. I think all of us ate better that year."

"And we took all those sexy fruit pictures!"

I cringed. "The one with the, uh, melons? And Ronnie with a sports bra on?"

"I should have made her buy that sports bra! I could never wear it again." Mia kissed my forehead. "You are an incredible friend, Dec. Think of all the times you've dropped dinner by when you knew we were busy. Or all the nights you've stayed up playing board games because Ronnie couldn't sleep."

"You're the only one who can stand Oscar when he's had another breakup."

"That's nothing," I argued. "I just ignore him when he's being an asshole."

"You're a fucking *saint*, man. He's lucky I don't punch him when he's being an asshole."

I shrugged. "I don't know. It's like he has all these feelings and he doesn't know what to do with them so he lashes out. I don't take it personally."

Mason squeezed my hands again before releasing them. "That's exactly what I'm talking about. Those are the qualities that make you a really good friend, you know?"

"That doesn't mean I can be...whatever Sidney wants."

"Why do you think they want something other than a really good friend? It seems like that *is* what they want."

"Plus," Mia said, tone super reasonable, "didn't you say the sex was good?"

"Yeah, but..."

Both of them just looked at me.

"But there's...other stuff. Like...like the inevitability of me fucking it up."

Mia nudged Mason. "I'll let you take this one. I have to pee."

"Girl, if I didn't know better, I'd think you were pregnant." He narrowed his eyes. "Wait—"

"No way! We just got married! We are not having kids yet." She slid off the bed and into my tiny bathroom.

Mason engulfed me in a hug that felt so good I wanted to move in and stay awhile. "Basically you decided you were eventually going to fuck up so you fucked up really hard as soon as you could?"

I sagged. "I hate this. I miss them so much. And it's not like with you and me. I thought it was going to be like that, that not being with them would be hard at first, but on some level I'd at least feel like it was the only thing I could have done."

"It took me a long time to feel that way, but I think I know what you mean. The sense that maybe doors were opening instead of closing."

"Yeah. Exactly. This… I feel like I drove straight into a wall. On purpose. And now I'm all, gee, being covered in glass shards and bleeding all over the place is super inconvenient, why didn't I think of that before?"

"Well, this is nothing like that because you can walk this back."

I pulled away. "You're joking."

"Um. No? What's your genius plan? Pretending none of it ever happened and hitting the dating apps?"

Mia emerged in time to hear the last half of the sentence. "But wait. You have to talk to them. Right? You can't *not*? Declan. You have to talk to them."

"And say what?" I demanded with way more vehemence than Mia really deserved to have shot in her direction. "Sorry. I just mean, what do I say about this? *Oops, sorry I accidentally dumped you while having a slight panic attack?*"

"Yes!"

"Excuse me—" Mason tugged me in for a brief, almost violent hug. "You ass. What panic attack? You had a panic attack and you didn't call me? Hi, your best fucking friend. What the hell."

"It was stupid."

"*You're* stupid."

I uttered a watery laugh and shoved at him. "Shut up. It was horrible. I thought I could push it down. Do the show like normal, pretend everything was fine, but then I was flipping out and babbling and Sidney was just staring at me and…"

"Dec…" Mia sat down again, expression troubled. "One of the things that's nice about having a person, like a relationship—and I know all relationships aren't the same, but in general—is that you don't always have to pretend with that person. But what if you'd gone to Sidney's and said you were super anxious and couldn't do the show in that exact moment?"

"But I'd said I would."

"I know, but you…couldn't." She'd gone all gentle. "You had a panic attack. It's not like you could just reschedule it for when it was more convenient."

"Sometimes I can cover it up for a while." Not forever, but it hadn't been dumb to think I might be able to do it for an hour.

"But you didn't *have* to. Right? What's the worst that could have happened if you'd been honest with them?"

It hadn't occurred to me. I wiggled under the blankets on the bed and pulled them up to my chin. "I don't know." Except that wasn't true. They would have been wonderful and compassionate. And probably not in a pitying way, either. If I'd said I couldn't do the show right then, Sidney would have told me it was fine. They probably would have invited me to stay and read a book or something. Because they liked it when I was around while they worked. And they cared about me.

When I looked at it that way, the last thing they would have wanted was for me to force myself to do the show when I was that anxious.

"I'm so dumb," I mumbled, sinking farther into the bed.

"You're not dumb," Mia said.

"No comment," Mase said.

I tried to kick him from under the covers, but I didn't have enough freedom of movement to do a good job. "But I can't talk to them. I have no idea what I'd even say."

"Hmm, let me think." He assumed a bastardized *The Thinker* pose. "You could start with *I'm sorry, really sorry, like I-will-be-your-hot-sex-monkey-for-a-week sorry.*"

Mia nodded gravely. "That seems reasonable."

I managed to hit both of them with one pillow. Hashtag skillz-with-a-z. "No, but seriously. If someone did what I—"

Mase put his hand over my mouth. It was not as hot as when Sidney did it. "You did way worse to me, son, and I got over it. Even if you weren't so hung up on them you can't see straight—which you are, by the way—it would still be a decent thing to apologize."

"But nothing's changed!" I whined. "I still can't be this person."

"What person?"

I did a whole big flapping thing with my arms. "This person who someone else can trust! This person who deserves to fall in love!"

"I'm taking that as a profound insult. I fell in love with you, and I felt lucky that you were in love with me."

"And then I fucked it up so badly, Mase. I fucked it up

so, so badly. I like *destroyed* you, and I loved you more than anything."

"Um, hi, do I look destroyed to you right now? Don't make me into the stick you use to beat yourself, okay?" He leaned in until most of my vision was taken up with his face. "Hate to break it to you, sunshine, but I got over your ass."

I laughed. It was a wet, exhausted laugh, but it was still a laugh. "Yeah, you did. But like… I don't want to do that again."

He shrugged. "So talk to Sidney. Look, Dec, you're my best friend in the world. I'm not even that pissed that you lucked out and found someone amazing, but I really will be pissed if you throw that away because you're scared." He shook me very gently. "I trust you. And if Sidney wants to trust you, you should let them. You definitely shouldn't decide they don't have the right to make that choice."

I looked at him, feeling all the years of our friendship, seeing all the love we'd had for each other etched in his face as clearly as he must see it in mine. "I don't think I could forgive me."

"You would forgive me, though. Or Mia or Ronnie or Oscar."

Which…yeah.

"So what makes you unforgivable?"

"I fucked up worse?"

He shook his head. "Not this time. This time it's a blip." When I opened my mouth he said, "Okay, a really *big* blip. And if Sidney doesn't want to take you up on hot monkey sex, fine, but I think probably they'd appreciate the opportunity to forgive you. Or maybe kick you. Either way."

"No kicking." Mia kissed my cheek. "Mase is right. Also maybe you should let us, I dunno, help or something next time you have a panic attack."

"It's not, like, a hobby of mine," I grumbled. "And help how? Hold my hand while I cry?"

"Uh...yes? Would that not be helpful?" She glanced at Mase, who shrugged again. "I think if I were having a panic attack that'd be comforting."

I rubbed my eyes. "Maybe. I don't know."

"You don't have to, but at least have it as an option. And I hope that whatever happens, Sidney comes back to drinks. I really like them."

"Me too."

Mason went to mess with my hair then made a face at it instead. "Cheer up, buttercup. And take a damn shower."

"You're not my mom!"

He grinned.

They stayed a little while longer, making sure I was basically all right. Mase offered to cancel the date he had planned so we could cuddle and watch TV, and Mia invited me over for a sleepover at her and Ronnie's house, but in the end I opted to stay home.

I spent a couple of hours cleaning, which you can only do in a tiny little room if you have hashtag-mad-skillz at procrastination and distraction, which I do. But by the time I went to bed I had done my laundry at the laundromat down the street, cleaned and put away all my dishes, changed the sheets on my bed, and swept the floor.

Not that cleaning cures depression or anything, but it at least made me feel like less of a lump. And it gave me something to do while I obsessed over texting/calling/emailing/sending a pigeon to Sidney. I could say I was sorry, but then what?

Going to sleep in a clean apartment was nice, but I was no closer to figuring out what to do. Cleaning: doesn't cure being a dumbass. Tragically.

Chapter Twenty-Seven

I conducted an aggressive program of self-care on Sunday, ~~still putting off actually talking to Sidney~~ because I totally needed it.

Luxurious bath complete with tea and a book: check.

Start carnitas in the slow cooker: check.

Add a bunch of people on Instagram who post beautiful travel pictures because I love looking at them: check.

Get a little weepy about a fantasy of exploring castle ruins somewhere in the world: check. (Technically not all that self-carey, but it was triggered by the pictures, and I went with it. I bet Sidney was fun to travel with… Sidetracked. Back to self-care.)

Leave a message for my old therapist to schedule an appointment (because it might help and it couldn't *hurt*): check.

Cut all my nails, like a grown-up: check.

Play with Toby in the sun: check.

Stay away from Twitter: check.

Talk to Mase about his date, which was good: check.

Send Oscar a text message with all emojis just to annoy him: check.

Contemplate whether "annoy your friends" counts as self-care and decide it does: check.

Take a nap: check.

Check on carnitas, run out for avocados: check.

Feast: check.

(In between those last two there was a long contemplation of inviting Sidney over for dinner, but I chickened out. Definitely not good self-care, but then again, I sort of had a date with myself, which is a legit item on your standard internet self-care checklist, so I win.)

Monday. I'd talk to them Monday. They had the show. I'd call them after the show. Or no, text. Or maybe email. Except I could email them at any point during the day, even when they were at work. Technically I could also text them while they were at work. Scratch that.

But Monday. Sunday was for self-care. Monday was for... dealing with what I'd done. Good plan.

The problem with putting something off is that most things you postpone don't get easier the longer you go without doing them.

Case in point: Monday morning, sitting in the fish bowl, drinking coffee and staring into space. Monday afternoon, me in the fish bowl, still staring into space like the good little permanent employee I was.

Monday at quitting time, sitting in my car, trying to decide what to do.

For six weeks I'd gotten out of work on Monday and driven to Sidney's apartment to film The Love Study. I wondered how many more weeks it would take before I no longer instinctively wanted to drive to their place on Mondays after work. Anyway, I should probably call them tomorrow. When they didn't have a show to shoot.

The show only took twenty minutes. Thirty if you add in all the after-show stuff.

Maybe they'd be too tired after the show to talk to me.

No, that was illogical.

Maybe they wouldn't want to talk to me at all, which was possible, and I would accept it. Might even be relieved.

There was always tomorrow...

Which was what I'd said yesterday. I should have called them yesterday after my day of self-care. That would have been super clever.

I could wait until next weekend and do a whole other day of self-care, which was probably a good habit to get into anyway, and call them then?

This seemed like a fresh and innovative idea until I realized it was a great big ball of anxiety and procrastination wrapped up with a *TREAT YOURSELF* bow.

I should do it today. If I was going to. And Mase would ask. So would Mia.

The show was about to start, because I'd been sitting in my car for the entire time it would have taken me to drive over there. Wow. Really good time management, Dec. Pro shit.

I pulled up Your Spinster Uncle on my phone (I was already subscribed) and waited for the notification of the livestream. When it pinged, I clicked.

Sidney looked good. Not good as in well rested or anything (and I bet there was a vegetable graveyard in their fridge) but good to me. I liked to see them.

"Welcome to Your Spinster Uncle. I'm your spinster uncle Sidney, and we're working through some Q and A backlog, so let's get to it. As always, you can message the message number while we're live, or you can call in."

It had been weeks since I'd seen an episode of their show, so maybe I was making it up, but it sure seemed like they weren't bringing the same level of energy they usually did. They sounded a little monotone. Not quite bored. Maybe numb?

Other than looking tired, though, they were in a typical Spinster Uncle outfit. Their hair was pulled back in a ponytail and they were wearing a black T-shirt with their rainbow choker. I bit my lip, looking at their neck, thinking about kissing them.

Would trade sex monkey services for forgiveness. Hands down. Would volunteer sex monkey services free of charge.

I watched as they worked their way through a few emailed questions and a text message. They were really good at the whole advice-giving thing, which I'd weirdly never considered until that exact moment, despite the fact that they'd given me legit advice a few times in the beginning of The Love Study, and all of it had been good.

My chest ached, thinking about that. Simpler times. We were so much more innocent then…or no. But I hadn't felt any pressure and I was a lot more fun when I didn't feel pressured to conform to some kind of mold.

The whole point of The Love Study was figuring out what I wanted, and then when I finally got it, I somehow fucked it up. Except what I'd wanted was to spend time with Sidney, not necessarily to become one half of a couple. I didn't even understand what that meant, and I wanted to talk to Sidney about it because they were the person I could talk to about relationship models and how they applied to real life.

They took a call from someone sounding young who asked

if Sidney's parents were divorced because the caller's parents were getting divorced and they were really sad.

"Divorce is hard in a lot of ways, especially on kids." Sidney's voice was low, careful now. They were looking right into the camera. "I think it's sometimes helpful if you think of what you're feeling as grief. Your family will change now, and that can be scary. You have a right to mourn for how things used to be. Do you have access to a counselor? Maybe at school? It helps to talk things out sometimes, if you find a person you can trust."

The caller could maybe talk to the school counselor (aww, this kid had to be young, that was middle school or high school lingo). Sidney rattled off a few websites and hotline numbers and kept the caller on for a few more minutes, their voices fading into the background while I sat in my car in a parking lot watching a tiny screen.

I had the worst idea.

The very worst.

It was so bad it might...curve back around to being good?

Or if not good, acceptable?

I could call in.

I needed advice, after all. And Your Spinster Uncle was an advice show. I checked the time. If I was gonna do this, I'd have to do it now.

They didn't publicize the phone number on YouTube ("That way lies madness and perverts—not the good kind," they'd explained when I asked), but I knew where to find it.

Was I doing this?

Would they be mad if I did? I mean, it might not be fair? But the last time I'd needed advice about them I'd asked them on the show, and they'd said it was a one on the not-messed-up side of the scale. They'd even said that being live let them think more clearly, so...maybe it was okay?

Or maybe I was just trying to justify doing a horrible thing.

Except Sidney wanted me to trust them. And I did.

I dialed the number.

They'd gone back to the email questions, but wrapped up and connected a call. My call? My heart was pounding. I heard a couple of clicks on the line.

"Hi, this is Sidney. How can the Your Spinster Uncle community help you today?"

"Omigod. Um." I cringed. "Um."

On YouTube, their face changed. They leaned toward the mic. "Declan?"

"I'm sorry. I mean, for everything, but mostly for being too chickenshit to call you like a normal person."

"You are calling me. We're literally on the phone." I thought, just maybe, they wanted to smile.

"The thing is, I need advice again."

"That's what we're here for. Right, commenters?"

Holy shit, the commenters. I was on my phone so I couldn't look. "Um, so. So I sorta… I fucked up."

"Everyone fucks up at one time or another. Maybe we can help you decide what to do now. Do you know what you want?"

The thing was, that's what they'd say to anyone. We'd talked about how they facilitated calls to make things go smoothly, to get to the point fast without people noticing they were being herded straight for it.

I was relieved to be herded. "Well, I want to…um…open communication. With someone. I mean I have this *friend* who fucked up and wants to open communication with the person their fuck-up most hurt. Theoretically. So, like, how do you approach someone you flipped out all over and then hid from because you were too ashamed to talk to them?"

"I think there's a lot to untangle there, but ultimately if you think you hurt someone, you can always offer an apology. Maybe they'll accept it and agree to talk to you. Maybe they'll accept it and want it to end there. Or maybe they'll be too hurt to accept your apology at all." Their eyebrows rose just a little. "You won't know until you try. But I think if you feel bad about how your actions affected someone, that's where you start."

It was a really good Spinster Uncle answer. I couldn't tell where Sidney came down on those options. "So you think I just—I mean my friend just…barges in and vomits apologies all over?"

Their lips twitched. "I'm not sure *that* would be appreciated. But I do think it's valid, as long as the behavior was within reasonably healthy bounds for a relationship, to request to be heard. And the only way to do that is to…do it."

"Right. Um. Yeah. Good points." I swallowed. "Is this a situation where you think I just text and ask if they want to talk to me? Would that be too intrusive?"

"I think that would be appropriate. One text. I would follow up by email if you get no response, and let it go completely if you get no response there either."

"Yeah, that…sounds good. I mean not the no-response thing. The having-a-plan thing. Thanks."

They smiled, said, "Thank you for calling," and disconnected me.

But because I was watching the livestream, I saw the breath they took, the pause that lasted a beat longer than you'd expect.

"Let's do one more question, this one by message…"

My heart was still pounding. My chest was still achy. But I'd spoken to them. And they seemed receptive. Ish. Leaving room for rejection later.

Fuck it. They kept their phone on silent for shooting. I opened a text, experiencing a pang of regret when I saw their familiar name and color scheme (yes, of course I have color schemes for different people, what kind of caveman doesn't color code their phone contacts?).

I stared at the screen and lectured myself. *Just do it. Do it right now. Do not pass go, do not collect two hundred dollars.*

What could I possibly say? Oh god. This was somehow harder than calling the show.

~~Hi, it's me.~~ Um, no.

~~How have you been?~~ What were we, business associates?

~~I'm so fucking sorry I can barely eat or sleep.~~ Okay, that was definitely not a healthy apology.

I'm sorry.

I stared at it.

Weak sauce? Yes. But wholly and entirely true. Without a doubt.

What, just that? Just "I'm sorry" like that could possibly make up for knocking on their door, losing my shit, and running away?

I hit send. That had to be the best place to start, anyway.

I'm so sorry. I would love to see you or talk to you. Or email, also fine. Any form of communication, dealer's choice.

I sent that too.

Um, this is where I stop texting so as not to be a creeper since I know you're still shooting. But I want it on the official record that I would really like to talk to you and my lack of spammed texts is meant to be respectful, not to…express lack of interest. Or investment. Or anything.

I didn't even reread that block of text before sending. Then I closed the app and put my phone in my pocket.

I took it back out to make sure it was on both vibrate and

sound. Now would be a good time to drive home, but what if I somehow still missed their reply? If they sent a reply.

I navigated back to YouTube, but the stream had ended.

Oh god.

The stream had ended.

They could be reading my texts right—

The phone vibrated and dinged.

I am open to calling, texting, email, or in person. I have time available in about fifteen minutes for any of the above.

Ding. *With a slight preference for in person, but no pressure.*

Fifteen minutes was just enough time to drive over there. I sent back, *I'm on my way.* Then added, *Do you have food or should I pick something up?* Which might be a little presumptuous, but I hadn't eaten since lunch and I knew they'd want to eat before going to bed.

That would be good. No preference on food.

I sent back a smiley. What the hell.

Okay, so, best takeout between my work and Sidney's: and *go*.

Chapter Twenty-Eight

I got Thai, because that seemed safe and neutral, until I was walking up the stairs to their apartment and remembered that the first time we'd had Thai food was after sex, standing in their kitchen, eating a meal so we could get back to banging.

Would they think I was insinuating something with my choice of food? No, right? We'd had it a couple of times and I knew their order, that was all. It was a logical and totally-not-based-on-sex choice. Right?

I stopped walking in the middle of the stairs and seriously considered going back out for something else.

But that was madness. I was here now, nearly to their door. Only a fool would squander this momentum.

I put my head down and kept marching.

They opened the door looking more tired in real life than on screen. "Hey."

"Hey." I held up the bag of food. "I would like to...offer

this food. As a token of my apology. And also as sustenance. And I'm absolutely not implying we should have sex tonight it's just the first food I could think of that I knew your order for," I finished in a rush.

"Noted. Come in." Their eyes seemed a little hooded behind their glasses, as if they were wary, or maybe just exhausted.

The apartment was exactly the same. Which made sense, since it had only been three weeks. I handed over the bag and stood there like a lump watching Sidney get us plates and utensils. It felt like my kitchen familiarity rights had been revoked so I couldn't do anything but watch.

Oh, and put my stuff down in a pile. As usual. That was probably still permitted.

Wow. We were really not talking. At all. Um. "So...how have you been?" I immediately wanted to take it back.

They shot an eyebrow raise at me. "Fine. You know. Tea with the vicar, that sort of thing."

I swallowed. "Yeah, that was a dumb question. Sorry." I took the offered food and followed them to the armchairs. "Things got...bad. For me. I mean what I did was bad. And the rest of the week. Though I took a permanent job at my work, so that's been okay."

"Really? What prompted that?"

"I'm...not sure. The event went well. And I guess I sort of...decided to take the opportunity. I can always quit later if it doesn't work out."

"A wise guiding principle for any endeavor."

"Um. Yeah. Wait, was that pointed?"

They shrugged. "That must have been part of what happened between us. Things weren't working out for you?"

"Um." Could I say *um* more in any one conversation than

I was right now? "I'm not sure. Honestly, I didn't know what I was doing or saying or feeling. I flipped out."

They made a dismissive arm gesture. "'*Flipped out*' is non-specific and potentially minimizing."

"Right. Yeah. I...had a panic attack." My shoulders hunched as I said it.

Sidney put down their food. "Are you all right?"

"Fine, fine, it was no big deal."

"Maybe we should...treat it as if it matters, though. Is that why you left so quickly?"

"I didn't want to—" *flip out* "—lose it in front of you. I'm sorry."

They nodded. "I understand."

I ate a bite of food, barely tasting it, while they looked at me. I didn't know what else to do. And I couldn't keep staring back because I felt too...too much. Too exposed. Too embarrassed. Too much like if I said the wrong thing I'd never get to sit here and eat Thai food with them again.

"Actually..." They took a deep breath. "Actually, while I do understand, I also felt really, really hurt. We could have done a lot of things at that moment, and any number of them could have included you having time to yourself for whatever reason, but just leaving and not talking to me at all was...awful. For me."

"For me too. Shit, I didn't mean to—I didn't mean that like I was trying to say it was the same kind of awful, just I missed you so much and I had no idea it was going to hurt so badly to not be able to talk to you and I'm really, really sorry."

"Okay. I accept your apology."

"I mean...are you sure, though?" I had to ask. I didn't want them to say they accepted my apology if they couldn't.

They picked up their plate again, setting it on their lap. "I guess it felt like all the other times people have faded away.

Except this time I'd tried so hard to not do that myself and I didn't think you would. It surprised me. Maybe it shouldn't have, I don't know. But I thought we could talk to each other if things weren't working, and then you just…left. I am sure that I accept your apology, though. I know you mean it."

"I do. I'm so fucking sorry I did that. And then, once I'd done it, I didn't know how to *un*-do it, how to take it back, especially because I still feel like the reason I did it is valid, so it's really hard to…to pick it all apart and figure out what the right thing is." I ran down, feeling weirdly winded and also still awful. If I'd thought saying all that would help, I would have been disappointed.

They looked at me for a long moment. "I felt like you'd decided I wasn't worth the trouble. That being with me wasn't…enough."

"Oh my god, *no*. Nothing like that."

"Yes, but…" Their brows drew down in their difficult-thinking expression and my heart kind of ached knowing I'd been the cause of it. "But you wouldn't talk to me. That was the issue. Not that you got worried, or anxious, or did something you wish you hadn't done. The problem was we didn't talk about it which meant we couldn't fix it. I guess I need to know what you want now that you're here."

They sounded so neutral. So uninvolved. It was ludicrous of me to wish they'd take a huge emotional risk right now—or more than they already had—but for a moment, I wasn't sure I could be the one who did that. I wanted to. Sort of. But if I opened myself up and asked them to take me back and they even hesitated for like a second (which they'd be sensible to do), I'd be crushed.

My hands were shaking. I could not do this. There was no way. We'd finish our food and part as friends and that was it, that was all I could manage.

Do you know what you want?

Except I did know. At least I thought I did. I kept my eyes on my food and said, very softly, "Would you mind holding my hand?"

They moved fast. Fast like they weren't worried about spooking me. Fast like they wanted nothing more in the world than to hold my hand. To be invited to do so. "I'm right here. Take your time." They took my right hand in both of theirs and just sat there, awkwardly bent over, like they could do it all night.

Which was too much for me and I started to cry.

They slid their fingers free to take the bowl away from me and set it on the table so they could grab both of my hands. "You already apologized. I completely accept. I swear."

"But you... I..." I sniffled. "You deserve better than me. I will fuck up again. I will always fuck up again."

"Didn't you hear me spinstering at you? Everyone fucks up. That's a fact of life."

"But I fuck up *massively*. And you stopped doing relationships because you couldn't find anyone who wanted to do it the way you did, and what if I don't? What if I fail you?"

Sidney took a breath. Their expression was...intent and serious and totally not repelled by me. I could tell. At least I hoped so. "This is the untangling. Like. It's not really...useful for you to be obsessed with failing me. When as long as you keep talking to me, as long as we're figuring things out together, you can't fail me. If we discover we want incompatible things, then we'll deal with that, but do you think that's true right now? Or are you afraid it might be later, like it was with Mason?"

I hunched a little. "Maybe that. I don't want to hurt you like I hurt him."

"Not to, um, doubt your gallant instincts, but do you

think you might also not want to be hurt like *you* were before?"

Ugh, I was terrible. I was a terrible human being. "I'm sorry."

"For what? Declan, that's…normal. It's normal to want to avoid pain. It's built in for evolutionary purposes, right? It's not like that undercuts your desire to save the people you care about from pain." They sort of choked. "Not that I'm saying—I mean—you haven't said—and I *wouldn't* say—"

"Oh my god, stop, I care about you so much."

Their cheeks lit like a sunset, all pink and rose. "I care about you too. But I need you to not disappear again because I can't do that. I really, really can't be okay in a relationship where I'm always afraid the other person is going to pull away and refuse to speak to me."

"I won't. I'm sorry. I freaked out and got scared and next time I will tell you if that happens."

"Okay. In that case, I deserve what I say I deserve, and you're…you're it. If you still want to do this."

I swallowed. "I do want to do this. More than anything. But I thought it would just feel right and it didn't. I mean, some of it did? But some of it didn't, and I don't know how to talk about that."

"I think in a way we both sort of tried to walk a path that wasn't ours." They took another deep breath. "I've thought a lot about this, and I wonder if maybe 'dating' as a conceptual framework just isn't really for us? Or I should say, I'm beginning to think it's not really for me. My favorite times with you are the times we didn't approach like they were dates."

I nodded slowly. "Like me hanging out while you worked. Or you texting me to be your sex monkey."

The flush deepened. "I'm pretty sure I didn't say it that way."

"Dude, I dig being your sex monkey. Don't steal my joy."

"Your sex monkey joy?"

"With bells on."

We both smiled, which felt good.

"So I don't know, but that's what I've been thinking about. While hoping you would talk to me. I have a lot of stuff to say, but I guess that's what it comes down to: maybe we should analyze the results of our past experiments and alter future experiments according to what seemed to be working?"

I leaned forward and whispered, "FYI, you're turning me on right now. Can I say that? I know we haven't worked everything out yet, but I just thought you should know the effect your hot analytical summary is having on me."

"It's less a summary and more a proposal."

I pretended to swoon a little.

"But what definitely won't work is if we don't talk about things when they're not working, so I propose we start from a standpoint of clear, honest communication from now on." They paused. "The cookie date seemed like a really good idea, but it totally fell flat."

Ouch. "Um. I think that was my fault."

"I think if we prioritize assigning blame we're not gonna get very far."

"Okay, fair enough. It did freak me out a little. Our Valentine's Date."

"Can you say how? I have theories, but I'd like to hear yours."

"Um." I chewed on the inside of my cheek for a few seconds. "I think the wedding was already sort of all up inside my head. Like I spent serious time hiding in bed the night before our date because I felt emotionally oppressed by my rental suit? And I thought we were going to do mad casual because of Valentine's Day, and you not being into Valentine's Day, and then you were so dressed up, and you had this amazing plan, and I felt so rotten for not being into it."

They were nodding. Continuously. "And I thought you were only doing casual for me, which is why I wanted to prove to you that we could do romantic Valentine's Date if you wanted us to, but it wasn't a natural fit to me, either."

The sheer relief of hearing that they hadn't been entirely comfortable with that night made me legitimately light-headed. "Really? You're not just saying that?"

"Saying the thing I think you want to hear would skew the results of our clear and honest communication experiment." They smirked. Gently, though. A soft, gentle sort of smirk, which is totally a thing. "Did the wedding end up... being triggering?"

"I guess so. And it was such a beautiful day, but Oscar, Mase, and I went back to Mase's after and felt sorry for ourselves. It brought back all those feelings, all that pressure. To be a player in that world. That narrative. And I think it got jumbled in my head until I felt like we—the thing we were doing—was part of that pressure."

"That honestly makes perfect sense to me."

I frowned. "It does? It makes me feel a little crazy."

"I'm grateful to The Love Study because it brought us together," they said slowly. "But I also think it kind of... shunted us into a dating metric that we wouldn't have otherwise gotten into as quickly as we did. Like, on our own I think we'd both be happy—I'm pretty sure I'd be happy—hanging out a lot, and sharing food, and watching documentaries, and listening to podcasts, and just talking. And having sex. Um. As much as we wanted, which for me is...more than a very little." That flush again, oh my god.

"Me too. The sex thing. Actually all of it. Like the 'date-friend' thing seemed really good for a minute? But ended up making me feel like we were in deep waters without a map. Wait. In the desert without a map? What would you need in deep waters, a compass?"

"And a boat, presumably."

"Deep waters without a boat! That's how it felt. Like flailing around while the waters got more choppy and I didn't know how to get out."

"Okay." They squeezed my hands, which was apparently a thing I was into, because it made me want to purr and press my head against them like a cat. "Next time you feel that way, if it happens again, I really need you to talk to me about it. I wasn't drowning, but I wasn't comfortable either. And I'll do the same."

"Next time. I mean...you mean..." I looked at them over my glasses, afraid to raise my head, afraid to commit. "So you think we should try again?"

"Yes. In the interests of discovery. And also because I miss you."

"I miss you too."

"Can I say one more thing, that's more...spinstering than deep feels relationship talking?"

"Sure. Yeah. Always."

They shifted a little in their armchair, eyes wandering over their books before coming back to me. "I think you have some internalized stuff going on with your anxiety that played a role here, and while I'm not going to make some kind of awful ultimatum about it, I also think, as your friend, that it might be a good thing if you...addressed that. In some way."

"Um, yeah. Me too. I made an appointment with the therapist I used to see, so...yeah. Working on it. I guess it usually feels like I can barrel through it if I try hard enough, but I couldn't this time. And Mase told me he'd kick my ass if I had a panic attack again and didn't mention it."

"Maybe the ideal would be not feeling like you needed to, uh, 'barrel through'? Which was probably Mason's point."

"I think his point was I better fucking not."

They smiled. "He's a good friend. I really like your friends. The, uh, Motherfuckers."

"Me too. They all want you to come back to drinks, by the way. Mia was basically like, 'Even if Sidney doesn't want hot monkey sex anymore, tell them to come to drinks again.' Paraphrasing."

"I'd like that."

"Um, Sidney?"

"Yeah?"

"I'm really sorry. I didn't know what to do and I hid, which was shitty of me."

"It's okay. I mean, yes, I agree, it was *really* shitty. It made me feel ugly and alone and like I shouldn't have even tried to be close to other people, but—"

"Omigod I'msosorry." I leaned over and pressed their hands to my forehead because I didn't quite dare to kiss them. "I hate that I made you feel that way. You're so amazing, and so smart, and everyone your whole life has totally missed out on being with you because you're one of my favorite people on earth and I know we haven't known each other that long but I think I can say this with certainty I totally love you." I shrunk deeper into myself and tried to disappear. "That was the absolute wrongest time to say that, sorry. But it's true."

They squeezed my hands. Again. "I have very deep feelings for you too. Arman assured me that if something happened between us it was your loss, but Declan, you're…also really amazing. Please, um, sit up again?"

"Sorry," I mumbled, knowing I was blushing.

"So I think we'll have some times like this, when we're trying to figure out our individual stuff and how that…goes together with our mutual stuff. Like gears, you know? Your gear and my gear and our friendship gear and when a gear jams we'll have to work it out."

"Except for the sex gear. I don't think anything's gonna jam that."

They shook their head. "It really might. Sometimes I get dysphoric and that makes sex harder."

"Oh. But you'll tell me if that happens? And if I can help?"

"I'm going to try. It's not an easy thing to talk about, but we have that communication project going, so I'll try. Maybe we should have called the show *The Communication Study* instead. That might be more accurate."

"But not as good for keywords or whatever."

"True. The SEO on *The Communication Study* would not recommend its use." They pushed up their glasses. "So just to put all the cards on the table, I would like to continue seeing you, and having sex with you, and texting you, and talking to you about random podcasts for no reason other than I enjoy hearing what you have to say."

"Ditto. Same. Amen." I worried for a second that I wasn't acting serious enough, but then they kissed me, and I decided not to worry about anything. "I really missed kissing you. And also talking to you. And I had all this stuff in my head and you were the only person I thought would understand it."

"Same."

We reheated our dinner and curled up in their bed with an archaeology documentary. When we'd put our plates aside it seemed kind of natural to do a sitting-closer-together thing. Which morphed into me asking if I could put my arm around them, and them asking if they could put their head on my chest. And then I was playing with their hair and snuggling in closer and…it was all so warm and felt so good. We didn't have sex, we didn't even make out. But this space felt…more important.

Being able to share food and lie in bed together, to laugh a little, to talk in low voices about ethical practices on dig sites (super fascinating stuff) was more vital in that moment than anything else we could have done. Then I went home, so they could get good sleep before work the next morning.

I felt so much lighter. Like I was walking on layers and layers of down comforters and if I stumbled, it would be okay, I'd bounce right back up.

Chapter Twenty-Nine

Here's how my friends introduce me to new people: "This is Declan. He left his last boyfriend at the altar, but he's reformed now." They think it's hilarious.

If Sidney happens to be in earshot when someone says that, we look at each other like we're sharing a secret, like we're getting away with something. Other people assume we're dating in some conventional way.

When really?

We're just doing everything we enjoy and nothing we don't enjoy.

We have better things to do for two hours in the dark with each other, so we don't go to movies.

I'm still wigged out by which fork to use, so we don't go to fancy restaurants.

Sidney still hates all the culturally dictated romantic stuff like flowers, so I don't send them flowers.

We love watching movies together, though, so we do that in one of our beds, or we buddy watch when we're both in the mood to be responsible and not stay out late on a work night.

We love eating fancy dinners (we even get dressed up sometimes), so when we want to do that I make an elaborate meal and they work in the background, or they sit on the counter and talk, or we listen to podcasts.

When we go to drinks we always sit together, even though we don't need to, because we like being just that close.

We love coming up with our own forms of romance. Sometimes one of us leaves a note on the other's car while they're at work. We have more than once exchanged sex toys just for fun, on an arbitrary day we picked a few weeks ahead of time. Sex toys are the gift that keeps on giving: you buy them once and then can use them in a variety of applications and combinations for years to come! Get it? *To come?*

Sidney laughs at most of my terrible jokes. And every now and then makes one of their own.

I dropped off breakfast-in-a-basket after they'd worked a few really long inventory days, even setting my alarm for oh-dark-thirty to get to their apartment in time for them to eat. Except they were so happy to see me we may have spent that time…doing other things. Oops. It wasn't a gift fail, so much as a…gift success in an unexpected direction.

They always say they're not that sweet, but I totally disagree. Sometimes they bring me a cup of coffee and we sit with the armchairs close together, our legs all intertwined, and when I look up from my book they're just kind of smiling at me. Whenever it happens they blush and look away real fast, but it makes me feel warm and gooey. In a good way. Melty. Like we could sit just like this for a long, long time.

When Sidney introduces me to people, they say, "This is Declan." And I can't help grinning at them like they're the only person in the world.

* * * * *

Reviews are an invaluable tool when it comes to spreading the word about great reads. Please consider leaving an honest review for this or any of Carina Press's other titles that you've read on your favorite retailer or review site.

To discover more books by Kris Ripper, please check out zir website at krisripper.com! You can also find more Ripper books at the usual places where ebooks are sold.

Acknowledgments

My thanks, as always, to the early readers who expressed their enjoyment of this book—and nudged me in the direction of publishing it when my nerve failed (as it usually does). Particularly Lennan Adams, KJ Charles, and Alexis Hall, badasses all three.

Deepest gratitude to the best of agents, Courtney Miller-Callihan, who never fails to support any path I want to take with a project.

And, world without end, my thanks to General Wendy, whose feedback is always snarky, clearheaded, and on point.

Simon Burke has always preferred animals to people. When the countdown to adopting his own dog is unexpectedly put on hold, Simon turns to the PetShare app to find the animal TLC he's been missing. Meeting pet owner Jack isn't easy on Simon's anxiety, but his adorable menagerie is just what Simon needs... and it's not long before their pet-centric arrangement sparks a person-centric desire.

Keep reading for an excerpt from Better Than People *by Roan Parrish!*

Chapter One

Jack

If you had told Jack Matheson when he woke up this morning that he'd end the day at the bottom of a ditch, he wouldn't have been terribly surprised. After all, his whole life *felt* like it was spent at the bottoms of ditches these days—what was one more literal one?

The nightly walk had begun as they usually did. As soon as he finished dinner and placed his plate and fork in the sink, the dogs had clustered around him, eyes hopeful and tongues out, ready to prowl. Bernard butted his huge head against Jack's thighs in encouragement while Puddles hung back, waiting to follow the group out. Dandelion pawed at the ground excitedly, and Rat vibrated in place, tiny body taut with anticipation.

The cats cleaned themselves or snoozed on various surfaces,

watching with disinterest, except for Pirate. Pirate twined her way through the forest of legs and paws and tails, back arched, sleek and ready.

"Let's head out," Jack said, clipping on leashes and straightening harnesses as he shoved his feet into worn boots and plastic bags in his back pocket.

Pirate led the way, trotting light-footed ahead of them, then doubling back like a scout. Huge, snuggly Bernard—a St. Bernard who'd been with him the longest—took turns walking next to each of the others, nipping and licking at his friends enthusiastically, and drawing back when he accidentally shoved them off their feet. Bernard didn't know his own strength.

Dandelion pranced along, happy as always to snap at the breeze or a puff of dust, or simply to be outside.

Puddles walked carefully, his soft golden face swinging back and forth, alert for danger, and he jumped at every sound. Twice, Jack had to scoop him up and carry him over the puddles he refused to step in or walk around.

Rat took the lead, just behind Pirate, her tiny legs going hummingbird fast to keep ahead of the others. She kept her nose to the ground, and if she scented a threat, she'd be the first to take it on.

Their leashes crisscrossed throughout the walk, and Jack untangled them absently as he kept one eye on the animals and the other on the sky.

Summer had settled into autumn, and the leaves of Garnet Run, Wyoming, were tipped with red and gold. The air held the first promises of winter, and Jack found himself sighing deeply. Winter was beautiful here. His little cottage was cozy, his fireplace warm, and the woods peaceful.

But this year, for the first time in nearly a decade, he wouldn't have work to occupy him as the snow fell outside.

Jack growled and clenched his fists against the fury that roared in his ears as he anticipated yet another night without a notebook in his hand.

Bernard snuffled against his thigh and Puddles whined. This—this right here was why animals beat people, paws down.

They were sensitive. They cared. They wanted to be loved and they gave love back. Animals never betrayed you the way people did. They were loyal.

"It's okay," Jack murmured. He scratched Bernard's massive head and ran gentle fingers over Puddles' tense ears. "I'll be okay."

Bernard gave his elbow an enthusiastic lick.

"I'll be okay," Jack repeated firmly, to himself this time, as a squirrel's over-enthusiastic labors dislodged an acorn from an overhanging branch. The acorn rustled through the leaves and fell directly onto the soft fur between Puddles' ears, where Jack's fingers had stroked a moment before.

Puddles, skittish at the best of times, reared into the air, fur bristling, and took off into the trees, his leash slipping through Jack's fingers.

"Dammit, Puddles, no!"

Jack tried to follow, but Bernard had plopped down on the soft grass at the tree line and was currently rolling himself in evening smells. It was useless to attempt to move Bernard once he was on the ground, even for a man of Jack's size.

"Stay!" Jack commanded. Bernard woofed, Dandelion flopped down beside him, Rat clawed at the ground, teeth bared. "Pirate, watch them," he called to the cat, even though Pirate had never given him any indication that she understood orders, much less took them.

Jack took off after Puddles. The thought of the dog afraid made Jack's heart pound and he ran full-out.

Puddles had been a trembling mess when Jack found him by the side of the road two years before, and it had taken a month before the Lab would even eat the food Jack offered from his hand. Slowly, painstakingly, he had gained Puddles' trust, and the dog had joined the rest of his pack.

"Puddles!" Jack called into the twilight. He heard a whine ahead and sped up, muscles burning, glad for his afternoon runs. Leaves crunched up ahead to his left and Jack zagged. "Puddles?"

Dark was closing in on the woods and Jack narrowed his eyes, hoping to avoid running smack into a tree. When he heard Puddles' soft bark from up ahead he threw himself forward again.

"I'm here!" he shouted, and was answered with another bark. Then, the sound of crackling branches split the quiet and a whine and thud stopped Jack's heart. He barreled forward to see what had happened, and heard the sound again as his legs broke through what he'd thought was underbrush, and found no solid ground on the other side.

His legs windmilled and his hands caught at the air for a second that seemed like forever. Then he landed hard and rolled down an embankment, stones and branches pummeling him on the way down.

Jack came to a sudden stop with a head-rattling lurch and a gut-churning snap. For a single heavenly moment, there was no pain, just the relief of stillness. Then the world righted itself, and with clarity came agony.

"Oh, fuck," Jack gasped. "Oh, fuck, fuck, fuck."

He bit his lip and lifted his swimming head just enough to peer down at his right leg, where the pain ripped into him with steely teeth. Nausea flooded him as he saw the unnatural angle of his leg and he wrenched his gaze away.

For three breaths, Jack did nothing but try not to puke.

Then a wet, trembling nose nudged his hand, and he opened his eyes to Puddles' warm brown gaze.

"Thank god." Jack sucked in a breath and lifted a shaky hand to the dog's side. "You okay, bud?"

Puddles sat down beside him and rested his chin on Jack's shoulder, a loyal sentinel.

For some reason, it brought tears to Jack's eyes.

"I'm fine, Charlie. Jesus, back off." Jack growled at his older brother, who was hovering over him, one large, rough hand nervously stroking his beard, the other catching on the over-starched hospital sheets as he tucked them around Jack.

After hours of pain, insurance forms, and answering the same questions for every nurse and doctor that came along, Jack's habitual brusqueness had morphed into exhausted annoyance.

"Yeah. When I got the phone call to meet you at the hospital after you'd been found crumpled at the bottom of a hill with your bones sticking out I definitely thought, 'He's totally fine,'" Charlie said flatly.

They looked alike—the same reddish-blond hair and hazel eyes; the same large, solid builds, though Charlie was bigger, muscles honed from his constant physical labor—and despite his brother's droll reply, Jack could see a familiar fear in his expression, and in the way he stood close, as if he wanted to be able to touch Jack and check that he was all right.

Charlie had looked after him his whole life, worried about him his whole life. It would be useless to expect him to stop now. Not that Jack really wanted him to.

"Sorry." Jack fisted his hands at his sides and closed his eyes.

Charlie eased his bulk down onto the side of the bed.

"I know I've been saying I wanted to see you more,"

Charlie said, making his voice lighter. "But this isn't exactly what I meant."

Jack snorted and punched his brother a glancing blow to the shoulder. He hadn't actually meant for it to be glancing, but it seemed his strength had left him.

On the table next to his bed something familiar had appeared: his sketchbook and three pens. His gut clenched.

"Where did those come from?"

"I brought them from your place. Boring in here."

"I don't want 'em."

Charlie's sincere and puzzled expression deepened.

"What? You've never gone a day without drawing in your life. I thought especially in here you'd want—"

"Well, I don't," Jack bit off. He closed his eyes. He hadn't told his brother that he hadn't drawn in eight months. Not since Davis...

Clearly confused, Charlie picked up the sketchbook and pens, huge hand dwarfing them.

Jack swallowed down his rage and fear and disappointment. He felt like every shitty moment of the last eight months had somehow been leading up to this: concussion, broken leg, cracked ribs, lying in a cramped hospital bed, with absolutely nothing to look forward to.

Darkness swallowed him as he realized that now the one thing he'd taken pleasure in since his life went to shit— walking with the animals—was off the table for the foreseeable future.

"Fuck." Jack sighed, and he felt it in his whole body. Charlie leaned closer. "What'm I gonna do?"

The app was called PetShare and one of the nurses had recommended it after a failed attempt to have Charlie smuggle the dogs into Jack's hospital room had led the nurse to enquire about Jack's situation. She'd taken his phone from his hand, downloaded it for him, then returned the phone and said sternly, "No dogs in a hospital. Obviously."

Now, home and settled on the couch with a pillow and blanket after basically being tucked in by Charlie and promising he'd call if he needed anything, Jack fumbled out his phone and made a profile.

Username? He hated usernames.

JackOfAllDogs, he typed. Then, with a guilty glance at the cats, he changed it to *JackOfAllPets*. Then he decided that looked too much like *Jack off* and changed it to *JMatheson*.

At the app's prompting he uploaded a photo of Bernard for his profile picture. Then on to the questions. He hated answering questions. When he got to the final box, which asked him to explain what he was looking for, he grumbled to himself as he thumbed too-small keys, wishing he could draw instead of type. He'd always been better with images than with words anyway. Somehow, people always took his words the wrong way.

That's why it had felt so fortuitous when he'd met Davis, who seemed to pluck the words he intended from his drawings and put them on the page. A perfect partnership. Or so he'd thought.

He banished all thoughts of Davis from his mind and mashed the Submit Profile button, then shoved his phone back into his pocket.

PetShare matched pet owners with animal enthusiasts who didn't have pets of their own. Some of the users were people like Jack who needed help with animal care. Others were just willing to let animal lovers spend time with their pets. But with four dogs (and a cat) who needed twice-daily walks, Jack wasn't optimistic about his chances of being matched with someone, no matter how enthusiastic they were. He imagined he might need three or four interested parties to meet his animals' needs.

Charlie had volunteered to walk them until he found someone, and he didn't want to burden his brother any longer than he had to. Charlie had the hardware store to run, and he spent long hours there and on construction sites.

Jack flicked on the television. He'd never watched much TV before the Davis debacle. The worlds he dreamt up in his head and the world outside his door had always been preferable to any he'd found on the screen. But over the past eight months he'd learned the numbing power of flickering lights and voices that required no response.

Wanting something mindless and distracting, Jack selected *Secaucus Psychic*. Maybe seeing people who'd lost family members to actual death would put a broken leg in perspective.

Hell, who was he kidding. He didn't want perspective. He wanted to sink into the couch and into his bad mood and sulk for just a little longer.

He'd banned Bernard from the couch because, though fully grown, the St. Bernard behaved like a puppy, flopping on top of Jack despite weighing nearly as much as him, and with a leg held together with pins and casting, and ribs and head aching, Jack didn't think he could take a careless flop. So instead, Bernard had piled himself on the floor in front of the couch, as close to Jack as he could get, and lolled his massive head back every few minutes to check if he was allowed on the couch yet.

Pirate curled delicately in the crook of his elbow, though, and he stroked her back, making her rumble.

An unfamiliar ding from his pocket startled both Jack and Pirate. It was the notification sound for PetShare. Jack thumbed the app open and saw that he'd matched. Someone whose username was *SimpleSimon* and lived 6.78 miles away from him had checked the *I'd love to!* option next to Jack's description of what he was looking for.

"I'll be damned," Jack said to the animals. "Either this dude is a saint or he's got no life at all."

Pirate yawned and stretched out a paw to lazily dig her claws into his shoulder.

"Fine, jeez, I know. I don't have one either," Jack grumbled, and resentfully clicked *Accept*.

It was a horrible night. One of Jack's worst.

Because of his concussion, he couldn't take a strong enough painkiller to touch the ache in his ribs and the screaming in his leg. He tossed and turned, and finally gave up on sleep, searching the darkness for the familiar reflective eyes watching him. After a moment, he lurched upright. The sudden movement shot pain through his head and chest and leg and left him gasping and nauseated, clutching the edge of the mattress until the worst of it passed.

Fuck, fuck, fuck.

Finally, having learned his lesson, Jack gingerly pushed himself off the bed and shoved the crutches under his arms. The pull of the muscles across his chest as he used his arms to propel himself forward left his ribs in agony. By the time he got to the bathroom, usually just ten quick steps away, he was sweating and swearing, teeth clenched hard.

Then, the drama of lowering his pants.

"Can't even take a damn piss without fucking something up," Jack muttered. At least, that's what he'd intended to mutter before the pain and exhaustion stole the luxury of indulging in self-deprecating commentary.

Humbled and infuriated in equal measure, Jack gave up on sleep entirely. Coffee. That's what he needed. Coffee was the opposite of sleep. Coffee was a choice he could make when apparently he couldn't control a single other goddamn thing in his pathetic, broken life.

The trip to the kitchen was suddenly rife with unexpected hazards. A squeaky dog toy sent him lurching to one side, groaning at his wrenched ribs and the shock of pain that shot through his leg. When he could move again, his crutch clipped the edge of a pile of unopened mail that had sat for weeks, which cascaded across the floorboards like a croupier's expert spread of cards.

Naturally, that got the attention of several animals and Jack stood very still while the envelopes were swatted at, swept by tails, and finally, in the case of the largest envelope, flopped upon by Pickles, the smallest of his cats.

Mayonnaise, a sweet white cat with one green eye missing slunk up to him on the counter and butted her little head against his arm.

"Hi," he said, and kissed her fuzzy head. She gave him a happy chirp, then darted out the window cat door above the sink.

Everything took four times as long as usual and required ten times the energy. The crutches dug into his underarms with every touch, bruising and chafing the skin there and catching on his armpit hair. His leg hurt horribly and the longer he stayed upright the worse it ached as the blood rushed downward. His head throbbed and throbbed and throbbed.

Though he'd gotten up while it was still dark, the sun had risen during the rigamarole of making coffee and eggs. Jack scarfed the eggs directly from the pan, afraid if he tried to sit down at the kitchen table he wouldn't be able to get back up.

He realized too late that he couldn't bend down to put food and water in the animals' bowls and began a messy process of attempting it from his full height.

His first try slopped water all over the floor. Swearing, he dropped towels over the spills, moving them with the tip of his crutch to soak up the water. Next came the dog food, and Jack practically cheered when most of it went in the bowls.

The cat food, smaller, skidded everywhere, and Pirate and Pickles looked up at him for a moment as if offended. Then they had great fun chasing the food all over the floor. When the dogs joined the chase it resulted in the knocking over of bowls of water, the soaking of food, the scarfing of said food by the dogs and a counter full of hissing cats.

Jack opened a tin of tuna and let them at it, staring at his ravaged kitchen. It looked like the forest floor on a muddy day and it stank of wet dog food. The prospect of trying to clean it up left him short of breath and exhausted.

Bernard, always one to lurk until the end of mealtimes, hoping to scarf a stray mouthful, shoved his face in the mess.

"Good dog," Jack said. He'd meant to say it wryly, but it came out with relieved sincerity.

Louis, the least social of his cats—he only liked Puddles—poked his gray and black head out of the bedroom, sniffed the air, and decided that whatever he smelled didn't portend well. He eschewed dinner with a flick of his tail and retreated back inside the bedroom. Jack made a mental note to leave a bowl out for him later.

Just as Jack sank onto the couch, the dogs started shuffling to the front door the way they only did on the rare occasions when someone was approaching. Jack groaned. He hauled himself back up and pretended not to hear his own pathetic whimper as he made his way to the door.

"Back up, come on," Jack wheezed at the animals. Then, in a whisper, "Be extremely cute so this guy likes you." Then he yanked the door open.

There, with one hand half-raised to knock, stood a man made of contrasts.

He was tall—only an inch or two shorter than Jack's six foot three—but his shoulders were hunched and his head hung low, like he was trying to disappear. His clothes were mismatched and worn—soft jeans, a faded green shirt, a peach and yellow sweater, and a red knit scarf—but every line of his body was frozen and hard.

Then he lifted his chin and glanced up at Jack for just an instant, and Jack couldn't pay attention to anything but his eyes. A burning turquoise blue that shocked him because after years of drawing he'd always thought blue was a cool color. But not this blue. This was the blue of neon and molten glass and the inside of a planet. This was the blue of fire.

As quickly as he'd looked up, the man dropped his gaze again, and Jack immediately missed that blue.

"Uh, hey. You *SimpleSimon*?"

His head jerked up again and this time there was anger in his eyes.

"On the app, I mean? I'm Jack."

Jack held out his hand and Simon inched forward slowly, then shoved his hands in his pockets and scuffed his heel on the ground. He had messy dark hair that, from Jack's view of the top of his head, was mostly swirls of cowlicks.

"You wanna come in and meet the pack?" Jack tried again, attempting to infuse geniality into his voice instead of the exhausted, pained, irritation he felt at every dimension of his current situation.

Simon tensed and scuffed his heel again.

"I won't bite," Jack said, shuffling backward to make room. "Can't say the same for Pirate, though. She's a little monster."

Good. A dad joke. Great first impression, Matheson.

But Simon gave a jerky nod and followed him inside. When Jack reached to close the door behind him one of his crutches caught and slid to the ground. Jack swore and grabbed for it, avoiding wrenching his ribs at the last moment by deviating to grab the doorknob instead, knocking into the man's shoulder in the process. Jack wanted to scream.

Simon immediately moved away and Jack had a moment of resentment until his crutch was retrieved from the floor and held up for him.

"Thanks. Damn things. Mind if we sit down?"

Jack dropped onto the couch with a groan but Simon didn't sit. He hovered near the doorway to the kitchen and crossed his arms over his stomach.

Jack saw his nostrils twitch and begged the universe that Simon wouldn't turn around and see the utter shambolic trough that was his kitchen floor.

They'd messaged last night to set up this meeting and their exchange had been perfectly friendly. All Jack could imagine was that his bad mood was so palpable that he'd put this guy off.

"So, uh. I'm Jack," he tried again.

The man's arms tightened around himself.

"Simon," he said, voice low and very quiet.

When nothing else seemed forthcoming, Jack launched into introductions to the animals and watched Simon unfold.

When Jack gave the signal to allow Bernard to approach, the dog cuddled Simon so aggressively that Simon ended up sitting on the floor. Bernard licked his face and snuffled into his armpit and Simon huffed out a sound that might've been a laugh. Jack caught a flash of fire blue through his dark hair.

"This is Puddles," Jack went on. "He's a neurotic dude. Hates puddles. Seriously, you'll have to pick him up and carry him over them."

Simon held out his hand, head still bowed. Puddles placed his chin into Simon's hand and then sat down right next to him, pressing himself against Simon's hip.

"Hey, Puddles." It was so soft Jack almost didn't hear it. Puddles kept leaning into Simon.

"That's Rat." Jack pointed to the tiny dog whose hairless tail whipped across the floor. Rat jumped over to Simon, then bounded away after something only she saw. "And Dandelion." The cheerful mutt wriggled happily when Simon pet her.

Simon was bookended by Bernard and Puddles, petting them both at once. His scarf had come loose and Pickles, who was one of Jack's newer arrivals, made a beeline for it, batting at it until his claws tangled in the yarn.

"Shit, sorry. Pickles, no!"

Jack moved to stand, forgot about his leg, and groaned, falling back onto the couch.

"Fuuuck my life."

Pirate slunk single-mindedly from her perch on top of the easy chair, making her way through the room to Simon.

He reached out a hand for her to smell and she gave him a dainty lick on the knuckle. Jack thought he saw a smile behind all that hair, but before he could warn Simon, Pirate pounced on his scarf, too, wrestling with Pickles over it and nearly garroting Simon in the process.

"Jesus, this place is a mad house," Jack muttered.

A creaky laugh came from the man currently buried under animals on his floor.

Simon unwound his scarf and wrapped it around Pickles and Pirate, hugging the cats to his chest with one arm. Then he got to his knees and slowly stood, patting Bernard and Puddles with his other hand. Jack could hear Pickles and Pirate purring in their swaddle.

"You okay?" he asked Simon.

"Mhmm."

"Okay, well… Still up for it? I know they're a lot, but…"

Simon shook his head and Jack's stomach lurched at the

thought of finding someone else who could help. But then Simon said, softly, "It's fine."

"Yeah?"

Simon nodded, all shoulders and dark hair and flash of blue eyes and slash of pale jaw.

"Oh, great, amazing, wonderful." Relief let loose a torrent of words, and Jack hauled himself off the couch to take Simon through whose leash was whose and where they could and couldn't go, what Puddles was afraid of in addition to puddles (sticks shaped like lightning bolts, grasshoppers, bicycles, plastic bags), which dogs they might meet that Bernard would try to cuddle to death and Rat would try to attack, what intersection to avoid because there was a fire ant hill, and why never, ever to grab Pirate if she tried to climb trees.

Simon nodded and made soft listening sounds, and every once in a while he'd jerk his head up and meet Jack's eyes for just a moment. When Jack passed the leashes, treats, and plastic bags over to him, Simon paused like he was going to say something. Then he put the treats and bags in his pocket, wrapped his unraveling scarf around his neck, and backed out of the door, head down and dogs in tow. Pirate leapt after them.

"Okay, then," Jack called from the door as Simon walked away, not wanting the animals out of his sight. "You have my number if you need anything, right?"

Simon held up his phone in answer, but didn't turn around.

"Okay, bye," Jack said, but there was no one left to hear him.

Chapter Two

Simon

Simon's heart fluttered like a wild thing and he sucked in air through his nose and slowly blew it out through his mouth, concentrating on the smells of the autumn morning. Pine and dew and fresh asphalt and the warm, intoxicating scent that seemed to cling to him after only ten minutes spent in Jack Matheson's chaotic house.

He rounded the corner so he knew he was out of sight, then led the dogs to the tree line and pressed his back to the rough trunk of a silver fir. He squeezed his eyes shut tight to banish the static swimming at the edges of his vision and willed his heart to slow after the encounter with Jack.

Shy. It was the word people had used to describe Simon Burke since he was a child. A tiny, retiring word that was itself little more than a whisper.

But what Simon felt was not a whisper. It was a freight train bearing down on him, whistle blowing and wheels grinding, passengers staring and ground shaking with the ineluctable approach.

It was a swimming head and a pounding heart. A furious heat and a numbness in his fingers. It was sweating and choking and the curiously violent sensation of silence, pulled like a hood over his entire body, but concentrated at the tiny node of his throat.

Shy was the word for a child's fear, shed like a light spring jacket when summer came.

What Simon had was knitted to his very bones, spliced in his blood, so cleverly prehensile that it clung to every beat of his physical being.

The huge St. Bernard called Bernard—apparently this Jack guy wasn't exactly the creative type—bumped Simon's hip and he opened his eyes. The cautious yellow Lab, Puddles, was looking up at him with concern in his warm brown eyes; tiny Rat was scanning the road looking for threats; easygoing Dandelion was happily yipping at birds; and Pirate the cat was daintily cleaning her paws as her tail swished back and forth.

Simon's breath came easier. He was right where he wanted to be: outside, spending time with animals. He dropped to a crouch and murmured to the little pack, letting them smell him, letting his heart rate return to normal.

"Hi," he said, trying out his voice. It tended to go scratchy from disuse. "Thanks for walking with me." Bernard smiled a sweet doggy smile and Simon couldn't help but smile back. Animals didn't make him feel self-conscious. They didn't make him feel like he was drowning. They gave and never required anything of him except kindness.

He'd discovered this as a child, around the same time he'd

discovered that other children could not be counted on to be kind. Not to him, anyway.

Pirate meowed and took off down the road and all the dogs mobilized to follow her, tugging Simon back onto the lane. As they walked, he basked in their quiet joy and the peace of simply being in the fresh air. In that peace, his thoughts drifted to Jack Matheson.

Simon had gotten himself to Jack's front door by sheer, knuckle-clenching force of will.

For the past two years, Simon had been saving up to get a bigger apartment so that he'd have space for a dog. He'd planned the walks they'd take and the parks they'd go to together.

When his grandfather died six months ago and Simon saw his grandmother's face—brow pinched with grief and eyes wide with fear—Simon knew what he had to do. He moved in the next week. His grandmother was his best friend and he didn't want her to be alone. But the cost of her company was the plans he'd made: she was terribly allergic to animals.

He'd made his profile on PetShare the week he moved in with his grandmother and for the last six months, he'd waited. He'd matched several times, usually with people who needed someone to stop by and feed their pets while they were at work, but that wasn't what he wanted. He wanted to spend time with animals, bask in their easy companionship.

So when he saw *JMatheson*'s profile pop up, with its picture of a huge, adorable St. Bernard and its description of his rather extensive needs, which managed to be both terse and self-deprecating, Simon's heart had leapt.

But when he stood outside his door, he hadn't been able to make himself ring the bell. It was like his hand ran up against a physical force when he tried. He stood there, trying to break out of the paralyzing fog.

And then the door had opened.

Stocking feet, worn sweatpants, a bulky cast on one leg—his eyes had traveled slowly up from the ground. A faded Penn State hoodie, broad shoulders, and biceps that bulged as they wielded crutches.

But it was the first glimpse of the man's face that had frozen Simon in place. He had hair the color of copper and gold, a strong jaw etched with copper stubble, a straight nose, and hazel eyes beneath frowning reddish-brown eyebrows. His full mouth was fixed in a scowl.

He was beautiful and angry and it was a combination so potent that it flushed through Simon with the heat of an intoxicant, then set his head spinning with fear.

He'd clutched his arms around himself in a futile attempt to keep all his molecules contained, dreading the sensation of flying apart, diffusing into the atmosphere in a nebula of dissolution.

Simon had been consumed by the conviction he'd held as a child: if he could squeeze his eyes shut tightly enough to block out the world then it would cease to see him, too. But when he'd opened his eyes again, there was Jack Matheson, still beautiful, but now looking at him with his most hated expression.

Pity.

Simon shook his head to clear the image of Jack's pitying gaze and picked up the pace, as if he might be able to outrun the moment when he'd have to drop off the animals and interact with Jack again.

"Grandma, I'm home," Simon called as he shouldered open the door, arms full of groceries.

"In the kitchen, dear!"

He deposited the bags on the counter, but backed off when his grandmother moved to kiss his cheek.

"You'll be allergic to me. One sec."

He jogged downstairs to his basement room and changed his clothes, giving a fond look at the fur of his new friends clinging to the wool of his sweater.

"How did it go?" his grandmother asked, sliding a cup of tea toward him on the counter. The smell of lavender perfume and chamomile tea would forever remind him of her.

"As well as can be expected?" Simon hedged, sipping the hot tea too quickly. She raised an eyebrow and he sighed. "He was fine. I just... Whatever. You know." Simon raked a hand through his hair.

His grandmother knew better than anyone how hard it was for him and how angry he got at himself for the hardship. She'd been the one he came to, red-faced and sweaty, when he'd nailed varsity soccer tryouts his sophomore year and then fled the field, never to return, when the coach noticed he hadn't shouted the team shout with the other boys and forced him to stand on his own and yell it with everyone looking.

She'd been the one who found him in the basement he now lived in, tear-streaked and reeking of vomit after his eleventh-grade history teacher had forced him to give his presentation in front of the rest of the class despite his promise to do any amount of extra credit instead.

Simon swallowed, overcome with affection for her.

"The dogs are great, though. There's this really big St. Bernard who's a cuddly baby and throws himself around even though he's probably two hundred pounds. And he has cats, too, and one of them comes on the walks. Her name's Pirate—she's a calico with a black spot over one eye—and she leads the group like a little cat tour guide."

Simon's grandmother squeezed his hand.

"It's so good to see you happy," she said wistfully. Simon ducked his head, but a nice, comfortable kind of warmth accompanied his grandmother's touches. She didn't rush him the way his father did, didn't try and finish his sentences the way his mother did, didn't try and convince him to *just try* and be social the way his sister, Kylie, did. The way his teachers and school counselors had.

"Yeah," he said. He gulped the last of the tea and put his cup in the dishwasher. "I'm gonna go get started on work. You need anything before I do?"

"I'm fine, dear. I'll be in the garden, I think."

Simon hesitated. His grandfather's rose garden was the place Simon still felt his presence most strongly, and it was where his grandmother went when she wanted to think of him.

"Is it bad today?" he asked softly. He wasn't sure if *bad* was the right word, precisely. After all, it wasn't bad to miss the man you'd spent your life with, was it? It was merely…inevitable. But it was the shorthand he'd used the first time he'd asked, when he'd found her at the fence, one swollen-knuckled hand pressed flat to the wood and the other clutching the locket with her late husband's picture in it, and it had stuck.

She smiled gently at him. "Medium." With a pat to his arm, she left him to make his way down to the basement.

After a year, the graphic design business that Simon ran from home had become sustainable. The ability to make a living had been a relief, but the bigger relief had been the opportunity to quit his job working for the company where he'd dreaded going every morning and the cubicle that had left him open to social incursion from all directions.

Now, he conducted all his communications via email. He made his own schedule, which meant he could take long lunches to spend time with his grandmother—or, more recently, take time to walk Jack's dogs. He didn't mind working on the weekends to make up for it if necessary. It wasn't as if he had anywhere he wanted to go. In the quiet of his basement office, without the anxiety of the company work environment, Simon could lose himself in color, shape, font, and balance.

Today, however, Simon was distracted. He'd get to see the animals again tonight and already his skin tingled with the promise of contact. After the third time he found himself staring off into space, he pinched his arm, hard.

"Stop it."

He told himself that it was pathetic to be this excited about getting to hug some dogs or cuddle a cat. He told himself that he was an adult and taking a walk should not be the highlight of his day.

He told himself a lot of things, but it still took him longer than usual to finish his work.

That evening, back in the clothes he'd worn to walk the dogs earlier, Simon stood once more before Jack's door. This time, he was able to ring the doorbell and the sound was met with yipping and barking from within. After a minute, he heard a groan that could only be Jack and then a stream of swearing.

When the door finally opened, Jack's hair was flattened on one side and sticking straight up at the crown.

"Hey," he said, voice rough. "Sorry. Fell asleep."

Simon glanced at his face and took in the shadows under his eyes, like someone had pressed thumbs there hard enough to bruise. He took in the creases on one cheek and the tightness around his mouth that might have been pain, and wondered what had happened to his leg.

He opened his mouth to say it was fine, but the words inflated in his throat until they were a balloon choking off his breath. There was the itch of panic and then he swallowed the words down and could breathe again. He nodded.

Suddenly, exhaustion hit him. He should've anticipated it, what with the effort it had taken to drag himself here this morning, the effort it had taken to go inside, and now the effort of doing it all over again. It was an exhaustion that sapped all his reserves and put a certain end to any chance of conversation that might have existed.

The anger rose and with it Simon could feel his chest get hot. The heat crept up his neck and his ears blazed. Before his face could turn red he clenched his hand into a fist and gritted his teeth. Then he closed his eyes, held out his other hand, and prayed that Jack would understand.

"Listen," Jack said, not understanding. "It's probably too much to ask. Twice a day. Maybe—"

Frustration consumed Simon and he drove his fist into the door jamb. It hurt. He held out his other hand without looking at Jack and, after a minute of shuffling noises and barks, felt the leashes placed on his palm.

Simon closed his fingers around them and nodded. Then he headed out into the cooling dusk without a backward glance, cursing himself silently all the way.

Away from the house he sucked in deep breaths. Again. Damn it.

"Your dad makes me nervous," Simon told the animals. He could hear the misery in his shaky voice.

Bernard woofed gently in reply and Dandelion trotted excitedly at his side.

"I'm kind of crap with people," he told them.

Rat snarled at nothing.

"It doesn't help that your dad's, uh…pretty hot. Even if he is kind of intimidating. But I'd be grumpy too if I broke my leg and couldn't walk you. Wish you could tell me how he broke it."

Simon went on chatting to the animals until Puddles stopped short. Simon peered at the ground, keeping Jack's list of the dog's fears in mind. It was a stick shaped like a lightning bolt.

He tried to guide Puddles to give the stick a wide berth, but the dog wouldn't budge. Simon studied the stick, trying to intuit what it was about it that made Puddles so afraid.

After a minute he snorted at himself. Who knew better than him that fear didn't have to have a reason?

"It's okay, sweetheart. I'll take care of it."

He picked up the stick and threw it deep into the trees. Puddles let out a yip of relief while the other three dogs surged forward in an attempt to chase the stick.

"Whoa, whoa!" He pulled on the leashes, and managed to corral the dogs back onto the lane, even though it was clear that Bernard could've dragged them wherever he wanted if he'd chosen to do so.

Puddles nuzzled Simon and he rested his hand on the dog's head, appreciating the softness of his fur and the warm press of his body.

"Maybe tomorrow I'll be able to talk to your dad," Simon told him softly.

Puddles barked.

"Yeah. Maybe tomorrow will be better."

Don't miss Better Than People *by Roan Parrish,*
out from Carina Adores!

www.CarinaPress.com

Copyright © 2020 by Roan Parrish

Also available from Kris Ripper
Runaway Road Trip

Copyright © 2019 by Kris Ripper

Just like Thelma and Louise, *but with
more boinking, and less dying at the end.*

Bored freelancer Doc has lousy taste in men. The most recent example steals his computer and ties him to his bed, which is where his bestie Rowe finds him. An hour later Doc's riding shotgun in Bertha-the-ancient-vehicle on the way to Los Angeles, where Rowe's about to start his Real Life As An Actor.

Since life after Rowe leaves will be all diplomatic client emails and dying alone Doc could use a good distraction, and a spontaneous road trip down the coast is the perfect thing. Yes, technically he's always had a little crush on Rowe, but it's no big deal. Right up until Rowe kisses him and the world turns topsy turvy—in the best possible way.

When Rowe confesses he hasn't been entirely honest, the betrayal sends Doc running. He doesn't need more crappy guys in his life and dying alone is way better than being with someone he can't trust. But losing Rowe is like losing a whole piece of his past and the best dreams he's ever had for his future, and Doc's not sure he can go back to boring after living something so much better.

To check out this and other books by Kris Ripper, please visit Ripper's website at krisripper.com/reading-order-book-list.

Discover another heartwarming romance from Carina Adores

Simon has always preferred animals to people. Meeting a grumpy children's book illustrator who needs a dog walker isn't easy for the man whose persistent anxiety has colored his whole life, but Jack's menagerie is just what Simon needs.

Four dogs, three cats and counting. Jack's pack of rescue pets is the only company he needs. But when a bad fall leaves him with a broken leg, Jack is forced to admit he needs help. That the help comes in the form of the most beautiful man he's ever seen is a complicated, glorious surprise.

Being with Jack—talking, walking, *making out*—is a game changer for Simon. And Simon's company certainly…eases the pain of recovery for Jack. But making a real relationship work once Jack's cast comes off will mean compromise, understanding and lots of love.

Available now!

CarinaPress.com

CARRPBTP1020TR